PENGUIN BOOKS

Dusk

EVE EDWARDS has a doctorate from Oxford University and thinks researching is a large part of the fun in writing historical fiction. She lives in Oxford and is married with three children.

eve-edwards.com

Books by Eve Edwards

THE OTHER COUNTESS

THE QUEEN'S LADY

THE ROGUE'S PRINCESS

DUSK

Dusk

EVE EDWARDS

PENGUIN BOOKS

PENGUIN BOOKS

Published by the Penguin Group
Penguin Books Ltd, 80 Strand, London WC2R ORL, England
Penguin Group (USA) Inc., 375 Hudson Street, New York, New York 10014, USA
Penguin Group (Canada), 90 Eglinton Avenue East, Suite 700, Toronto, Ontario, Canada M4P 2Y3
(a division of Pearson Penguin Canada Inc.)
Penguin Ireland, 25 St Stephen's Green, Dublin 2, Ireland (a division of Penguin Books Ltd)
Penguin Group (Australia), 707 Collins Street, Melbourne, Victoria 3008, Australia
(a division of Pearson Australia Group Pty Ltd)
Penguin Books India Pvt Ltd, 11 Community Centre, Panchsheel Park, New Delhi – 110 017, India
Penguin Group (NZ), 67 Apollo Drive, Rosedale, Auckland 0632, New Zealand
(a division of Pearson New Zealand Ltd)
Penguin Books (South Africa) (Pty) Ltd, Block D, Rosebank Office Park, 181 Jan Smuts Avenue, Parktown North,
Gauteng 2193, South Africa

Penguin Books Ltd, Registered Offices: 80 Strand, London WC2R ORL, England

penguin.com

Published 2013
001

The moral right of the author and illustrator has been asserted

Typeset in 12.5/16pt Bembo Book MT Std by Palimpsest Book Production Ltd, Falkirk, Stirlingshire
Printed in Great Britain by Clays Ltd, St Ives plc

British Library Cataloguing in Publication Data
A CIP catalogue record for this book is available from the British Library

ISBN: 978-0-141-33739-5

www.greenpenguin.co.uk

Penguin Books is committed to a sustainable
future for our business, our readers and our planet.
This book is made from Forest Stewardship
Council™ certified paper.

ALWAYS LEARNING   **PEARSON**

In loving memory of Jennifer Lovell

And each slow dusk a drawing-down of blinds

– 'Anthem for Doomed Youth', Wilfred Owen (1893–1918)

PART ONE

Ticket

I

The Somme, forward medical station,
near Albert, 1 July 1916, 2 a.m.

'Nurse, I'm ready for the next patient. What do we have?'

Helen checked her hastily scribbled notes for the surgeon. Dr Cameron was one of her favourites among the medical staff, a cheery Scot, short of stature, whose balding crown glowed in the operating theatre lights with a steady and reassuring beam. Absurd, but she'd learnt to look at it whenever she felt adrift or scared, drawn to flutter at his side like a moth to the collector's lantern.

'We've a lung, a knee and a head wound, doctor.'

'Head wound – will he pull through?'

Helen swallowed, remembering the deep injury she had seen on the scalp, blood against dark hair like the red stripe on the dark wing of the cinnabar moth. 'Unlikely, doctor.'

'Best leave him then. Bring me the lung.'

Helen signalled to the orderlies, two elderly labourers with whom she communicated in her schoolgirl French. '*Celui-là. Vite, vite!*' The 'lung' in question was a poor private no older than her; he had taken shrapnel in the chest on a ration run, according to the tag on his toe.

The old men heaved the stretcher up and bounced the boy into the operating theatre. Helen had already cut off his bloody uniform, but it was nigh on impossible to keep the place as clean as she had been taught. The surgeons had stopped demanding it of the nurses, seeing they were fighting an impossible battle when the casualties came in so fast.

And tonight had been a 'quiet' night.

Dr Cameron probed the injury. 'Two holes. Thank God he's insensible. Chloroform.' Helen, who had received the extra training required to administer the anaesthetic, gave the boy a light dose to keep him under as Miss Kelly, an experienced nurse in her fifties, moved closer to assist the surgeon.

The doctor tutted, annoyed by the insult of the injury to the young victim. 'We'll have this sorted at the double.' With the deft touch of someone with too much experience of grave injuries, the surgeon repaired the damage and sewed the boy up, humming as he did so. 'That'll have to do. Lord, I'm hungry. Can't wait for breakfast. Bring the knee and tell me how the head is doing.'

Two operations later, the surgery was over. The head had died on the table – a merciful release, Dr Cameron had told the nurses as the man was taken away. You could not save everyone. The knee had become an amputation, but the patient was expected to pull through.

The Scot stripped off his bloodied gown.

'Good work, Nurse Kelly, Nurse Sandford. Go and

get some rest, my dears. We've orders to clear the beds. Pass the word on.'

Helen nodded. 'Yes, sir.' She exchanged a grim look with the other nurse. He didn't need to say any more. That order meant another assault was planned, casualties expected. The day shift would have their hands full. She would have to snatch what sleep she could before going back on duty. 'I'll tell Sister, shall I, Miss Kelly?'

The older woman gave her a grateful smile. 'Thank you. If you wouldn't mind. I'm dead on my feet.'

Pausing at the head nurse's station in Ward One, Helen passed on the message to her section leader.

Sister Richards received the news with her usual stoic acceptance, her face strangely waxen, reminding Helen of a weather-worn marble angel in Highgate Cemetery, each drop of bad news sliding over her face, taking a little more of her identity with it every time. 'Thank you, Sandford. I'll see you back on duty at six unless you are required.'

Helen left Sister Richards looking despairingly at her list of patients, calculating who would survive the removal from the forward medical station to one of the units further behind the lines. Helen was thankful she didn't have to make these life-and-death choices, her junior position sparing her some burdens. There were too many decisions to make as it was. Should she have said the head wound might pull through? What if they had operated on him first?

She hurried out of the hut, running away from the

night's work. You couldn't think like that. Helen's teachers in nursing school had warned her that she had to stick with her decisions, not unpick them afterwards. Do what you think is right. Prioritize. Read the medical evidence and draw conclusions based on fact not fancy.

She paused in the doorway to allow her eyes to adjust to the dark. In a few hours, dawn would flush the horizon, bringing a false rosy glow to the dead world. Night was kinder, veiling the ugliness, but she could still see it in her mind's eye. At heart a nature lover, Helen had spent much of her life as a child out of doors on tramps through the countryside, seeking out the hidden world of hedge and copse, avoiding her home and her father for long, happy hours. This place had once also been a landscape of lush meadows and slow rivers; now the fields around the River Somme had undergone a thorough and complete beating. Though it was high summer, this area had been so pounded by artillery that nature had been whipped into a retreat. The churned mud was a dirty bone-white due to the chalky soil. The odd stray drift of flowers among the network of wooden duckboards was the only proof that things could still grow. It was haunting how the stubborn blood-red poppies and bright dandelions clung on where other flowers had given up. During the day, chalkhill blue butterflies still hung from stems, flexing their wings, bravely pretending life as normal could proceed. Helen had no such hope. Most of the trees were amputees, the last remaining sprays of leaves waving their surrender.

British lines, the Somme, 1 July 1916, 2 a.m.

The ticket lay flat on Sebastian's palm, slightly damp like everything else in the trenches. Creased down the middle, folded and refolded so many times, it was threatening to make a permanent division into two parts.

He knew every single curl on that elaborate font, the sloping S, the roundness of the Os.

> The Palace Theatre of Varieties invites you
> to an evening of Patriotic Songs
> 'Your King and Country want You'
> We don't want to lose you, but we think you ought to go!
> 23rd October 1914, Row F, Seat 14

He ran his finger over the middle, knowing he risked further degrading the thinning pale pink paper, delicate as butterfly wings. The ticket gestured to a life beyond mud-and-plank walls, his talisman, something solid in contrast to the holder who felt so insubstantial. Since orders came down for the attack on the German lines in the morning, Sebastian had been going about his duties as if he were dreaming but not able to wake. Full consciousness was too dangerous – that way lurked insanity. The 1st Somerset Light Infantry, or what was left of it, had been asked to steel themselves to do the unthinkable so often, he was no longer sure he had any courage left, having expended it all on other days, other raids. Tired – so tired. If he could manage in this semi-aware state, he might get by. It was the men who dwelt too much on things that got the shrieks. A bit of emotional lobotomy was the only way to survive.

He could not, would not, lose it in front of the men.

Find an anchor and hold steady. Sebastian fixed his gaze on the music-hall memento, a paper skin overlying his lifeline, forcing his mind away from the danger zone. The ticket was his link to the first time he met Helen. Now, near the likely end of things, perhaps he need not fret too much about tearing it. Life was dissolving around him, a tablet in a glass of water, fizzing away to nothing but bubbles and a bitter taste. Would something as fragile as romance survive or would that too crumble to meaningless pieces? He no longer knew.

'Have you ever been to Germany, Doodle?'

Sebastian looked up from his notebook, slipping the worn ticket back between the covers. He had earned his nickname – in its full form Yankee-Doodle – thanks to the happy coincidence of his habit of sketching in his book or on any scrap of spare paper, and his American blood. Private Cook, the unit's clown and fixer, had christened him a few months back and the name had stuck – now everyone used the friendly moniker.

'What was that, sir?'

'Germany – have you visited?' Sebastian had thought his commanding officer had been snatching a few moments of sleep before tomorrow's assault. Instead, Captain Williams lay staring up at the stain of sleepy, fat bluebottles that covered the plank ceiling of the dugout, hands laced across his chest like a medieval tomb effigy. The captain had had little enough rest since the orders had come through to prepare the company, but, like Sebastian, he was probably unable to close his eyes even though they were supposed to be off duty, the other officers in the company standing the watch. The constant artillery fire from their own lines to clear the wire from no man's land made them all strangers to sleep. The returning barks from German guns were unnerving. Sebastian pushed away the thought that an unlucky hit could bury them alive; at least in the dugout they were safe from shrapnel.

'Germany? No, sir. I never had the chance.'

'I forgot — you're so bally young. You were what? Sixteen when this madness blew up in our faces?'

'Seventeen, sir. Nineteen now. I did travel but not to Germany.'

'I had friends in Berlin before all this.' Williams waved his hand in the direction of the Germans hunkered down in the ruined village of Serre. 'Spent the summer of eleven there. A fine country. Damned fine.' His words were punchy, but his tone lacked energy as if he too felt half rubbed out of existence.

'So I've heard, sir.' Sebastian wondered at this strange mood that had come upon his captain. He needed his leader to show no cracks if he was going to maintain his own determination not to fail in his duty.

Williams scratched the bites on the back of his hands. 'I can't help asking myself if any of my friends are over there.'

Sebastian couldn't think of a suitable answer. Despite the best attempts of the propaganda back in London, it was a rare Tommy at the front that held any personal grudge against Fritz, but neither did they think too much about him as a person. If you did that, it became next to impossible to take the shot or go over the top. 'Best not to wonder, sir.'

'You're right, as always, Doodle. You've an amazingly level head on your young shoulders.'

Sebastian took the compliment, undeserved though he knew it to be. He was only calm because all the alternatives were worse. He faced the dawn with dread, haunted by the thought that there was little or no point to their courage as this stalemate in the trenches had gone on for too long. For all the pep talks from top brass, their knowledge gained from poring over maps at headquarters, it was hard to believe that yet one more push would break through the German lines. He could see what they were trying to do – it wasn't as if there were no strategy behind the orders. The whole hellish situation was like one of those interminable rugby games at school where the scrum had been too evenly matched. For all the shouting of the sports masters, neither side could do more than splatter each other with mud until some lucky heel scuffed the ball free. He sometimes wondered if the generals thought that their troops were actually teams to be pitted against each other, not considering how their bodies were being blown up, sliced apart, gassed to death.

Christ.

Best not to think at all.

Helen retreated to the cocoon of nurses' huts, a small collection of iron-roofed buildings hastily assembled on the site of what once must have been a prosperous farm. Some of their equipment was housed in the shell of the barn; the house itself was roofless. Even so, several of the male orderlies had taken to bedding down there, preferring it to the huts that could become either freezing or like ovens, depending on the whim of the weather.

She envied the men their freedom to choose. For decency's sake, the nurses did not have such latitude. Many people back home found it shocking to have women so near the front, not because of the danger, but the risk of fraternization between the sexes. The nurses countered possible accusations of loose morals by chaperoning each other in this masculine world of doctors and soldier patients. Helen shared her cubicle with Mary Henderson, another sister in her section, but they were rarely there together, working opposite shifts. As anticipated, the little enclosure was empty, her bed ready for her. Eating could wait until after she had slept. She took off her headscarf and apron and hung them on a peg. Starched cuffs, collar and blouse followed, then she filled the enamel basin on the box washstand. She couldn't bear the idea of taking anything from the theatre into her bed. Checking the door was firmly closed and the curtains pulled, she finally took off her underclothes and soaped her face, arms and chest briskly. She fell into a kind of standing doze, exhausted by the night's work.

The suds smelt medicinal, not like the rose perfume that her sister, Flora, had favoured back in the days when they could afford a few luxuries. The water trickled cool down to her elbows, then to the tips of her little fingers, before dripping to the linoleum. The shivery sensation brought back the memory of someone running a stalk along her inner arm. She closed her eyes to savour the brief escape.

A picnic. Young people stretched out on a riverbank, young gods come to the mortal world to play. Sebastian leaning over her and tickling her awake with the feathery bluegrass. Yes, that was what he had called it, the faint trace of America in his accent, as light as the touch of the seed head against her skin. She would have called it plain meadow grass until she met him, but now preferred the name he used as it captured the faint blue wash of the ripening stem. He had insisted on sketching her as she lay on her back, her sleepy smile the definition of spring, he had claimed, full of promise.

But he didn't want her near him now.

Helen shivered and grabbed a linen towel, quickly drying herself, a burst of frustration at his last letter fuelling her movements. She had thought he understood her, but instead he had tried to send her home.

'Stupid, stupid war.' She glared at her reflection. She was still pondering her reply, knowing better than to post the first impassioned response. How could she make him see that her sacrifice was as worthy as his? That women were not butterflies to be kept in a glass house?

She pulled a nightgown over her head. Perhaps he thought she had no common sense – a sweet face but no brains? Strange really. It had always been the other way round before, her intelligence praised to make up for what she lacked in looks. Sebastian was the first man to say she was pretty, but she had decided long ago it was the artist in him who saw interest in forms that others thought quite ordinary. He had made her feel desirable, her with her unfashionably full figure and long, straight brown hair. He'd claimed it shone with golden highlights, but, as she punished it now with a brush, she could see nothing special about it.

'Far too heavy and dull, Helen,' she told herself, unembarrassed to be talking aloud as there was no one to overhear. Her tone turned mocking. 'Not like *Flora's blonde curls*.' Lord, how many times had she heard that comparison when she was growing up? She was used to playing the ugly sister to Flora's Cinderella.

Looks had promised to determine the sisters' destiny. Their father had been blunt: he declared Helen a wasted effort of a girl when she left school at fourteen, fit only for service or teaching; Flora, the family jewel, was destined for great things. Helen had stumbled over the threshold of adulthood where others glided.

Bending closer to the little mirror, Helen brushed her fingertips over her skin. She had suffered from a bad complexion in her last year at home, but it had cleared up with age. Still, her father had never forgiven her for daring to be so plain.

Helen dropped the brush and twisted her hair into a loose plait. Not her father. She did not want to think of him.

But the recollection had already forced its way in — refusing to leave. Dad would have mocked her to see her pretending to be a competent nurse. Every time she dropped something — and her natural clumsiness always increased tenfold around him — he had clouted her, shouting into her face that she was a disgrace to the Sandfords. It was so unfair. He blamed her faults on her mother's German blood, an Abendroth from Dresden before marriage, because, of course, nothing bad could come from the Sandfords, good Suffolk folk with ne'er a smudge on their family reputation. She had come to hate the sound of those stodgy farming folk, grinding their women down into the mud.

Helen picked up the ribbon curled like a centipede on her nature diary and secured her plait in preparation for bed. Amazing that her parents had ever met considering her father's stay-at-home nature; he didn't trust the people in the next village, let alone from another country. Yet in his younger days he must have been different for Geerta had been introduced to Harvey Sandford by mutual friends while on holiday at Brighton and they had married only weeks later. Helen had seen the wedding photograph — her parents looking happy and painfully young. She had imagined how it must have been: the country solicitor's clerk pretending to be a man of the world in the gay holiday atmosphere of Brighton, with its fluttering flags and Punch and Judy shows; the pretty, shy German girl, unable to read the nuances of the English tongue she was learning, translating his fumbling words into the romance of the lover she had created in her imagination. It had not started out so badly, but, as the war clouds gathered, her father had become embarrassed by his wife's origins and found an outlet for this in his inadequate daughter.

'You're useless!' her dad had yelled in Helen's face once when she'd fumbled the coal scuttle.

'Please, Harvey, let the girl alone,' her mother pleaded. 'She does not mean it. Here, please, drink your tea.'

'That makes it no better, Mother.' He snapped the paper straight, his movements having crumpled the pages. 'I don't know what we're going to do with her. Spinster material, she is. She'll be the bane of our lives, you mark my words.'

And Helen supposed he had been right because she was the reason why Flora had upped and left for London, taking her little sister with her, a flurry of righteous white-blonde hair and red coat, the drab little sister in brown hurrying to catch up. Harvey Sandford had lost his golden girl the same day he had got rid of his curse.

Served him right, nasty, selfish man. Leaving had the effect of wrenching the telescope from his grip and allowing Helen to look at him through the other end.

He shrank to a petty dictator, his inadequacies even clearer.

Footsteps approached the nurses' dormitory at a run. Helen tensed, half expecting a summons to the operating theatre, but the messenger passed by. A reprieve. She still had time for sleep. Helen gathered up her hairpins and tucked them in the Chinese box by her bedside. She ran her finger round the rim. It was a beautiful object that an admirer had given Flora and then been passed on to her. Cardboard covered with a silk embroidery of creeping tigers in an ink-black forest, it folded up like a fan, so was easy to transport. Yet, when you pulled it out and pushed the base flat, it formed three hexagonal compartments, like a little bit of honeycomb. It was the only thing she had with her that belonged to her sister, but she doubted Flora even remembered it: she had been given so many gifts over the years and discarded them easily.

That thought wasn't so satisfying. Flora's attitude to life was like that – throw out anything or anyone she did not want with her.

My nature is more like the box, thought Helen whimsically, tipping out the pins and playing at folding and unfolding the honeycomb a few times. *Memories springing out at a touch*.

Sebastian had once told her that he thought memory worked like a Russian doll, one leading to another, but that was too tidy. Hers brought the recollections side by side, jostling for attention, the *now* having to compete with the *then*. Flipping the boxes open a final time, she replaced her pins and slipped between the bedcovers, leaving the tigers to guard her little treasures.

The reply to Sebastian's letter would have to wait.

Sebastian flicked through his notebook, reviewing his sketches. There was a portrait of his servant in the trenches, Ted Atkins, killed last week and not yet replaced. He missed the old campaigner's steadiness and fussy ways. One page had a perfect thumbprint on the corner – in mud rather than ink.

'What would you have been doing, if it hadn't been for this blasted war?' Captain Williams propped his head up on one arm.

'Me, sir?' They had been serving together for three months and this was the first time the captain had broached the subject of his private life.

Williams rolled his eyes. 'You had a future, didn't you, even though you were barely in long trousers?' He sighed and flopped back. 'Nineteen fourteen. I was on a rubber estate in Malaya, saving up a nice little nest egg, planning to marry and settle down out there. Never imagined I'd end up in charge of a rabble of cockneys and public school boys.'

Sebastian found it hard to picture the captain in such an exotic place; the redhead's pale complexion must have made the equatorial sun a torture. It would have been a life of sunburn and peeling skin.

Two years back. What had his own future held?

'I'd just won a place at the Slade.'

Williams raised an inquisitive eyebrow.

'It's one of the art colleges in London. Even did a few terms. I was going to be an artist.' Sebastian grimaced at the memory of his old self striding so confidently through the West End, drunk on being young, feeling he had the world at his feet and believing love conquered all.

Williams laughed. 'Bloody good thing the war intervened then. Can't let a good man like you go to waste.'

Sebastian had heard this dismissal of his chosen career too often to bother to argue. It no longer hurt.

A shell whistled overhead, exploding some distance away. Williams warmed to his subject, thankful for the distraction. 'Modern artists haven't a clue how to draw. Look at that Cézanne fellow. Saw one of his pictures once – couldn't tell the sky from the sea.'

A second shell landed short, rocking the trench with a percussive *whump* as the mud absorbed the impact. The candle on the ledge next to Sebastian puffed out. He fumbled for the matches, swearing under his breath. Neither of them commented on the near miss as the occurrence was too frequent to surprise. Outside there was a shout from the men, telling the bleeding artillery to point the effing guns in the right effing place. Sebastian wrenched his thoughts back to the ordinary world of artistic endeavour, which now seemed as fanciful as Shangri-La.

'I was planning to return to New York last summer for an extended holiday – if the war hadn't intervened. I grew up there until I was eleven.'

'*An extended holiday*, eh?' The captain's tone was amused rather than mocking. 'Ah, how the other half lives!'

'My father's family are from the States. I had ideas of going on a sketching tour of New England.'

'Good Lord, a sketching tour!' The idea tickled Williams. 'But what have you done with your accent, Yankee boy?'

'I'm only half American. The English side — my mother — insisted her boys went to Eton — it was where all her brothers went. Ironed out most of the accent, don't you know.' Sebastian put on an impossibly posh voice.

Williams snorted. 'Cut it out, Doodle, you sound like the bloody colonel. I'll be wanting to salute you next. So where's your old mum from?'

His mother would faint to hear herself referred to with such disrespect. 'My "old mum" is from Somerset. Daughter of an earl.'

'Blimey.'

'Not an important one.' Sebastian wondered why he was confessing so much to Captain Williams. The prospect of imminent death did that to a man. 'Bit of a ramshackle lot, truth be told. Disgrace to the House of Lords and all that.'

'Still, grandson of an earl,' chuckled Williams. 'And I'm the son of a coalminer. If you want any more proof that the world is barking, there you have it.' He yawned. 'I'm so bally tired, I can't sleep.'

Sebastian passed Williams his flask. He still had half his ration of rum left: he'd tipped it into his flask to make the chlorinated water palatable. 'Maybe that will help take the edge off.'

'You're an A1 chap, Doodle, even though you are an offence to common sense. Yankee blue blood, just fancy that.' Williams gulped down the contents of the flask and lay back on his camp bed.

Sebastian slipped the notebook inside his right puttee, rewinding the wrapping round his leg, relieved Williams hadn't mentioned the forbidden sketches even though he must have noticed Sebastian doing them. Soldiers weren't supposed to go into battle with anything on them which could reveal details of the allied operations to the enemy, including casual drawings like the ones Sebastian did in his spare moments. Williams must have decided on his own authority that they posed no danger. Life in the trenches was a strange mixture of intimacy and restraint. It was hard to have a heart-to-heart with a chap who you were likely to see buy it the next time you advanced towards the enemy guns. Sebastian had learnt to think of the men around him as comrades, as distinct from friends. Comrades fell, you mourned and moved on. The loss of a friend would be too gutting to contemplate. He knew: he'd already lost too many.

As Williams' gentle snores rumbled, a distant steam train going through a tunnel, Sebastian closed his eyes and leaned back against the plank-lined wall, collar turned up against the incursion of rats that liked to lick the Brylcreem from a chap's hair. He tucked his hands inside opposite sleeves to stop them nibbling his fingers. He felt like ninety, not nineteen. So weary, his bones ached. He wondered if he would ever feel young again.

Helen. She always made him feel happy. He'd think about her; he would refuse to let this bonfire of all that was good and decent incinerate his stubborn hope that love did count and could survive. What point would there be in fighting if there were nothing better than this, if life were just a battle of tooth and claw, animals seeking to be the fittest? That wasn't enough for him.

So where was she now? Sebastian knew she was posted to a forward medical station somewhere behind the front line, but he wasn't sure where, thanks to the censors. They had last met up a few weeks ago when he was on leave, before her move to the front. She hadn't written since his last letter two days ago. He couldn't blame the postal service as it was the one thing that was miraculously efficient in the whole fumbling war operation. The soldiers may not have boots that fitted, or uniforms in the right size, but they nearly always got their personal mail, thanks to the bravery of the messengers. He could hardly fault her for refusing to answer as he had just received word she had taken a position so close to the front and he had let rip his opinion of her risking her life. No one liked a scolding, least of all Helen, who despite her sweet appearance had the obstinacy of the proverbial mule. She had taken no notice of his protests when she had decided to come to France, so why had he been surprised when she took the next logical step closer to danger? Still, he hoped she had come to her senses and asked for another assignment, preferably back in Le Havre or better still one of the hospitals in England. He did not want her caught up in this mess.

Williams shuddered and turned over, the planks squeaking beneath him. A rat scampered over the bed, but kept running when Sebastian threw a stone. The dugout returned to its counterfeit peace. Sebastian replaced the blanket that had slid off the captain's legs. He had not done that for another man since he went camping with his brothers. Neil, the eldest, had been a terribly restless sleeper in a tent, arms flung out like a starfish, freckled face squashed against the canvas. He had gone down in the Mediterranean with Des.

No, not that memory, not now. Tears stung Sebastian's eyes, but he knuckled them away, his nose and throat burning with the effort of choking off the emotion before it could get hold. He swore under his breath, bringing himself back under control. War was a dirty business — but it was a business that had to be done by someone and their generation was the one selected. The bigger principles no longer seemed important; what mattered to him now was his loyalty to the other men and a desire not to fail in his duty. He could not let his brothers down.

But that didn't change the fact that the battlefield was no place for a girl, no matter how determined to do her part.

2

Picking a shaft of evening sunlight streaming through the window as his spot, Sebastian settled down to read the papers in the library of the Junior Athenaeum Club. The leather armchairs squatted on the dark parquet floor like thrones for fat potentates; the air smelt of beeswax polish and fresh newsprint. The only noise was the hum of low voices, the softened tread of the well-trained staff and the rumble of traffic outside. What bliss. A quiet pause before the storm when his brother, Neil, arrived on leave for the weekend.

'Seb, just the man I was looking for!' Desmond Packenham strode across the room, his hand outstretched.

'Des! Don't tell me that the navy's had enough of you already?' Sebastian threw *The Times* aside with its talk of a German invasion to shake his old friend's hand vigorously. 'Or does it mean we've beaten the Boche already?'

'Not likely. Got Jerry on the run though. I came down with Neil on the train. He told me where to find you.' Des collapsed into the armchair opposite him. With his florid complexion and unruly fair hair, Des always looked

23

permanently exercised about something. Naval uniform suited Des, thought Sebastian. He had always been a scruffy dresser, even when he had been at Dartmouth, the training school where he had teamed up with Neil, a like-minded, devil-may-care cadet. Now they both had commissions on the HMS *Irresistible*. Their captain must have taken them in hand and finally instilled some discipline because Midshipman Des now looked very dapper. 'Can you do me a favour?'

'I was supposed to be meeting Neil here,' said Sebastian, experiencing a familiar inner groan. His older brother was forever landing him in scrapes and this one was approaching like a navy warship steaming into port.

Des signalled for the waiter to bring him a drink. 'He said he'll see you later. He ran into Jack Glanville and his sister at King's Cross.'

Sebastian coughed. 'Say no more. Neil's desperately in love with Jilly. Has been for years. I imagine he went off like a hound on the trail of a fox.'

'And left me high and dry.' Des's pale green eyes twinkled as he pulled two pink tickets out of his breast pocket. 'And here I am with the two best seats for the Palace of Varieties tonight.'

Sebastian raised an eyebrow. The shows at the Palace verged on the saucy as the management specialized in *tableaux vivants* of chorus girls clad in flesh-coloured body stockings, skirting just under the line of indecent. Not that he was embarrassed by seeing bare skin: the Slade concentrated on drawing skills and he spent many hours observing the unclad forms of life models, male and female, pencil in hand. But still, it was all a bit vulgar. 'You require company for your excursion? I would've thought you'd only have eyes for the stage.'

Des took out a slim gold case and lit a cigarette. 'There's this girl.'

'Ah.'

Des leaned back, a dreamy smile on his face. 'She's a Venus, Seb.'

'Of course she is. All the fairies and fluff girls at the Palace are goddesses or they wouldn't have a job.'

'But she's different. New. Fresh. Amusing.'

'Then go ask this paragon to dinner.' Seb looked at his watch. 'Your leave will be over before you know it. No time to waste.'

Des puffed on his cigarette. 'I know.' He leaned forward, resting his arms on his knees, ready to share a confidence. 'But she has a sister.'

Seb feared he knew where this was heading. 'Really?'

'A sweet little thing – not so little actually. On the plumper side. Not a traditional looker – I have to be frank with you.'

'And why should I be interested?'

'Flora won't leave her on her own. Some family trouble; the girl is very timid so won't travel back after the show alone.'

'This ugly sister is part of the chorus then?' That made no sense.

'Lord, no!' Des chuckled. 'No, she's some kind of

dresser to the chorus in the evening. Training as something or other during the day. Forget what.' His cigarette sketched a vague circle like a priest's blessing. 'Teacher, nurse or something. It's a few months since I last saw them. The pair live in some ghastly digs in Canning Town. Or was it Forest Gate? Can't remember. The point is they stick with each other for protection. One won't go out without the other after dark.' Des subsided, not quite making port with his remarks. Did he realize, Sebastian wondered, that he had developed the habit of chopping up his conversation into short sentences like a telegraph operator? Too much time working signals perhaps?

'What's this to do with me?' Sebastian cast about for a plausible reason to wriggle out of the request that was about to be made.

'Would you be a brick and keep the sister company while I escort the Venus to supper after the show?'

'Des —'

'I'll be eternally in your debt.' He grinned, showing a tiny chip in his front tooth, given him on the cricket pitch years ago. 'I think she might be the one, you know.'

Every girl Des fell for was 'the one' according to him. Sebastian doubted very much that a chorus girl would make the finish line, not if Des's stockbroking father had anything to say about it. He'd be after a young lady with a private fortune from the Home Counties for his son. 'Do I have to, Des?'

The expression in Des's eyes took on a steely glint. 'I'll

let you borrow my motorbike while I'm at sea. I know you've always lusted after it.'

'By George, you must be serious if you're willing to let me near your pride and joy.' Sebastian made a quick calculation: an evening of small talk in exchange for weekends of freedom roaring round the countryside. Surely he need not be shy of charming a girl unused to attention; his own social ineptitude with the opposite sex might not be noticed by such an undemanding audience. 'All right, I'll be your second.'

Des stubbed out his cigarette. 'Good man. We'd better hurry. I wouldn't want to miss Flora's first entrance.'

Helen fastened the last hook and eye on Flora's costume and patted her sister on the back. 'You're ready.'

Flora turned, surveying her appearance in the mirror, pursing her lips critically. She looked like a calla lily, shapely and slim in her pale, skin-tight costume, long blonde wig covering her golden curls. Tonight's theme was the recruitment drive: Britannia surrounded by Valkyrie maidens encouraging the boys to go off to war – in other words, scantily clad Viking girls wearing strategically draped furs and carrying toy weapons. Helen considered the whole parade to be in very bad taste, but knew better than to offer her opinion to Flora. Her sister was still in love with the idea of performing before an adoring public and had few demands when it came to artistic standards. It wasn't Shakespeare, that much was certain.

'Do you think he'll be here tonight?' Flora leaned towards the mirror to apply a fresh coat of red lipstick.

'He', of course, was Desmond Packenham, the young naval officer who had been showering her sister with lovelorn letters. Flora had fallen for the idea of being the girlfriend of a noble suitor in one of the services and even quite fancied the chap himself, as far as Helen could judge. 'I'm sure he'll be here if he can.'

'Sandy dear, could you do something with this dratted feather for me?' Toots Bailey called from the other side of the dressing room.

All the chorus called Helen 'Sandy', having picked up the nickname from her sister. Helen didn't mind: it made them feel like family. She waved that she was coming, picked up her sewing kit and hurried over to deal with the last-minute costume emergency. A couple of stitches and the headdress was saved from disaster. Toots, a vibrant brunette, kissed her cheek. 'Thank you, sweetie. Oops, now I've smudged you.' She delved in her beaded clutch bag to find a handkerchief, but there wasn't time. The stage manager was already calling for the chorus.

Helen ushered her out. 'Don't worry, Toots, I'll sort it out while you're onstage.'

The dressing room emptied as rapidly as suds from a bath, a swirl of peach-toned girls in sequins and feathers spinning away for their opening positions.

Helen took a deep breath and sat down on her sister's chair. She liked the dressing room at these moments. A sense of life happening close by, but not sweeping her away. She could find her feet, centre her spinning self like a child wobbling on shaky legs in the school playground after a vigorous attempt to get dizzy. For weeks now she had felt she was lurching from one shock to another.

Picking up after her untidy sister, Helen cleared a space on Flora's eighteen inches of shared dressing table, tucking the spare hairgrips into the Chinese box Lord Gordonstone had sent the older girl, tigers growling on the tail of the one in front. She then inspected the lipstick smear, rubbing it away with a smidge of cold cream. Her fingers lingered on her cheek for a moment. Her complexion had cleared up over the summer. She could date that happy fact from the moment Flora had finally packed their bags and marched them both to the station to find their fortune in London, like a latter-day Dick Whittington, as Flora had optimistically put it.

I suppose that made me the cat. Helen smiled and smoothed her hair back with a feline flick.

Their departure had happened the morning after their father had given Helen a black eye. Flora had refused to be witness to any more abuse and anyway, she had told Helen, snapping shut her suitcase, she had always planned to leave for the big city so now was as good a time as any to put that plan into action. Being away from the threats and fists of her father had worked wonders for Helen's well-being. Though they were as poor as church mice, at least she didn't have abuse raining down on her at unpredictable intervals. She owed her sister for so much.

The music began outside, the gust of audience applause

beating against the door, a storm heard from under the covers. Helen sniffed at the bottles of perfume on the table, finding she liked Toots's light lavender scent more than Flora's heavy French concoction (another gift – Helen forgot from whom). She dabbed the smallest amount behind her ear, knowing Toots wouldn't begrudge her the luxury. As Helen had only just turned sixteen, all the chorus girls treated her like a little sister that needed mothering. They'd plucked her brows into a more pleasing shape, advised her on her clothes and even dressed her hair – not that they could do anything about the fact that she just did not have their sparkle. It was a tough test for an ordinary-looking girl to be dresser to a gaggle of the most gorgeous women in London. The only thing she had to match theirs was her generous figure which made her seem older than she was – an asset that had enabled her to get herself a place on nurse training without a blink at her claim to be eighteen.

Seized by a sudden impulse, Helen ran her fingers down the row of costumes and grabbed a feather boa from the costume basket. She draped it over her shoulders, adjusting it to hang just so. Mincing before the mirror, she did a little shimmy as she'd seen the girls do. It didn't work in her practical high-necked gown. She just looked a fool.

A door banged behind her. Mortified to be caught prancing about, Helen dropped the prop and spun round, expecting a sniggering stagehand. What she saw was much worse. A large man with dark hair slicked ruthlessly in place blocked the door. He was wearing his old evening suit, spats polished to a high gloss, the middle-class man's attempt at appearing well-to-do. He said nothing, just fixed her with his vicious hunting-dog glare.

Helen found her voice. 'Dad!'

'Surprised to see me, Helen?'

She could feel herself shaking in her shoes – until now, she hadn't known that this could be a literal description of the effects of fear. 'How . . . how did you find us?'

Harvey Sandford invaded the room and looked around with puzzlement at the gaudy trappings, the silks and satins of a lady's boudoir. Did he know that his golden girl was onstage at that moment wearing not very much at all? He'd be livid if he found that out. 'Flora wrote to your mother to tell her how you were managing. Didn't want to worry her, she said.'

'Oh, I see.' Helen had thought they had agreed to withhold their address from their mother, but it seemed Flora had forgotten that Geerta never kept anything from her spouse, or conveniently overlooked the fact, which would be more in character. Their mother was from the strict school where wives obeyed their husbands no matter what.

'Where's your sister?'

Helen could tell from the way he avoided meeting her gaze as he prowled that he was trying his utmost to keep his temper in check. He had to be furious with her for depriving him of his favourite daughter, but this was not the privacy of their home where there was no one to remark on his violence. Just beyond the door were witnesses aplenty. 'She . . . she's singing. There's a recruitment drive tonight.' There, he should approve of that.

He smiled briefly, teeth showing. 'That's my girl. I knew she would fall on her feet. Talent like hers won't let her down. Even when she defied me by leaving home, I admired her spirit. She's a true Sandford.'

Helen dared to let go of a little of her fear. He seemed mollified by news of Flora's success; perhaps this visit could pass off peacefully. 'Yes, she's very . . . um . . . popular.' Helen did a quick calculation as to how long they had before the chorus would sweep back in wearing their scanty costumes. 'But this is a shared dressing room, Dad, they'll be along for a change any moment now, the girls, I mean. Men aren't allowed. You'll have to see her after the show.'

Harvey Sandford nodded, the female unmentionables scattered on every surface a better defence of their territory than any number of barricades. 'I've got a seat in the gallery. Just wanted to check you were both here.'

'Yes, yes, we're here.' He was going to watch? This was a disaster.

Then he lobbed his grenade on his way to the door. 'Flora may be old enough to leave home without my permission, but you forget, Helen, you are still under my authority. You'd better get used to the idea of coming back to Haverhill tomorrow.'

'But . . . but I've a place training as a nurse. I can't just leave.'

Harvey Sandford snorted. 'You, a nurse? God save your patients. Anyway, your mother wants you. She's had a fall and needs some help around the house. You can nurse her.'

A fall or had been knocked down? It wouldn't be the first time. But Helen wouldn't put herself back in that house just to give him another target for his fists, even to help her mother. She knew how that would end – her running away again, but with no Flora to aid her. 'But Flora needs me too, Dad.'

He frowned. 'We'll talk about it later. Tell Flora I'll meet her at the stage door after the show.' He and half of Flora's admirers, but he wasn't to know that. Saints alive, this was a Titanic of an evening heading full speed towards the iceberg.

'Yes, yes, I will.' She'd have to warn Flora, stop her appearing in the second half. Perhaps they could leave early, say Flora had been taken ill?

Hand on the doorknob, he paused. 'You're looking well, Helen. I see that you've grown up a bit. Flora was right to let you spread your wings a little.'

Of course it would be Flora's doing, not hers. 'We'll see you later then?' Why was her voice always so weak around him? 'Bye, Dad.'

Harvey Sandford closed the door behind him.

Still trembling, Helen backed up against the wall and wrapped her arms round her waist, imagining she was folding her wings like the hawkmoth dropping from the path of a predator. This was not fair, so not fair! She could not go back with him – would not. Once upon a time, she had hoped her father had depths of compassion she would eventually access, some place where a meeting of minds might be possible, but the years had disappointed her. He had no hidden depths. He lived a life where only he could be king; he was cock of the walk, top dog. Flora would have to persuade him she needed Helen in London. Yes, he would listen to her.

But not if he was incensed at Flora's unsuitable occupation. He mustn't see her. Helen's head spun with the horrible dilemma.

The rapid fire of heels on the stairs warned her that the chorus was stampeding back for their costume change. Helen stood frozen to the spot. This was too awful.

Flora glided in, discarding her fur tunic with a practised hand. 'Helen, he's here!'

She closed her eyes. 'I know. He called by while you were onstage.'

'Don't be silly. I saw him sitting in the stalls. We exchanged one of those glances – the *significant* sort. He'll ask me out tonight, I'm sure of it.' Flora placed her wig on a peg by Helen's head, the strands brushing her in passing, then ran her fingers through her own hair to fluff it up. 'Where's my Grecian robe, Helen? Weren't you altering the hem for me?'

Yes, from short to barely there. Helen shook herself and took it off the hanger. 'Flora, Dad's here.'

Her sister paused in brushing her hair, face leached of colour. 'You saw Dad?'

'He knows you're performing. You told Mum where to find us.' Helen clenched the white fabric in her fist, wishing she could scream her complaints at her sister, but she owed Flora too much and could not be so brattish.

Flora's hand shook as she replaced the brush on the table. 'I wrote in German and I told her not to tell him. You can't blame me.'

This wasn't an argument worth pursuing right now. 'He has a ticket for the show. He'll be watching the next song. Please, you can't go on.'

Flora tugged the robe out of Helen's grip. 'Don't be a fool. I have to work or we won't make enough for the rent. I'm not ashamed of what I do. Dad will just have to lump it.'

Helen was aware they had only a minute to settle this and she had so much to say. 'He's come to fetch me. Says Mum is ill again and needs me.'

'Damn the man: can't he keep his fists under control?' Flora shook open her powder compact and took the shine of perspiration off her nose. 'Well, he's not having you back, you needn't worry about that.'

'But legally he's my guardian.'

Flora dropped the compact back in her cosmetic box. 'Sod the law, Sandy. I'll make such a fuss, he'll creep back to Haverhill with his tail between his legs.' She patted Helen's cheek. 'Don't worry. That man has no power over us any longer.'

Flora flounced out, leaving her area in its usual mess. Helen forced herself to pick up and lay out the next costume as if nothing unusual was happening onstage. Would their father hang on in the gallery until the last song or would he storm back in here as soon as he realized what kind of performer Flora had become? Well, there was something·Helen could do about that. Slipping out of the dressing room, she passed word to the doorman that Flora Sandford wanted no more visitors, friends or family, backstage that night.

3

The Somme, 1 July 1916, 5.15 a.m.

Sebastian checked his kit for the last time before emerging from the dugout that he had shared with Captain Williams. He did not have much with him as they had been ordered to leave all spare belongings and private correspondence behind in anticipation of marching to the front yesterday morning. He had dumped everything but his notebook from which he refused to be parted and he certainly did not want it to survive if he went down in the attack. Better it perish with him than be sent to his family and cause them distress. There were too many personal thoughts inside. Pruned of the stuff of his private life, his pack was weighed down with rations and water, his belt heavy with ammunition and grenades.

A real little soldier, he thought wryly, picking up his Lee-Enfield rifle. He preferred this to his revolver as it did not mark him out as an officer to sharp-eyed German snipers, unlike the sidearm. Both sides targeted senior officers. A thread of remembered music drifted through his mind, passing across it like one of the swifts swooping above the Somme on the hunt for flies, the carnage below none of its business. *Now your country calls you to play your part in war.* The tune returned, refusing to give up its hold, trilling as it snagged another line out of his memory. *We don't want to lose you, but we think you ought to go.*

Sebastian crackled with impatience. *Yes, thank you, brain, you can shut up now.* He had thought that, when facing extreme danger, his mind could have come up with something loftier than a foolish musical-hall song, but no, he would have to face death with a tuppenny ditty meandering through his head. Had other war heroes had this lowering experience? Had Nelson really been thinking of his breakfast, or a sea shanty, or the itch he couldn't reach on his back when he had died expecting every man to do his duty?

Not that I'm putting myself in the same bracket as Nelson, Sebastian quickly amended. *God, just listen to me — or don't, please. I need to get my head straight or that bullet will find me before I even get halfway to the German lines. Inadequate to the task doesn't even begin to describe it.*

Sebastian pushed the sacking aside and blinked in the half-light, dazed like a bear coming out of hibernation. In a moment the sun would rise, sending its beams streaming horizontally across the fields.

'Stand-to!' came the order from Captain Williams. All the men lined up at their positions, weapons ready. It was a ritual observed at dusk and dawn and could last for an hour or more. Sebastian was conscious that every soldier, from the Swiss border to the sea, stood to attention at this time, like some vast religious ceremony, their nerves strained, eyes and ears bent on the enemy. It marked the beginning of the new day – one that would be murderous and hellish but unavoidable. He inspected his own little contingent, finding no fault in their preparations. Guns were clean even if the men were not.

At last the order to 'stand down' came – a brief pause before the hour allotted for their big push forward; time enough for a quick breakfast. The sun sat full on the horizon. One thing was bloody obvious: attacking eastwards, they would be blind in their assault while the Germans would have them spotlighted. Had the commanders thought of that? Daylight raids were always carnage.

No sooner had he framed the question than the first British smoke bomb exploded in no man's land.

'Ready the smoke candles!' shouted Captain Williams, already up and patrolling the stretch of trench under his command.

Yes, they had. They were trying to hide their manoeuvres behind man-made clouds.

Private Cook, a cheeky bugger of a cockney, was manning the lookout on the fire step, a notch cut into the turf higher up the trench wall. He turned and grinned down at Sebastian. Filling in for Sebastian's missing servant, they had become quite close over the last few days. Cook wore the dust and grime like a coalman in his element. 'Morning, sir. 'Ad your beauty sleep then?'

'Morning, Cook. Yes, I slept like a baby.' Sebastian took his place with the men at his post, nodding to Bentley, Norton and Whitworth.

'Like a newborn, I bet, what with that barrage poppin' away all night. Awake every two minutes like me.'

'Effing guns,' murmured Norton, a taciturn farmer's boy from Sussex who rarely dropped more than two words at a time like a precision seed drill in the furrow of conversation.

'My missus swears our latest keeps 'er up all night, squawlin' and squeakin'. Says I'm lucky to be out of it.'

Thick billows of smoke mimicking a London fog rolled across the barren landscape.

'Gawd, will you look at that: a lovely pea-souper. Now I feel right at 'ome.'

'Glad someone's happy.' Sebastian adjusted his pack. 'How's Fritz this morning?'

'Quiet. I reckon our guns have done for 'im.'

Private Bentley, a lanky recruit from Coventry, had formed a tight bond with Cook from their first deployment, behaving at times like a music-hall double act; he now snorted with derision. 'Not a chance, Cookie. He's just waiting for us to go for our stroll.'

In a lull between explosions, a burst of birdsong – more a screech really – took them by surprise.

'Look at that bugger,' marvelled Cook as the swift swooped low overhead. 'Would've thought he'd pick somewhere else to fly this mornin'.'

'I think he's hightailing it out of here.' Whitworth, a quiet seventeen-year-old from Shrewsbury, shaded his eyes, watching the bird's progress. 'What is it? A swallow?'

'A swift,' said Sebastian.

'Nah, it's a swallow.' Private Cook rubbed his chin. 'I 'eard they don't 'ave legs, on account of 'em not ever landin'.'

Sebastian and Bentley exchanged a look. Both decided life was too short to take on the stubborn cockney's misapprehension of the facts. They let it go.

'What, never?' asked Whitworth. 'Not to sleep even . . . or mate?' He blushed, causing the other men to hoot. They all rather enjoyed his bashful nature and took every opportunity to tease him for it.

'No, son, they don't even stop to –'

'So how *do* they lay their eggs?' Whitworth asked hastily, interrupting Cook's gleeful and colourful response. He had quickly learnt not to flinch when a Tommy launched into the foulest language.

'Well, now, there you've got me. 'Ow do you think they manage it, sir?' Cook turned to Sebastian, doubtless hoping to scare up a blush from him too.

'With great difficulty,' offered Sebastian, prompting the chorus of laughter he had aimed for.

'Blimey, if I get out of this alive, I want to see that.' Cook wiped his eyes. 'A swallow dropping an egg like a bleedin' bomb, aiming for a soft landin'.'

'Everything all right there, lieutenant?' Williams asked, hearing the hilarity from the other end of the trench.

Sebastian stood up from his slouch. 'Yes, sir.'

'That's right, lads, keep up your spirits. Let's not let the Germans think we're afraid.'

'Yes, sir!' the men barked in reply.

But they were all afraid, Sebastian knew. They would be fools not to be.

Helen woke up with a start. Something was wrong.

Light slanted through the chink in the curtain spotlighting the chair with her uniform draped on the back. It was far too early to get up – she must have snatched only an hour's rest – yet her body was primed for action like an arrow fitted to a bowstring.

It was all right, she told herself. The courtyard was quiet. Casualties had not yet begun arriving.

So why was she so tense?

Sitting up, she reached for her tiger box and took out the worn photograph of Sebastian in his lieutenant's uniform and caressed the edge. The chances were that he was on rotation behind the lines; she persuaded herself he would be safe. The events of the day would be someone else's problem – at least that was what she prayed.

It was unfair but sometimes all she could do was hope the bullet went past Sebastian, the shell fell a hundred yards away, the gas cloud blew in the other direction.

Did that make her a horrible person?

She stared up at the ceiling for a long time.

The Palace Theatre, London, 23 October 1914

Sitting bathed in the half-light spilling from the stage, Sebastian was frankly a bit annoyed by the performance.

Pretty spectacles though they were, these patriotic pageants made no secret of their desire to manipulate young men into signing up for the great fight before it was all over.

> *'We watched you playing cricket and every kind of game,*
> *At football, golf and polo you men have made your name.'*

It was hard to concentrate on the shallowness of the words when trilled by attractive girls wearing very little. The English Roses, as they were called, floated across the stage like a flock of exotic birds.

> *'But now your country calls you to play your part in war,*
> *And no matter what befalls you*
> *We shall love you all the more.'*

Sebastian folded his programme into a fan. *Well, that's very good of you. So when I come back missing a leg, or don't come back at all, you will sigh more deeply over my photo? What a steaming pile of tosh.*

Des elbowed Sebastian in the ribs. 'There she is again — the one in the white dress. Isn't she a peach?'

Sebastian murmured something suitable in reply, but he found it hard to distinguish Des's Flora from the dozen or so beautiful blondes and brunettes striking artistic poses on the stage while the soprano belted out the lyrics. Flora's smile was just as false, perhaps even more strained than those of the girls around her.

Then finally, thank the Lord, it was over.

At the end of the encore, the soprano interrupted the applause with a modest wave, dismissing it as if the performers were not worthy.

'Ladies and gentlemen, we have a number of our brave boys on leave in the audience tonight. In recognition of their courage, I am sure you will all want to join with me in a special round of applause – for it is their bravery that we wish to salute this evening. Stand up, the army boys!' She gave a delighted wriggle that did interesting things to her sequinned bodice as a scattering of men got to their feet. 'Not to forget our lads in the navy – hoist your sails, seamen!' Des and a few others in the stalls rose out of their seats to a robust cheer. 'Ladies and gentlemen, I give you the flower of England's youth!'

Sebastian joined in the tumultuous clapping that followed. Despite his blush, Des was lapping up every moment of this adulation. Good for him. Yet it made Sebastian feel guilty to do nothing but applaud. He realized the evening was all staged to make him uncomfortable, but perhaps he should give a thought to joining up. Could he continue to let Neil and Des defend Britain when he was doing no more than fiddling about with paints and canvas? That wasn't real men's work, was it?

The applause died down, the servicemen took their seats with much sheepish shrugging and slaps on the back from neighbours and the soprano made her final announcement. 'If any of you boys sitting there have been moved to do your duty, then go to the officers waiting for you in the foyer. Sign up quickly as it might all be over by Christmas before you've had a chance to prove your worth. You can find the officers under the Union Jack by the saloon bar.'

Should he? Teetering on the edge, Sebastian suddenly remembered how he had felt during a particularly fervent sermon given in Eton Chapel by a past pupil who had become a missionary. He had sat transfixed in his pew, wondering if really he should cast aside art and dedicate his life to the natives of Nyasaland, before coming to his senses. God had not been telling him to do something so beyond his capabilities – it had been his own imagination whipped up by well-chosen, evocative words. And how could he tell anyone else about God when his own grasp of the deity was distinctly feeble? Instead, he had decided never to take a decision when under the sway of someone with powerful charisma, recognizing that he would be in no condition to judge if what was being peddled was snake oil or the elixir of life. Being a missionary – or a soldier – could be the right thing, but not if the decision was taken because certain keys had been pressed like on one of those typewriting machines. He suspected that in most cases the letters typed on the sheet of paper would spell out 'gullible fool'.

True to form, Des had not noticed Sebastian's private moment of crisis as his thoughts were on getting to that stage door first. As soon as the curtains closed and the house lights went up, he was running for the exit like a horse out of the gate on Derby Day.

'Come on, old chap, *broom-broom*!' he called over his shoulder.

Sebastian took that to mean that he should both hurry and remember the reward that awaited him. He sighed and excused his way past the line of people slowly filing out, catching up with Des as they made it first out of the doors. It was very dark outside. The tops of street-lamp globes had been painted black to confuse German airships, leaving only a little feeble light to spill down on to the pavement. He thought he might lose Des in the gloom, almost as bad as a fog, but his friend had waited for him.

'It's just round here,' Des said, walking what was evidently for him a well-worn path to the stage door. They were not quite the first to get there though: a rough-looking fellow was arguing with the doorman.

'Flora Sandford. I tell you she'll want to see me!' the man bellowed.

'Miss Flora ain't receivin' no visitors inside tonight,' the man said pertly. 'You'd best wait for 'er out 'ere, sir.'

'But you let me in earlier, you cretin!'

'Orders 'ave changed.' The doorman cracked his knuckles, sizing up his opposition in case it came to violence. 'She won't be long. Just 'old your 'orses.'

Des made a sound of disgust. 'Lord, Seb: he's old enough to be her father. Poor Flora, having to fight off the attentions of people like that.'

A small crowd began to gather, Des's early start proving false the adage about the bird and the worm. A whole flock of them were pecking about, trying to catch a chorus girl or two for the evening. The angry man was pushing and shoving them out of his way, growling at anyone who dared to encroach on his position at the front.

'Who do you think you are, sir?' said one young gentleman, prodding the older man in the ribs with his cane. 'I have an appointment within.'

'If I'm not allowed in, then no one else is! No one goes near my Flora.'

'She's not yours,' sneered the toff.

'Yes, she is!' Spit sprayed from his lips, driving the gentleman back more effectively than the shoving. Sebastian feared the older man was on the verge of apoplexy: his neck and face were scarlet. 'She's my daughter, you filth!'

Well, that put a damper on the crowd as nothing else could. It seemed fine to lust after the fantasy girls on the stage, but not in the presence of their very prosaic fathers.

'Somehow I don't think she'll be pleased to find out he's outside, do you, Seb?' murmured Des.

'I'd say that was a sure bet.' Sebastian wondered if that meant he would not have to go through with this ridiculous double dinner outing. He was sorry if the girl had family problems, but really it would release him from an unpleasant duty.

Des must have learnt something about thinking on his feet in naval battle training for he had already come up with an alternative plan. 'Come on, Seb, back to the theatre.' Retracing their steps, they re-entered the foyer.

A cluster of men was still gathered round the recruiting tables, the bar doing good post-performance business as so many toasted 'Devil take the Boche!'

Des tapped an usher on the shoulder. 'Take a message backstage for me, old chap?' A shilling appeared, pressed into the man's palm.

'Of course, anything to oblige the navy.' The usher tapped his cap.

'Tell Miss Flora Sandford that Desmond Packenham has a solution to her problem at the back door. I'll wait for her here.' The messenger hurried off.

Sebastian raised a querying eyebrow. 'Solution?'

'Whisk her out the front of course.'

'Ah. That's positively Machiavellian of you. Why hasn't the First Sea Lord put you on his staff already?'

Des smiled, but he was too worried that he would miss his chance with Flora to reply in kind. They did not have to wait long. Two girls accompanied the usher to the foyer, both muffled in coats with the collars turned up, doing their best to disguise themselves. Flora ran to Des with a little squeak of relief when she saw him.

'Oh, Des, it is too, too awful. Our father's come to drag poor Helen back home. He won't give us a moment's peace and I do so need her.'

The Helen in question hung back, looking away as her sister clung to the naval officer's arm.

'I know you need her, Rosebud. Don't worry your pretty little head about it.' Des tapped her nose. 'He's out the back. We can jump into a cab and be away before he suspects.'

She gave a little moue of disappointment. 'But that doesn't solve anything, darling. What am I to do about Helen?'

'We can talk about that later. Let's take this step by step, eh? Rome wasn't built in a day and all that.'

'Oh, Des, I'm so glad you're here.' Flora's bright blue eyes flooded with an attractive sheen of tears. Sebastian did not like it – talk about pushing the right buttons. For genuine emotion, he preferred the quiet sister's pale cheeks and drawn expression. She was not as plump as Des had led him to expect; in fact, she looked rather thin in the face, her eyes dark and shuttered by long lashes. The rest of her under the coat was anyone's guess. Not a beauty by modern standards, she looked . . . well, interesting, in a Mona Lisa way. He felt less reluctant to spend an evening trying to work out what was going on behind that closed expression.

'Des, if you are planning to put your escape plan in action, then you'd better look sharp,' Sebastian reminded Des. 'The young ladies' father will probably work out that they are not going to walk right into his arms and might think to try the front like you did.'

Tearing himself from Flora's worshipful gaze, Des signalled the same usher who had already earned himself a shilling. He held up a second. 'Find us a cab, will you?'

The man darted outside and practically threw himself

in the path of the first black cab to circle Cambridge Circus.

'There's our lifeboat, ladies. Follow me.' Des swaggered out of the theatre, thoroughly enjoying his chance to rescue his lady love. Not quite a white charger – and he had the annoying details of her sister and Sebastian in tow – but very nearly the perfect evening for his knightly instinct.

Sebastian stood at Des's shoulder as he offered his hand to assist the girls into the cab. The usher had summoned one of the petrol versions rather than a horse-drawn hackney; it had a wide seat at the rear, the driver up front behind a glass partition. Sebastian thought again of the father waiting at the stage door. 'What now?' he asked in a low voice. 'You've only put off the problem, not solved it.'

'Putting off the unpleasant to do something very pleasurable makes a lot of sense to a man on forty-eight hours' leave,' Des said blithely. 'Where to? The Cavendish?'

Sebastian shrugged. 'This is your party.'

But the party would have to wait, for Mr Sandford appeared at the corner. 'Stop!' The two girls ducked down and buried their heads in the seat. 'Flora! Flora Sandford! Come back here!'

'Quick, man!' Des barked the address at the driver, then jumped in the cab, Sebastian on his coat-tails.

'Flora!' shouted her father, running after the moving vehicle. 'It's me – it's your dad!'

But the motor car was already heading down Shaftesbury Avenue and Mr Sandford had to give up his pursuit.

'That's that, eh? Safe and sound, sweetheart, as I promised.' Des helped Flora to a seat, squashing up his body against the far door. This left Sebastian the tiny space next to the other sister. Apologizing, he manoeuvred himself into the gap. She said nothing, staring at her hands linked tightly in her lap. A working girl's fingers – nails short, skin slightly reddened from frequent immersion in water – the exact opposite of his mother's which had probably never seen a wash tub and harsh soap, the manicure always perfect.

'So I understand, Miss Sandford, that you have a training position?' Sebastian purposely ignored the very obvious subject of the angry father, hoping to help her calm down with talk of ordinary matters.

Big chocolate-brown eyes darted to his face like some wary wild creature. She glanced behind, fearing to see another cab in pursuit. There was no sign of one.

'You're safe now. He won't have followed us.'

She turned her attention back to him. 'What was your question, sir?'

'You have a training position.'

'Yes, I do. How did you know?'

'Des told me. Nursing or teaching, he thought.'

'Nursing. Queen Charlotte's Hospital, Marylebone.' The conversation flagged when she gave no more information. Sebastian tried to ignore the warmth radiating through his trousers where their thighs were touching.

'I'm sorry,' she said suddenly, 'but who are you?'

Sebastian re-ran the conversation since they arrived in

the foyer and realized that, in the flurry of the escape, Des had neglected to introduce him. 'I beg your pardon, Miss Sandford. I'm Sebastian Trewby, a friend of Des's, as you no doubt guessed.'

'Are you in the navy too?'

'No, nothing like that. I'm in training, but as an artist.'

Her eyes widened as if he had declared himself the Sultan of Zanzibar. 'Gracious! I don't think I've ever met a real artist before.'

He smiled. 'I meet rather too many of them so I think you're lucky. I'm at the Slade, a college for us aspiring Rembrandts and Constables. Do you like art, Miss Sandford?'

But the little flash of interest from her had been bottled up again, like a genie afraid to emerge from the lamp. 'Doesn't everyone, Mr Trewby?' She looked past him out of the window, the faint glow of the streetlights flickering across her face like the end of a newsreel.

'No, actually, they don't. My brother Neil thinks the only good painter is one with a bucket of whitewash.'

'Oh.' Her lips formed a perfect little circle lifting at the corners. There, he had summoned up another smile.

'And my mother doesn't understand why I can't confine myself to gentle landscapes and still life, the sort of thing she did as a girl in the schoolroom. I tell her that that isn't art; that is passing the time with watercolours. We have fearful arguments on the subject.'

'Fearful?' She wrinkled her nose at that. Sebastian wondered what she would consider 'fearful'.

'Yes, the usual thing.' He imagined the Trewby rows as a series of caricatures. 'Father burying his head in his soup, brothers deserting the table – or going under the table if we reach the throwing-bread-rolls stage – servants taking sides and laying bets on who is going to come out on top.'

'And who does?'

'It's always a stalemate. You see, we are as pig-headed as each other: an immovable object meeting an unstoppable force.'

'Which are you?'

'Sorry?'

'Object or force?'

'My mother is definitely the object. Definitely.' He grinned. This was an oddly frank discussion to be having with someone he had only met a few moments ago, but he was enjoying himself.

'Sounds lovely.' She nestled down in her coat, only the tip of her nose and eyes now visible.

He chuckled. 'You wouldn't think that if you had dinner with us.'

4

The Somme, 1 July 1916, 7.20 a.m.

Only ten minutes to go until the attack. Sebastian wished the wait was over. If he had any more time to consider exactly what he was about to do, he feared he might go mad. Sweat trickled down his back, his expression locked in a fake smile for the sake of the men.

And then all the air was sucked from the world.

Boom!

An enormous mine exploded under the Hawthorn Redoubt to the right of the 1st Somerset Light Infantry. They threw themselves to the floor of the trench, hands over ears. The earth vibrated like the surface of a bass drum. Chalky soil trickled to the ground from new cracks in the mud walls.

'Jesus, what was that?' asked Bentley, shaking his head to clear dulled hearing.

'Our sappers have been busy, clever buggers,' commented Cook, drilling his own ears with a grubby forefinger.

Sebastian closed his eyes briefly, kicking away the thoughts of the devastating effect of a mine on the men in its vicinity. The crater was now a new objective for the neighbouring 29th Division to dominate before the Germans recovered. Their own division, the 4th, had been ordered to go straight forward across no man's land and capture the trenches of the first line of German defence and hold them until the next wave came to sweep on the second and third lines. That was the plan; somehow, Sebastian knew reality was not going to be as simple as the arrows he had seen on the briefing map.

Next to him, Whitworth began to mumble a prayer, his hands trembling on the stock of his rifle. Sebastian felt sick and sorry for both of them, neither yet twenty and the private relying on him for leadership.

'So, Whitworth, ready to take on the enemy?' he asked, pulling the boy to his feet. He tried to remember what he had been told to tell the men in these situations. To think he had once worried if he had the courage to ask a girl out; now he was seeking the strength to urge men to hazard their lives.

'I . . . yes, sir.' Whitworth's pale blue eyes were round with terror.

'I've done this before. Just keep your head down. You go up, walk forward steadily as fast as you can. Hopefully, our artillery will have cleared the barbed wire from our path. When we reach the enemy, we take on any survivors and then occupy their position.' Listen to him: didn't he sound just like the commanders he no longer trusted? But what good would it do Whitworth to be unclear about their orders?

'Yes, sir. I've got it.'

'Stick with us, lad,' said Cook with more warmth than Sebastian had managed. 'We'll show you where to go. Bloody shootin' party out there, with us as the grouse, but we'll get through, you'll see.'

'Righto. Yes, yes. I can do that.' Whitworth mustered up a passable smile and took his position with more confidence.

'Thanks, Cookie.' Sebastian gave the older man a nod.

'Just doing my bit, Lieutenant.'

'And doing it well.'

Private Cook grinned, displaying a gap in his yellowing teeth. 'Then, if we get out of this in one piece, sir, p'rhaps you can mention it. Always fancied making lance corporal. Wife would be chuffed.'

The wind changed slightly, driving the smoke-mist into their eyes. Cook wiped his with a grubby handkerchief. 'Won't be long now, lads.'

Cavendish Hotel, London, 23 October 1914

The cab drew up outside the restaurant in Jermyn Street. Sebastian swiped his hand across the misted window, little droplets of condensation racing each other down to the door frame. The roads were noticeably quieter than before the war, but the Cavendish was still popular enough to draw the crowds. The hotel was really a number of town houses knocked together to create a single building so kept to a domestic scale in the rooms.

The front door was modest so you could imagine you were entering a private residence rather than one of the most famous dining rooms in London.

Des paid the driver and led their little party inside. The popularity of the kitchen presided over by society's most celebrated caterer, Rosa Lewis, meant they had to wait ten minutes before being shown to their table. It was an awkward pause: Des and Flora were absorbed in each other; the younger Sandford girl stood apart, rubbing self-consciously at the fabric of her brown dress. Sebastian played with his cigarette case, more to look as though he were at ease than from any wish to light up. It was situations like this that made him acutely aware of his age. At seventeen, he was still not quite used to being treated as a young man rather than the boy he had so recently been. He knew how to act the sophisticate with his brother's older friends, like Des, but inside he felt a fraud. Would the girls sense that?

He could sympathize with the younger Miss Sandford's unease. She clearly felt out of place: the other women – her sister included – were wearing much more fashionable clothes in gay colours, those ridiculous hobble skirts, with fancy turban hats. Her sombre clothes suited her simpler Raphael Sistine Madonna looks. The gown fell in the straighter silhouette women had adopted the last few years, but that did not disguise the fact that she had curves, which was what had brought to mind the painting that once hung in the Vatican chapel. He shared Raphael's appreciation of a girl who looked womanly rather than like a stick. He wouldn't mind sketching her if he thought for one moment that he could persuade her to sit. In contrast to her sister's modern prettiness, her face had a timeless quality, the sort that he would not be surprised to find in a medieval or Renaissance painting. How old was she exactly? Her figure and her face were at odds.

'Come this way, ladies, gentlemen.' The maître d' led them to a table not far from the fireplace. Sebastian held out the chair for Miss Sandford while Des performed the same service for Flora. Des ordered a bottle of champagne.

'Now, Flora, tell me about the situation with your father,' Des said. The waiter popped the cork and deftly served them each a flute of fizz before leaving the bottle in an ice bucket. 'How can we help?'

We? Sebastian had not signed up to anything but dinner. He glared at the menu.

'Oh, Des, he is a most difficult man.' Flora took a swallow of champagne. 'He isn't very *kind* to Helen, if you understand me.'

Helen swirled her drink, but did not take a sip, seemingly fascinated by the bubbles winking out of existence as they reached the brim. 'Flora, please.'

'No, Helen, Des is on our side: we can trust him. And I'm sure he can vouch for his friend.' She dismissed her sister with a turn of an elegant shoulder, the silk of her emerald-green gown moving smoothly over her ivory skin. 'You see, Des, he has a temper. I'm afraid that if

Helen is forced back home,' she lowered her voice, realizing the Cavendish dining room was not a place to mention such things, 'he'll start taking it out on her again.'

Sebastian went cold, the feeling catching him unexpectedly like a stroller on a beach misjudging the waves and receiving a wet slap on the ankles in payment. This was not a simple matter of a family falling out over something trivial. There was precious little anyone could do when the head of the house decided to discipline his wife and children with blows. It wasn't unusual: his own schooling had included a few appointments with the cane. Yet, from the sound of it, Flora was hinting at more than ordinary corporal punishment.

Flora sighed, playing the martyr with attractive pathos. 'That's why we left when we did, abandoning everything to make our fortune here. She is better off in London, with me.'

Des raised her hand to his lips. 'Of course she is, Rosebud. We'll make sure nothing happens to her. Put it away for now. Try to enjoy yourself.'

Sebastian knew then that Des had no intention of getting involved in this tangle. His only interest was enjoying his girl's company for a few hours before he had to go back to his ship. That sat uneasily with Sebastian: Des had promised help when he had nothing to offer. There had to be something they could do.

'Miss Sandford, is there no one you can appeal to among your relatives?' Sebastian asked the younger girl.

'Please, Mr Trewby, it really is nothing for you to worry about.' Her cheeks were flushed with embarrassment.

Flora cut in like a yacht tacking in front of a little steamer, forcing her to give way. 'Our mother is from . . . from abroad, our father an only child. We have no relatives in England. I am the only person Helen can turn to. So here I am – and I will protect her.'

'And she is very lucky to have you.' Des signalled the waiter over to take their order. 'Now, are you going to have the pork or the beef? I've heard good things about the Beef Wellington.'

'Then I'll have that.' Flora smiled adoringly at him. Was her affection real, wondered Sebastian? He turned back to the younger sister.

'Miss Sandford, what would you like?'

Flora giggled. 'Miss Sandford? Lord, that sounds so formal!' She had assumed the airs of a hostess trying to enliven a flagging cocktail party. 'She's not some old society biddy. Do call her Helen – or Sandy if you prefer.'

Sebastian gave Flora a tight smile, not liking how the older sister rode roughshod over the younger. 'If she doesn't mind.'

'No, I don't mind,' Helen said quickly. 'But call me Helen please, not Sandy.'

'So, Helen, what have you chosen?' Sebastian had set his mind on the lamb.

Helen scanned the menu. 'I'm . . . I'm not feeling

hungry.' The poor girl looked as if she would rather be anywhere other than this dining room.

'But you haven't eaten all day, Helen, not if I know you.' Flora addressed herself to Des. 'She came straight from the hospital after an early start. She'll fall asleep in her soup if we're not careful.'

'I did eat. I'm just tired.'

Des closed his menu with a snap. 'Oh, you should have said, Helen! Here we are – dragging you about London when doubtless you would prefer cocoa and your bed. Look, Seb told me earlier that he had already eaten.' *He had?* 'Why don't you let him escort you home in a taxi – on me, of course – and I'll bring your sister later.'

Helen did not look thrilled with that plan either. She pleated the linen napkin nervously. 'Flora, did you tell Dad where we lived?' she asked in a near whisper.

Flora shook her head, face arranged in a hurt expression. 'No, you ninny! Of course I didn't.'

'And you don't think anyone at the theatre will tell him?'

'No! They wouldn't without first asking me if I minded and I would never give permission, you know that.'

The waiter arrived to take their order. Des smiled pleasantly and explained that two of their party would be leaving. He then ordered the beef for himself and Flora. Sebastian wondered if he should protest. But then he did not want to stay if Helen left. He stood.

'Miss Sandford, Helen, shall we go? I think we've been given our marching orders.'

She rose, looking uncertain, a passenger on a sinking ship debating whether it was better to jump or cling to the wreckage. 'If you are sure.' She was still talking to her sister, not trusting that Flora had kept the secret of their address.

Flora tutted. 'Go, Helen: you know you have an early start tomorrow morning. Des only has another day of leave.'

Helen looked down, taking to heart the reminder that she was spoiling everyone's plans by her resistance. The two lovers wanted time alone so she and Sebastian were being packed off, children sent to bed without their supper. 'Yes, of course. What time will you be back?'

Flora laughed. 'Good Lord, are you my mother now? Don't wait up for me.'

Des finally remembered that Sebastian wasn't his servant. 'Thanks, Seb. I'll see you before I go about . . . well . . . you know.'

The motorbike. Sebastian's spirits lifted. 'Yes, absolutely.'

As they left, he heard Des lean over to Flora and reassure her. 'He's a good fellow. A1 at Lloyd's, as they say. You can trust him with your sister.'

Helen wished she had just said farewell to Des's friend once they had left the Cavendish and made her own way home. Her skin felt as if it did not quite fit her under his gaze and he looked at her far too much. She was used to men glancing at her then moving on to the far more eye-catching, vibrant Flora. Sebastian had not just looked, he had studied her: a scientific curiosity, reminding her of a bookplate of Mr Darwin on the *Beagle*, establishing the characteristics of a new species. *Sister Drabius.* Now they were stuck together for the long dark drive back to Whitechapel – the other side of the city, miles from the West End. The cabbie had almost refused to take their fare until he realized he could nip home to Stepney, calling it a day thanks to the lavish tip Sebastian had promised him. She should have seized that chance and fled before the driver reconciled himself to the trip up east.

'Do you think there's any risk you might find your father waiting for you when we arrive?' Sebastian asked, writing his initials in the misted window. He seemed fascinated by the patterns made by the faint streetlight through the condensation.

Helen shook her head, but he would barely be able to make out her movements, sitting as she was in the shadows as far from him as she could get on the rear seat of a hackney cab. 'No, Mr Trewby, I don't imagine he'll get anyone at the theatre to talk; we're like a family.' The proper sort of family – that kept each other's secrets and watched out for trouble. 'And my landlady will be awake. She'll make sure I'm safe.'

He turned to her, his dark hair and eyes making him a study in contrast when set against the hazy white window – a photographic negative. '*Mr* Trewby again, not Sebastian? I guessed that you did not like your sister and Des forcing you into my company. I'm sorry.' He gave a charming, self-deprecating smile. 'For what it is worth, I really do not pose a threat to you. Girls scare me to death.' He laughed at himself, which made her feel much better.

'I do not consider you a threat.' But that was far from the truth. Instinct told her that he threatened her peace of mind. Wary though she usually felt towards men, even she was not immune to a romantic daydream and could weave many thoughts around someone with those poet looks – dark, intelligent eyes and a tumble of mahogany hair. Face perhaps a little too long for perfection, but that only made him seem more, well, *collectable*. She had always been drawn to the rare, the unobvious in nature, which was why she particularly liked moths, more so than their garish cousins, the butterflies. Seeing Sebastian reminded her of a euphoric sighting of the Convolvulus Hawk-moth as it danced along Bird Brook one summer evening, so big and determined that she could hardly believe it belonged to the Suffolk countryside. A natural spectacle.

Helen smiled to herself, imagining netting him for closer inspection – if she dared. She too had done her fair share of studying him when she thought he wouldn't notice. She hovered, uncertain whether to call him the more formal, and proper, Mr Trewby again or Sebastian: each choice seemed loaded with implications. So she said nothing.

A few more faintly-lit streets passed before Sebastian broke the silence. 'What are you going to do about him, if you don't mind me asking?'

Strangely, she did not. Unlike Des, who clearly only had thoughts for enjoying his brief time on leave, Sebastian had seemed genuinely concerned about her predicament. 'There's not much I can do. I'm just sixteen. He has the law on his side.'

His eyebrows winged up. 'Only sixteen? But I . . .' He stopped himself mid-sentence, working out there was no polite way of ending that remark.

'I know I might look older — and Flora is quite a bit older than me, six years in fact — so people are often surprised.' And she felt well beyond her age, never having had a carefree childhood like she had read about in books at school. Nursery teas, gardens to play in, fussy nannies with a heart of gold — all the sentimental kinds of stories they now judged suitable for girls. Her life had always been fraught with rules that changed on a despot's whim, sentence handed down before the verdict was given, as Alice found in Wonderland.

'You're going back with him?'

Helen appreciated the fact that he was really listening to her, not assuming anything. 'Well, no. I'm going to avoid him.' She smiled at her lap.

'Is that possible?'

She shrugged. 'I hope so. I won't go to the theatre again until he's left London. He doesn't know where I'm training so, as long as Flora doesn't give anything else away, I should be safe.'

'Oh yes, your protective sister.'

Helen understood how Flora might seem to someone

like Sebastian; she had noticed his narrowed eyes and sarcastic expression as Flora had turned her full array of fluttering and sighing on the naval officer. Sebastian would scorn the surface play of emotions, not realizing that, while part of it was a show, Flora was much more complicated than the fragile blonde beauty she pretended to be. Helen had always regarded Flora's displays as part of her instinctive behaviour as a female of the species responding to the signals of the male – so common in the natural world she had observed and recorded in her diaries – the dance, the preen, the flutter. Yet humans were more complex than birds and bees; Flora's greatest strength, as well as her weakness, was to believe in the emotions she acted out, falling for her own illusion. She really was worth much more than Sebastian's dismissive tone suggested. 'Flora can be quite persuasive when she wants. She might even be able to talk our father out of taking me home, once he has got over his shock of seeing her in the show.'

Sebastian returned to swirling his finger across the pane. 'Not exactly something for fathers, is it?'

'Or anyone with any taste,' she joked.

He laughed. 'True.'

The rest of the journey passed in silence. They were almost at her road when he suddenly spoke up again.

'I wondered, Miss Sandford . . . Would you be interested in sitting . . .' He stopped. 'No, it was foolish of me to even think of asking.'

Her heart beat just a little faster, wondering what that

cut-off sentence had hidden. An invitation to a social event, a dinner party or theatre even? Had his courage failed before he asked her out? She would have refused of course, but it would have been nice to have been invited just this once. 'There's my door. By the privet hedge.'

He got out first to open the cab door for her. Her street was one of the better ones in Whitechapel, a neat row of two-up two-downs, but even darkness could not disguise the poverty of this district, the smell of badly maintained privies and people living in close proximity. Nearly all her neighbours were Jewish immigrants, only just finding their feet in a new country, whole families crammed into tiny rooms. 'You will be all right now?'

'Of course. I'm sorry to drag you all the way out here.'

'No trouble.' He shook her gloved hand – their first proper touch as she had managed to avoid taking his arm throughout the evening.

She pressed her palm lightly against his, then quickly pulled away. His fingers were long and she could see they were only slightly roughened from the wear and tear of paint and charcoal – an artist's hands. 'Thank you.'

'My pleasure.' He waited until she had her key in the lock of the front door then climbed back inside the cab. The vehicle puttered away, rousing the neighbour's springer spaniels to an enthusiastic round of barking.

Helen closed the door and leaned against it. What had he wanted to ask?

5

The Somme, 1 July 1916, 7.30 a.m.

Captain Williams strode down the trench, tapping the men on the shoulder as he passed. 'This is it: zero hour. Time, gentlemen.' He nodded to Sebastian and then took his position at the centre of their line.

'Bloody hell,' muttered Cook, but he was the first up the fire step and on to the scaling ladder they had leaned against the wall of the trench. He slithered over the top on his belly. Sebastian followed, keeping low as the cockney had done; the decision to go over was easy now when he had men looking to him to lead. His first thought as he reached ground level was that the watery morning light seemed so much brighter out here even though it was filtered through the smoke clouds. He had a flash of memory, washing brushes, watercolours swirling through the jar in curling formations as he changed colour from pale blue to green. Then the guns started firing from the German lines, a harsh rattle like stones in a tin box. He stumbled forward a few paces, taking cover behind a slight swell of earth, the remains of an old wall. The sheer amount of metal in the sky was terrifying, like a swarm of bee-bullets, the noise unimaginable.

A state he recognized as his battle-readiness took over. In extreme danger, his brain played a kind of trick on him, dividing into two — one part aware of what he needed to do to survive, coolly calculating, able to take decisions in fleeting instants; the other cobweb self floated in a detached state of confusion and terror. He could sense the men coming up behind him, waiting for his signal, so he gestured for them to move forward. They started across no man's land, head and shoulders hunched down, but keeping up a steady jog forward until they met with the first tangle of barbed wire that had not been cleared.

'Feckin' useless artillery,' mumbled Cook. 'Do we go on, sir?'

'Have to.' It had become quickly apparent that the plan to clear the path for the soldiers with the overnight bombardment had not worked. They were going to be rabbits caught under the gardener's raspberry nets, picking their way through their own wire and then the enemy's as the Germans took potshots at them. 'Like Peter Rabbit and Mr McGregor,' muttered Sebastian, kicking off the wire caught on his boot. 'Murder to get through.'

Whitworth gave a shrill laugh, getting the nursery-book reference. 'Loved that story, sir.' The sound was cut off abruptly as he grasped his throat, blood welling through his fingers, a look of astonishment on his face. He fell against Norton.

They had barely advanced fifty yards.

'Damn it, Whitworth, don't you do this to us.' Training took over. 'Norton, take Whitworth back to our lines, make sure he gets seen to.'

Norton nodded, slung the boy's arm over his shoulder and half carried him back to the trench, feet bumping on the ground.

'Cook, Bentley, the rest of you with me.' Sebastian pressed on, leading his squad of fourteen while noticing that the others from his division had crept ahead of his little section, threading their way through the traps they themselves had laid for defence. Right and left, soldiers fell randomly, like conkers dropping from a chestnut tree as the breeze of bullets took them. So much for the German defences being beaten by the bombardment. He barely heard the clatter of the machine guns. Could something be too loud to hear? His boots slid in the churned earth, wet from the brief shower in the night. The heat of the hidden sun hammered on the front of his helmet. There had to be several hundred yards until they reached their objective and a third of the men were down.

Terrified, he wondered how he kept on going.

Then the German artillery joined the party, big guns behind the lines trying to find the right range to annihilate the oncoming wave of troops. By common consent, the men scattered for cover. Sebastian, Bentley and Cook took refuge in a large shell hole, the size of a bunker on a golf course, greasy with mud and fouled by human remains.

'I think us grouse might be losin'.' Cook wiped the sweat from his brow.

'Game birds always lose. What they're bred for,' muttered Bentley darkly.

As much as he agreed with the sentiment, Sebastian had to keep them moving. 'All right, it's clear the enemy is picking us off at will. We'll move forward in stages. As far as the next shell hole.' He gestured to the shallow rampart thrown up some twenty yards away. 'Cook, can you see anything?'

Nearest to the rim, Cook gingerly peered over the top. 'Nah, sir. Not a sign. Nothing to shoot at.'

'The worst of the fire is coming from our right. Let's make for there and take the machine-gun position.'

A body landed in the shell hole just behind them with a thud.

'Christ, Norton, you've taken years off my life,' joked Cook as their comrade crawled on his stomach towards them.

'Whitworth?' asked Sebastian.

'The medics have him. Bullet caught him in the side of the neck. Might live,' Norton said tersely, his blood-stained hands wrapped round his rifle stock and barrel. 'Orders?'

Whitworth was lucky to have fallen so close to aid. From here on, Sebastian would have to abandon any casualties. 'We're going to take down that machine-gun crew. We cover the ground to the next shell hole fast, then grenades at the ready. There's a gap in the wire at two o'clock. We'll run for it, lob a few presents at Fritz then follow in after. Pass the word to anyone within earshot. Understood?'

The three soldiers touched the brim of their tin helmets.

By God, Sebastian was proud of them. They all knew the chances of beating the bullets were slim. 'Go!'

Whitechapel, London, 24 October 1914

Flora did not come home until the small hours. Helen had been unable to sleep, anxiety swirling with mild panic, an ugly pairing, waltzing through her consciousness every time she tried to close her eyes. She knew better than to say anything when Flora finally slid between the sheets in their shared bed. Her sister smelt of smoke and brandy, masculine scents at odds with the usual feminine atmosphere of the spartan room. Able now to relax, Helen finally dipped into sleep, confused dreams splashing about in her mind. She woke when their landlady tapped on the door.

'Miss Sandford, it's six o'clock,' Mrs Glock whispered, knowing the elder sister did not like to be disturbed so early.

Helen slipped out of bed and padded in bare feet to the door. 'Thank you, Mrs Glock. I'm much obliged.'

'It's a pleasure, love.' The motherly lady bustled back down to her rooms on the ground floor.

A chilly morning, Helen dressed quickly, then braided

her long hair in a tight coronet as required by matron. She enjoyed the simplicity at the heart of nursing. There were rules which, if you obeyed them, earned you praise; make a mistake and you were sharply corrected, but it was always fair. You never had to guess what was coming your way. Her delight in observing the minute regulations had made her one of Sister Hardwick's favourites. Strange that she felt no guilt at breaking one of the more important rules concerning the age of trainees, but there it was: Helen never experienced a moment's regret for her choice to lie about that.

'Off already?' mumbled Flora, face buried in a pillow, a shield against the grey morning light, a daisy with petals folded.

'Yes. I'll have to run for my train.'

'See you later then?'

Helen sat on the side of the bed to pull up her stockings, her last good pair, clipping them to her garter belt. 'I won't come to the theatre again. I daren't risk it.'

Flora turned her head, eyes peeking out of her fall of golden curls. 'I'm sorry, Sandy. You won't be too lonely?'

Helen smiled. 'No. I've plenty of books to study.' She brushed the locks off Flora's cheek, noticing a red mark on her sister's neck, but made no comment. Her sister did not like being quizzed about her evenings with her beaux.

'Ask Mrs Glock to feed you,' murmured Flora. They normally dined together near the theatre with the other girls.

'I'll be fine. I can look after myself, you know.'

Flora shifted her hand from under her head to brush Helen's arm. 'I do know, but that won't stop me worrying. I'll talk with Dad if he turns up again.'

Helen nodded, biting her lip. 'I'm not going back.'

'Of course you aren't.'

'Will you be out again tonight?'

Flora stretched languorously, a cat-got-the-cream smile on her lips. 'I think I might. Des has invited me to a dance at the club of an acquaintance of his.'

Helen leaned forward and placed a light kiss on Flora's cheek. 'Have fun.'

'I will. Love you, Sandy.'

'Love you too, Flopsie.'

Flora giggled. 'You haven't called me that in an age!' Her expression clouded. 'Don't let anyone else hear you: it sounds so childish.'

Helen buckled her sensible shoes, slipped into her coat and picked up her handbag, sad that the door back to one of the few pleasant memories of her childhood had closed behind her. She did not feel ready to grow up. 'I won't. Your secret's safe with me.'

She had her hand on the latch when Flora thought of a last question. 'You got home safely? Des's friend looked after you?'

Studying eyes, thick red-brown hair, a natural wonder. Helen cleared her throat. 'Yes, he was a perfect gentleman.'

Flora smiled sleepily. 'Good. I thought he might be a little bit smitten with you. He kept looking at you.'

'He was very kind, but I don't think there was anything more than that.' Used to quelling hopes for her own prospects, Helen did not dare mention she had thought that maybe there had been something special in the way he regarded her.

Flora turned over with an amused hum.

'Sleep well.' Helen closed the door softly.

On arrival at the hospital, Helen was instructed to report to the sister in charge of the men's ward. Most trainees hated working there, complaining that the old, broken-down fellows who made up the majority of the patients were dirty and smelly. Modesty was frequently challenged and there were no longer any surprises left for Helen when it came to the male anatomy. Yet she enjoyed nursing the men. She found them without exception polite, however much pain they were in. They tended to treat the nurses like angels, unlike the female patients who erred on the side of regarding the younger ones as servants or daughters at their beck and call.

Sister Hardwick greeted Helen with her usual measured smile, which turned swiftly to a frown. An older woman with iron-grey hair and skin lined like an apple left over from autumn, the nurses whispered that she had trained under the great Florence Nightingale herself. Helen doubted that: even Sister Hardwick wasn't that old. 'Miss Sandford, you look exhausted. I will not have my nurses too tired to do their job.'

Helen rubbed self-consciously at the shadows under

her eyes. 'I . . . I was not well – had a stomach ache last night. I apologize if I look tired.'

The matron now looked concerned. 'If you are ill, my dear, you must stay at home and send word.'

'No, no, it was merely a monthly trouble that has passed.' Helen dared not breathe a word about her father. For a naturally truthful girl, her predicament was winding her in an uncomfortable maze of lies. She would have to remember her claim when her real monthly arrived; Sister Hardwick had a memory like a mousetrap, snicking closed on the least irregularity.

'Very well. We'd better get to it then. Today I will be teaching you girls how to change a dressing. We have a coalman with a nasty leg ulcer. It has been lanced, but we must keep the incision clean and prevent infection. The doctor ordered strict bed rest and he has to keep the limb elevated. First, please give the patients in beds three and four their baths and then change the sheets. Let me know when you are done.' She gestured to the right-hand side of the ward, to the arched windows set high in the wall.

'Yes, matron.'

Sister Hardwick checked her watch. 'Where's Miss Juniper got to? I swear that girl can never arrive on time. *She* will be scrubbing the bedpans.' As she dropped her pocket watch so it swung back on its chain, Molly Juniper burst into the ward, already gabbling her excuses, hobbling with dramatic flair.

'So sorry, matron. I missed the omnibus, then tripped over the kerb and scraped my knee . . .'

'Miss Juniper –'

'Then I got tangled up with this lady's umbrella – have you seen how the weather has taken a turn for the worse? – and that caused quite a furore, I can tell you . . .'

'Molly.' The single word was said with solemn emphasis. 'What have I said to you before?'

Molly squeezed her hands together. 'Not to go on so. To apologize without elaboration because there is no excuse for lateness.'

'Exactly.'

'I'm sorry.'

'Bedpans.'

'Yes, matron.' Sister Hardwick turned away. 'But it's always worth a try,' muttered Molly under her breath, giving Helen a sly smile. Helen wanted to laugh but dared not. 'Morning, Helen.'

'How's the knee?' Helen asked with an arch of a brow.

Molly stuck out her tongue and skipped away, her limp mysteriously vanishing as she called out cheery greetings to the men. She was a favourite with them, her passage down the ward acting like a beam of sunshine breaking into their dull lives.

Washing someone was a strangely intimate experience. Helen had trained herself to keep to her task, not thinking too much about being so close to flesh when polite society claimed to be shocked if girls so much as hinted at any knowledge of the private parts of the male body. Usually her patients were elderly, in their fifties, worn down by a hard life of manual labour, and it was easy to regard them dispassionately; but the coalman turned out to be young, in his twenties, and Helen could tell he found receiving the bed bath as embarrassing as she did giving it. When it came to what Matron briskly called his 'operative parts', he stilled her hand and took the sponge from her.

'I think I can reach that meself, miss,' he said gruffly, going every shade of red. Even the skin under the rough dark hairs on his chest was flushed.

Helen relinquished the task with relief. As ever, she was grateful that the men did not take up the obvious chance to make crude remarks about the care the nurses gave them; the uniform protected the young women and put them on a pedestal that, by common consent, none of the patients wanted to rock.

Helping him into a newly-laundered gown, she then called Molly over to double-team the sheet change. Tricky with the patient lying in the bed, but there was a knack to it as there was to most things in nursing. Roll him on his side, free the sheet, reverse the manoeuvre and remove the linen, repeat the process to make the bed. Helen had a sharp thrill of satisfaction when she saw her coalman sitting propped on the pillows, clean and comfortable. At least there was some good she could do.

She took her tea break with Molly after the demonstration of the correct dressing for an ulcer – clear the dead matter, dress to put some pressure on the wound, but not too much. Neither Helen nor Molly suffered from squeamishness so they had watched the procedure with close attention. The coalman had been admitted because his neglected ulcer had nearly gone gangrenous. He had to endure a scolding from matron on the subject, but fortunately it looked as though that horrible fate had been avoided.

'Handsome man, that fellow, particularly now his leg won't rot off,' Molly observed, nodding to their patient from the nurses' station. 'Shame he's already married.'

'Molly, you are completely shameless!' Helen poked her in the ribs. 'I can't see you settling down with a coalman.' Her friend was from a well-to-do family in Sevenoaks; no one from the lower classes would be allowed to court her if her brothers had any say in the matter, but it was a life too confining for their outrageous youngest sister.

'Who said anything about settling down?' Molly grinned, showing the gap between her two front teeth. She tugged a stray piece of her dark blonde hair moodily. 'But I have my own rules about trespass. Can't break them. More's the pity.'

Helen nibbled on a biscuit, deciding no comment would be appropriate.

'How was last night?' Molly asked. She loved hearing tales from the theatre, assuming it to be much gayer and brighter than it was in reality.

The mouthful Helen had just taken went down slowly and painfully as she gulped. 'The usual.'

'Oh.' Molly looked disappointed, then brightened up as a new thought struck her. 'Do you ever meet any eligible men with Flora? I mean, I know you don't want them — you live like a nun — but if you don't and I'm free . . .'

'No, no new men.' Helen washed up her cup. At least none that she wanted to share. Helen was surprised by a flash of jealous protectiveness for her new discovery; she wanted to keep him to herself for the moment.

6

The Somme, forward medical station, 1 July 1916, 8.30 a.m.

The growl of the approaching motor ambulances woke her. Helen lay for a moment, confused. She must have fallen asleep still fretting about Sebastian. Her dreams were always more vivid when she was exhausted, strange fragments of old and new, a rag rug of her thoughts. The shouts in the old farmyard outside warned that this was a new influx of casualties; it would be all hands on deck even for those like her who were off duty. She tumbled out of bed and dressed, shoving her feet into the rubber boots she wore in surgery, unconsciously acknowledging that she would be wading in blood.

Breakfast? She hadn't eaten since the previous night. Not that she was hungry, but she knew when she needed to keep up her strength. She grabbed a handful of biscuits from the tin she kept on the rickety table next to her Chinese box. The worn pattern of a smiling lady in a big hat and frilly white dress on the lid looked out of place in the nun-like quarters, a survivor from the pre-war world. Did she have everything? Cramming a biscuit in her mouth, she pinned her scarf in place and left the room at a run.

This was going to be bad: the courtyard was already full of stretchers, the orderlies overwhelmed as the ambulance men quickly unloaded their vehicles. Coming on behind them were the horse-drawn wagons, filled to capacity with the wounded, many propped up against the sides as there was no space to lie down. Helen ran for the operating theatre.

'Nurse Sandford, excellent. I was just going to send for you.' Sister Richards gestured to the closed theatre doors. 'I've assigned you to Dr Barnett. He is waiting for you to proceed with an abdomen.'

Her least favourite doctor and her least favourite injury, if one were allowed to rank wounds. 'Yes, Sister.'

Scrubbing her hands before entering, Helen shouldered her way into the room, hands held up like antennae, making sure not to touch anything.

'Miss Sandford!' snapped Dr Barnett, a fierce grey-haired man with the character of a hornet. 'I haven't all day!' His hands were already bloodied. There was something operatic about his stance, like a tenor about to sing his sorrow over murdering his lover.

She passed the other two surgeons already deep in their first operations. 'Doctor.'

'He's out but, if he comes round, administer the chloroform. Not too much. I don't want to lose him to a clumsy hand.'

With that reminder, she pulled up her face mask to keep her own nose and mouth far from the scent and dampened the cotton pad. Her fingers shook. *Let me get this right*. Her room-mate, Nurse Henderson, a pale, bespectacled girl with the quiet, neat demeanour that reminded Helen of a librarian, was assisting with the removal of shrapnel from the stomach. The smell, as with any abdominal wound, was horrendous.

'He'll lose a bit of gut but, if I can stop the bleeding, he might pull through.' Barnett glared at the injury as if it had personally insulted him.

Helen took the man's pulse – beating strongly, thank God. The patient looked so vulnerable, his dark hair flopping back from unnaturally pale skin. Barely a bristle on his chin, plenty of mud and blood though. Despite the lines around his eyes, he could not be more than eighteen. He could have been at a dance with his sweetheart or beginning an apprenticeship if the war had not swept him up.

'That's all I've time to do.' The surgeon let Nurse Henderson cut the thread to the last stitch. 'Next.'

A leg lost to a mine. A chest wound. Bullet in the back – this caused Dr Barnett to tut. 'Either cowardice or stupidity from our lines.' An arm that had to be amputated. Groin injury. The terrible list went on and on. After two hours, they had made no impression on the numbers stacked in the waiting room and overflowing out in the yard. At eleven, they paused for a drink and to allow a deeper clean of the tables and floor. Orderlies carried away the tub of spare human parts for burial. Helen gulped, trying not to think of the hands that had caressed, legs that had run swiftly, now no more than unidentifiable carrion.

Barnett slumped against the wall, head in his hands. 'Lord, oh Lord,' he groaned and Helen began to feel warmer towards the man. He was human after all. She coped by going numb; unable to think through all the tragic things she had seen on the table, instead she locked on the task that needed to be done. She leaned over the next patient, another young soldier with a dressing bound to his throat. *Whitworth, 1st Somerset Light Infantry.* Sebastian's regiment.

Her numbed serenity fractured, panic seeping through the cracks. That meant Sebastian was at the front too. She had been hoping that he would be on rotation behind the lines.

The casualty feebly gripped her wrist. The gurgle from his massacred throat and frantic movements indicated that he was desperate for water. Recalled to her duty, she returned the pressure.

'Can't give you anything now, soldier, but soon,' she whispered. 'Very soon.'

The Somme, 1 July 1916, 9 a.m.

Hell could not be as bad as this. For an hour now Sebastian had been stuck with his men behind a low rampart of earth thrown up by a shell, tantalizingly close to their objective of the machine-gun emplacement. The air was thick with missiles, dust, smoke – it was impossible to guess where the death blow would come from. It was doubly dangerous to stay still as the German artillery might find their range and blow them to kingdom come or a bullet cut them down. For the moment, the shells were falling to the rear, pummelling the ground they had already crossed, but the British shells were now landing too far forward, assuming the attack was running like clockwork and the men were already in control of the first line of trenches. That left the troops boxed in on no man's land by deadly fire. The screams and cries for help for the wounded had to be ignored, but it broke Sebastian's heart to abandon them.

After pretty continuous use, Sebastian's rifle barrel was scorching in his left hand so he had taken to wrapping his palm in the webbing that was used to sling it across his chest. Cook had improvised with a handful of grass and leaves. The sun had come out from the clouds, bringing with it a plague of flies and a stench of decay of biblical proportions.

Rolling on his back, Sebastian took a gulp of rum from his flask. The sharp hit of the alcohol drove out the taste of dust and smoke from his mouth. He had to break this stalemate. Death to stay here, court martial and execution if he retreated, almost certain death to advance. Not that he had any thought of falling back into that rain of shell-fire. The Germans were doing a fine job of making any British soldier think twice about retreat.

'Grenades at the ready.' He pulled his own supply from his belt.

Cook held up a German-made stick bomb which he must have scavenged off a body en route. Amazing –

Sebastian had not even seen him do it. "Ow about this, sir?' The long handle made it perfect for lobbing over longer distances.

'Got any more of them?'

Bentley pulled out another three from some secret stash.

'Can anyone throw it that far?' Sebastian gestured to the machine-gun emplacement, protected by a redoubt like some tiny medieval castle. *We're spinning back in time; soon be going for each other with stone axes.*

'Surrey Young Farmers' hay bale throwing champion,' muttered Norton, stringing more words together than Sebastian had ever heard him use.

Cook snorted. 'Should've guessed.'

Bentley passed him the first of the stick bombs.

'We'll provide you with covering fire.' Sebastian was surprised at how cool he sounded. 'On the count of three. One, two, three!'

Cook, Bentley and Sebastian targeted the redoubt as Norton sprang from the ground to lob the stick bomb. It fell short, exploding against the mud wall, splattering them with earth. The machine gun opened up again with a bark of scornful fire. The other men in Sebastian's squad returned the compliment, bullets coughing against the mud walls, hoping to find a peephole or weakness.

'Just getting my eye in,' muttered Norton.

Cook laughed, managing somehow to find black humour in their position. 'Take your time, mate. Not like we 'aven't got all day.'

'Again,' Sebastian ordered. 'Three, two, one!'

This time the explosive sailed sweetly over the lip of the redoubt and burst with a muffled crack. Taking advantage of the pause in firing from the Germans, Norton chucked the final two on the same trajectory.

'Forward!' shouted Sebastian, tossing his rifle on his back, revolver in hand. They crossed the final yards and scrambled up the sides of the redoubt and dropped down the deeper incline on the other side, boots slipping on the sandbags. Sebastian fully expected to have to engage in hand-to-hand fighting to win the position, but Norton's bombs had done the job for them. The gun crew were dead. He could not even tell how many of them there had been as the redoubt resembled a slaughterhouse, body parts scattered across the collapsed embankment. The unmistakable tang of fresh blood – acrid, sweet – mixed with earth. The gun itself had been blown off its mounting, but had survived better than those who had used it.

'Bentley, Cook, defend the entrance.' The rest of his squad were pouring over the edge; there appeared to be about twenty men left, some of his losses made up with stragglers from other units. Not too bad, considering. 'Norton, good throwing. Disable the gun.' Sebastian wiped the sweat from his forehead. July had once been a time of holidays, long, lazy days spent in the country. He was spending it in the country all right, but in a landscape more suited to Dante's vision of hell. *Stupid thought. Keep to the very real danger you are in, idiot.*

'Do we hold and wait for relief, or advance?' asked Bentley.

That was the question, wasn't it? If the tide turned, they could get bottled up here at this forward position of the German lines. They were supposed to push on if they could. 'We will take the next trench and hope to meet up with the others.' If Captain Williams was still alive, he might have taken the positions to their left. Others from the 1st Somerset Light Infantry had been on their right. They surely were not the only ones to get this far as the counter-attack from the Germans had been desperate, the act of a few survivors, not overwhelming force. The majority must have fallen back to the next line of defence, giving up this exposed part of their trench network. So perhaps the much-maligned British artillery had done some good overnight, weakened them at least?

'We go forward.' Sebastian turned away as Cook scavenged an epaulette off the remains of a German uniform. Trophy hunting was second nature to the men and it was pointless to protest. They fully expected their own bodies to be so desecrated were they to take their turn being the victim. It seemed only a mildly ugly fact amid so many more shocking sights. Yet Sebastian couldn't shake the image of the pale Saxon, back of head caved in by the explosion, sprawled on the ground like a starfish, mouth a circle of surprise, eyes sightless. The boy had been alive two minutes ago. Sebastian wanted to honour the dead, cover him with a blanket, but there was no time, no covering to spare.

'Right you are, sir.' Cook peered round the corner leading into the trench network. 'All clear.'

Sebastian would have given his firstborn for decent intelligence of what lay round the bend. 'Norton, Havers, Smith, guard our rear; Cook, Bentley, the rest of you, with me.' Sebastian led the way down the duckboards, boots thudding on the wood echoing like the thunder of a Tube train coming into a station. So far, their luck had held, but for how long?

Metropolitan Line, London, 15 March 1915, 6 p.m.

Sebastian hefted his portfolio from his right to his left hand as he stood in the queue for a ticket to the Underground. His weekend visit home to Taunton had gone as well as could be expected: his mother had liked his studies of hands and heads; his father had resisted making his usual jokes about the endowments of the various life models; his younger brother, Steven, had actually admired Sebastian's new geometric approach, influenced by an exhibition he had recently attended of Vorticist painting. Steven, a bright-eyed fourteen-year-old, was curiously eager for anything that was 'all the go' in the capital, finding life as a schoolboy in Eton stifling. Poor boy: still three more years to endure. He had looked decidedly glum when he had got off at the Windsor and Eton branch line.

Reaching the booking clerk's window, Sebastian handed over three pennies and received a ticket in return, slid across the brass tray with a chirpy 'Thank you, sir' from the clerk. How many times a day did the man say that, Sebastian wondered? What kind of life was that? Men turning into machines.

He took the stairs down to the platform, following the other passengers heading east. The tunnel smelt of engine oil and cigarette smoke, leather and damp tiles – a scent peculiar to the growing Tube network. Not exactly dirty, not exactly clean – the strange in-between character of public spaces in the metropolis. He overtook a woman with two children in hand, the youngest one with a stocking slumped round one ankle, dragging her feet. His own mother would not be seen dead down here. The very thought of sitting on the same bench as the lower classes would shock her to the core. She only travelled first class – the Tube was far too democratic for her taste – but Sebastian revelled in it. Evidence of his American half perhaps? He smiled at his reflection caught on the shiny wall tiles. He found much to please the artist, not least the modern design of the new circular sign, so different from the elaborate signage favoured by Victorians a few years back where one could never have enough curlicues. Perhaps he could sketch something, life from the train window, stuttering past in frames?

The little girl wailed as her mother tugged up the slumped sock, the sound breaking into Sebastian's daydream. What was he doing? Did he have to turn everything into art? Since the recruitment drive at the Palace, Sebastian had felt oddly redundant, a sensation that had travelled home with him. So much of the conversation was dominated by news of Neil, his letters from sea read out with great ceremony at dinner so the staff could also hear his much-edited exploits. As the middle son, Sebastian's art had always been something of an embarrassment to his parents. If he had been a girl, they would in all likelihood have been pleased. An artistic young woman sounded so much more reasonable than a man; girls were allowed to dabble in stuff like that before knuckling down to the serious business of marriage. He felt the unspoken pressure that he should be out doing something more practical, but all he wanted to do was draw. How long would he be able to ignore the challenging looks of the people on the streets when they saw a young man out of uniform?

He glared at the poster half flopping off the wall, beckoning more young recruits to step forward. He would join up when he was ready, not because he was ashamed.

That was easier said than done. He would challenge anyone who said he did not love his country as much as the next man, but he supposed he had just been hoping that the bloody thing would be sorted out before he had to make a decision.

The train drew into the station, the gatemen opening the doors for the passengers to get on and off at either end of the carriages. Sebastian stood back to let the ladies enter, then climbed aboard. Just as the carriage attendant was about to close the doors in their car, a young woman scrambled on.

'You'll get me in trouble, miss,' grumbled the gateman as he delayed ringing the bell to give the all-clear to the next car.

'Thank you!' the girl said, out of breath from her sprint from the stairs. She turned to find a seat in the busy carriage, coming face to face with Sebastian. The girl from the theatre. Flora's sister, Helen Sandford.

Sebastian got up to offer his place before any of the other gentlemen beat him to it. 'Miss Sandford?'

The girl looked up at him in surprise. She had bundled herself on to the train without really taking in any of her fellow passengers, still in a flap from her last-minute dash. 'Mr Trewby?'

Sebastian smiled. 'Well remembered. Please, do take my seat.'

'Thank you.' Helen sat down and arranged her battered black handbag on her knee.

It was hard to converse when you were a strap-hanger and the girl you wanted to talk to was seated. Besides, the clatter of the train through the tunnel meant any remark would have to be shouted. He contented himself with smiling at her when she dared raise her eyes to catch him watching her. The desire to sketch her had come rushing back, bursting into his mind like she had into the carriage, forcing open the doors of memory. That curving neck and harmoniously spaced features that recalled the face of a Renaissance Madonna. He had almost asked her to pose for him when he had left her at Whitechapel that evening, but had bitten his tongue in time.

Conversation impossible, they contented themselves with the shy smiles of almost strangers when their eyes met. Then, at Portland Road, the seat next to her became vacant and Sebastian took his chance to sit down.

'On your way to the theatre?' he asked.

Helen played with the ugly fastening of her bag. 'No. I don't go there any more.'

'Oh? Has your sister got a new position?'

'No, nothing like that. It was just that my father developed the habit of turning up unexpectedly and I no longer felt safe.'

'I see. He hasn't found you then?'

She shrugged, signalling that she had no more she wished to say to a mere acquaintance. Sebastian feared that his chance to talk to her was fast ending and he was not finished yet. Something about her drew him in and he had not yet worked out what it was.

'Well, if you have no plans for the evening, perhaps you'd like to join me for a spot of supper?' He felt shy making the request; asking girls out was not his forte.

'I . . . I'm not sure.' She did not seem opposed to the idea, just as unsure as him. Somehow that made it easier for him to assume a confidence he did not feel.

'Please. I would really enjoy the company. I know an excellent little restaurant in Soho, *Le Rendez-Vous*. You can get a decent meal for two shillings. Keep me from being too melancholy – I've just come home from a visit to my family and am feeling lonely.' He winced at the half-rhyme, hoping she had not noticed.

She looked up, a smile in her eyes. 'That sounds . . . well, that would be lovely. Yes, thank you.'

A broad grin stretched across his face. He had successfully asked a girl to supper – the first time he had ever done the thing cold, not at a dance or as part of a group of friends. Sebastian felt he deserved at least a round of applause. 'Well then, perhaps we had better work out how to get there.' He checked the Underground map pasted to the wall of the train.

'Change at King's Cross and catch the Piccadilly Line,' she said.

She was quite right, but somehow it did not feel quite right for a girl to be quicker at maps than a man. 'I see you know your way around.'

Helen shrugged. 'Necessity.'

'Do you still live out at Whitechapel?'

She shook her head. 'No, I'm sharing lodgings with another nurse trainee. In Highbury.'

They had reached their stop. More news would have to wait. Sebastian offered his arm. 'Shall we?'

Placing her small hand on the crook of his elbow, Helen let him lead her off the train.

7

The little restaurant in Dean Street was quiet on a Monday evening. A table by the window was available without them having to wait. Helen was thankful because she did not want time to regret her impulse to accept Sebastian's invitation. At home, she only had a cold supper and Molly's company to look forward to – if Molly had not also gone out with one of her young men. She spent more nights on the town than she did studying their medical books, teasing Helen for being so devoted to her work.

Helen relaxed, sipping her glass of water as Sebastian ordered cottage pie for them both – good English fare that disguised the lack of meat by adding plenty of vegetables. Molly would approve that she had seized the opportunity to have an evening off.

'So, Miss Sandford, how is your sister?' Sebastian straightened his knife and fork, evidently a little awkward even though he had been the one to pursue and get her here. That made her happier, more equal to him in this situation.

'She's well, thank you. I see her when I can.' Helen

watched a serviceman on leave saunter by with a girl on each arm. The threesome was laughing uproariously, laughter gusting like the brawling calls of rooks in the elms near her home. By contrast, Sebastian and she sat either side of the table like hedgehogs sharing a bowl of milk and bread, wary companions with defences ready to spring. Helen wondered if she would ever find ease in the company of a man like the rook-girls; her father had crushed that in her.

'What's she doing now?'

'She's in the new revue at the Palace, but my father followed her home one night and, well, I decided I had to find somewhere else to go.' The scene had been grim, poor Mrs Glock having to bar the door against his loud protests that she had kidnapped his daughter. In the end, despite the icy December conditions, Helen had climbed out of the back window, on top of the lean-to outhouse and made her escape through the yard. She had climbed enough trees in her nature rambles to think scraped knees and broken fingernails a small price to pay for avoiding recapture. Flora had sent her things on the next day when Helen found shelter with Molly. So far, her father had not discovered the hospital in which she was training so had no more leads as to her whereabouts. Flora, for once, was keeping mum. It was stressful though, always half expecting their father to leap out on her from some dark corner. Enough. He had taken too much of her life already without her thinking about him now. 'And how is Des?'

Sebastian folded his hands, elbows on the table, propping his chin as he studied her. 'Doesn't your sister know?'

Helen shrugged. Her sister had been strangely quiet on the subject the last time they had met up at a corner house for tea, closing up like a water-lily bud on a shaded pond. 'She hasn't said.'

Sebastian waited until the waiter had placed their meal in front of them before replying. 'He's more my brother's friend than mine. They are the same age and serve on the same ship. As far as I know, they're well. Neil mentioned him in his last letter. I take it the course of true love is not running smoothly?'

Helen picked up her fork and stirred the potato topping into the gravy. 'I wouldn't know. She really is devoted to him, you know. She isn't all flash, despite outward appearances. She just wants to believe in the possibility of love.'

'And I am sure she will never be without her admirers.'

'That's not love.' She was sharper with him than she intended, but he clearly still dismissed Flora as being without substance.

Chastened, Sebastian sighed. 'I suppose not. Sorry.' He suddenly smiled and topped up their wine glasses. 'My word, Helen, we do have the most extraordinary conversations, don't we? No shallow waters for us. Within five minutes, we are contemplating the nature of families, or love. Tell me more about yourself: do you enjoy your work?'

Serious subjects put to one side, they chatted on inconsequential matters for the rest of the main course. The food was excellent as he had promised and the waiters friendly. Sebastian was exposed as a regular patron. Helen was thoroughly enjoying herself for the first time in a very long while. She was pleased to discover they shared the same taste in reading – Dickens, not Thackeray – and that they both enjoyed the theatre, particularly the comedies of Oscar Wilde.

'I've never been entirely convinced by Gilbert and Sullivan,' Sebastian confided. 'Bit too silly on occasion.'

'Oh, that's what I like about their operettas! The words trip along in sublime nonsense, sometimes with a bite. What is there not to like about them?'

'There's a quality of smugness to them that I can't abide. Perhaps it's my American half coming through, but I sometimes feel they're just too pleased to be English. You, as a good Englishwoman, wouldn't understand.' He winked.

'Actually, you're wrong about that. My mother is German and she's their biggest admirer in our household. Knows all the words which she sings with her heavy accent – it's absolutely priceless when we get her going at Christmas.' A wave of homesickness tumbled through Helen. This December just gone, she had spent the holiday with Flora, celebrating with a very meagre dinner. While their mother was hopeless at protecting her daughters, they realized that she was more of a presence in the home than they had thought, always pulling out all the stops at Christmas, insisting on a tree, carols and a plentiful table. Helen wished Geerta could be a stronger person or in a different marriage.

Sebastian was quick to pick up the change in mood. 'You miss her?'

'Naturally. But I can't have her without him, so regrets are futile.' She gave him a flick of a smile. 'You're not shocked that she is from . . . well, you know?'

'How can I be? Our own royal family is related to the Kaiser and that doesn't stop me being a loyal subject. I hate it when I hear that ordinary people are being attacked just because of their nationality.'

Helen had known Sebastian would not hold her origins against her. He just wasn't the blinkered sort. 'There are whispers that the government might intern all Germans if this war goes on for much longer.'

'I've heard this too. A Bavarian baker near my lodgings in Goodge Street had his windows broken last week, his wife insulted at the market when she went shopping. The mob can turn ugly very quickly, particularly after bad news from the front.' He seemed to regret raising such a grim topic. 'But that won't affect your mother, I hope. Or you and Flora.'

'We'll see. My father finds us all an embarrassment now. Probably rues the day he married out of England. I think it has only served to strengthen his prejudice against foreigners.'

'More fool him. When this stupidity is over, we'll be friends again with Germany, I'm sure.'

'I hope so.'

After the meal, Sebastian ordered coffee for them both.

'May I see your drawings?' Helen gestured to the portfolio leaning against his chair.

Sweetly, he looked flustered by her interest. 'You don't have to, you know. They're nothing special.'

'No, I'd really like to see them. Please.'

He cleared a space on the table and took out a sheaf of paper. 'Just a few bits and bobs of my latest work.'

Helen picked up the first sketch. An old man lay stretched out on a bed, his skin wrinkled like a walnut, his ribs gaunt and stomach concave. The lines were strong, confident.

Sebastian nearly choked and reached out to take it back. 'Perhaps I should have edited them first.'

She shook her head. 'Don't be foolish. I'm a nurse, remember. This is fabulous. I can sense the bones beneath the skin, the wear and tear of life.'

Sebastian relaxed slightly, warming to her praise. 'I really enjoy sketching figures. He was a fascinating old cove. Took to posing like a duck to water and jolly pleased to see himself on paper.'

Helen drew the next picture towards her. This was very different — a landscape but all chopped up into geometrical shapes, tall rectangular trees and boxy houses.

'That's an experiment.' Sebastian waited, expecting a sneer.

'Can you explain it to me?'

'I try to draw the atmosphere of the place, not reproduce it like a photograph. Modern life is breaking up the landscape with roads and railways, houses and pavements. And this war – all those trench defences south of London – cutting up the earth. I can't draw lyrical smooth lines any more; I have to add these edges and fractures.'

'I see.' She ran her finger lightly over a tree, tracing the line. She could tell from the shape that it was a crack willow. The twigs would break with a snap if taken from the branch. A tree given to falling to pieces – he could not have chosen a better symbol.

He gave a sheepish smile. 'And it is all the go too, as I told my little brother. I'm not the only one experimenting in this fashion.'

She turned back to the portraits. He hadn't chopped at these, leaving the people whole. 'I think I like these best.'

'You'd be right to. They are more me, more original. With the landscapes, I think I'm playing with style rather than finding my own expression.' He reached out and placed a finger on the back of her wrist. 'I'd like to draw you.'

Helen flushed. 'Oh.'

'Not like that.' He put the old man away, taking the mortifying image of full nudity out of both their sights. 'Just head and shoulders. I've wanted to since we first met. You have a Raphael look to you. What do you think? Will you consider it?'

No one had ever looked at her quite like Sebastian and now she knew why. 'You think I look like someone from a painting?'

'Yes. Raphael's Madonna to be precise. Renaissance master so you can't get much better than that.'

'Well then, yes. I'm interested to see you work.'

'I have a little room I use as a studio in my flat. Would you come there? It's quieter than college.'

She wondered if it was wise to arrange to meet him alone – it felt rather daring. Looking across the table at his earnest expression, the humour dancing in the depths of his eyes, Helen decided she wanted daring at least once in her life. 'I suppose I can.'

'Saturday afternoon? It's too dark in the evenings to get good light – I've had to black out the skylight – you know, the war regulations.'

'I see. Yes, Saturday – that suits me.'

He grinned. 'I tell you what, I'll take you to the tea dance at the Ritz afterwards to say thank you.'

'Goodness, you must be flush to afford that! I thought artists made it a point of honour to starve in a garret.'

'Not when they're sons of American financiers. Do not fear, Helen, I'll still be able to afford to feed myself next week.'

'Then I'll look forward to it.'

The Somme, 1 July 1916, 1 p.m.

The bullet missed Sebastian by a hair, hitting the mud wall by his head.

'Sniper!' he roared, diving back round the turn in the trench. If you caught the report, then you knew you had lived. The bullet that hit you was the one you never heard in time.

The angle had been high. The German must be under-cover somewhere close by. Snipers liked to lodge in the most unlikely places – up in trees, camouflaged in shell holes. Christ, the man might even be behind them now they had made their advance. Wherever he was, he had turned the next stretch of trench into a death trap. 'Anyone catch the flash?'

The boom of the big guns on the allied side fractured his remarks. The shells wailed overhead and exploded far behind the German lines.

'Up there!' shouted Bentley, pointing to a stump tangled with a mess of barbed wire. Two bodies, one British, one German, dangled on the barrier, ghastly scarecrows.

Sebastian pulled the rifle from his back. 'Cook, poke a helmet round the corner on the end of your bayonet. Rest of you, aim at the tree.'

Cook grabbed a helmet from a corpse at the side of the trench. The poor man looked as if he were praying, having taken his fatal wound and slumped to his knees. Cook wrapped the victim's jacket round the end of his rifle and stuffed the helmet on top, a rapidly fashioned decoy. He then reached forward, letting it lean round the corner like a man warily taking a peek.

Flash-crack from the left side of the trunk. Sebastian's squad all leapt up and fired at the spot. A soldier tumbled to the ground, his leaf camouflage fluttering like wings.

Without waiting for the order to be given, the squad advanced down the next stretch. More gunfire. A man behind Sebastian fell.

Dammit, there had been two snipers, not one. A second soldier down.

Too late to retreat, Sebastian hunched his shoulders and ran on, rushing to get out of range. They couldn't stop to deal with casualties this far forward. The men would have to take their chances until this merry expedition was over and they could send stretcher-bearers for survivors. He could now see the far side of the tree, the uneven shape of a man lying at the fork of what was left of the branches, still firing on the soldiers following behind. Sebastian took aim. The sniper suddenly went slack like a puppet with strings cut, rifle falling from his hand.

'Got 'im, sir. Well done.' Cook stumped past, blood seeping from his upper arm.

Sebastian cast his rifle over his back again, drawing out his revolver – his preferred weapon for close-quarters fighting. 'Did he get you first?'

Cook spat. 'Just a scratch. Not even a Blighty wound. I'll live.'

Just then a hoarse shout came from up ahead. 'Doodle? Is that you?' Captain Williams emerged from a dugout accompanied by a soldier wreathed in German helmet souvenirs.

Sebastian felt almost weak with relief. 'Yes, sir.'

'We hold this line until reinforcements arrive. Can't

risk moving too far beyond our supply lines. Set your men to converting these trenches to face the enemy.'

'Yes, sir.'

Williams came right up to him and clapped him on the back. 'Glad to see you survived. Lost near two-thirds of my men in that first dash.'

Sebastian did a quick head-count of the men he could see. 'I'm down by half. We took out a machine-gun emplacement. I have wounded left behind.'

'As do I. All the same, excellent work. Send two messengers back to company HQ with news of our position. Signals should be catching us up, but until they do the messengers will have to go. They can take any walking wounded with them as long as it doesn't hold them up too much. Tell them to try not to get themselves blown to bits by the German artillery.'

'Sir.' Sebastian saluted.

Williams turned to leave before adding, 'Good job with the snipers by the way. Had me pinned down on this side for near an hour. He played merry hell with my men before we twigged his position. Just couldn't get a bead on him.'

One less German to go home to his wife or mother. It wasn't the first man Sebastian had killed in this war and it did no good wondering about him. It was kill or be killed. 'Thank you, sir.'

With a nod, Williams walked wearily away, a hitch in his step from a wound in the calf. Sebastian checked himself over. No marks except a few barbed-wire scratches. Remarkable considering what they had come through. He turned his attention back to the job in hand, his exhausted troops slumped against the walls. 'Take a breather. Two men either end of this trench on guard, rest of you fifteen minutes' rest but keep alert. Use grenades if you see hide or hair of Fritz coming up on our position. Then we need to turn this round to face the new German front line – fire steps, loopholes – you know the drill.'

They set about their orders. Cook emerged from the dugout where Williams had been pinned down.

''Ere, sir, cop a look at this. These Jerries 'ad electric light and all sorts of comforts in there. Even a little stove. Cuppa tea anyone?'

'I think I love you, Cook.' Sebastian shook his head in amazement at the man's energy.

The cockney laughed. 'Better not tell the missus – she's a jealous sort. Tea coming right up.'

PART TWO

Sketch

8

Sebastian gave his studio a final inspection. Sprigs of winter greenery and pale jasmine stood in the jam jar on the mantelpiece. The red velvet cloth on the couch had been shaken and twitched into place. He could do nothing about the paint splatters on the bare boards and grubby whitewash, but then Helen was expecting an artist's workspace not a parlour. Should he invite her to sit on the couch or the single upright chair? He decided on the sofa; he would need the chair for himself. Catching sight of his mussed-up hair in a mirror he used for self-portraits, he quickly got out a comb and smoothed it straight. That would have to do.

A tapping on the front door three flights down announced his guest's arrival.

'I'll get it!' he called to his landlord as he bounded down the stairs. Mr Thomas had a shifty, troglodyte air which would doubtless scare her off if he answered the door. He made it in record time, undoing the attempt to smooth his hair in his haste. 'Hello.'

Standing two steps down, Helen lifted her chin to look up at him and smiled. 'Hello. Am I on time?'

'Perfect. Come in.' He stood back. Lord, he felt a twit. 'Shall I take your coat?'

He had to admit that it was not very warm in the hall so he was unsurprised when she shook her head. 'I'll keep it on for the moment, if you don't mind.' She did take off her hat though and he hung that on a peg by the front door. It stood out against the row of men's hats.

'You see we are a bachelor establishment.' He cleared his throat. 'So, er, follow me.' He glared at the crack in the door to his left where his landlord, Mr Thomas, was spying on him, one bloodshot brown eye unblinking as it took in the pretty visitor. He shifted to hide Helen from Thomas's suggestive leer. 'Would you like tea first, or shall we begin work directly?'

Helen dug her hands in her pockets. 'Tea would be nice.'

'Let's go into the kitchen so I can make up a tray.'

Sammy Jenkinson happened to be in the room when they entered, darning a sock by the hearth. A slightly built fellow with pale fair hair, he did a double take when he saw a lady in the house. He stood up, pulling his braces over his shoulders in an attempt to make himself decent. 'Miss.'

'Oh, Sammy, sorry to disturb you. This is Miss Sandford. She's sitting for her portrait.'

Sammy stuffed the sock in his pocket and held out a

hand for her to shake. 'So he's conned you into it, has he? Seb's had a go at all of us. Must say his taste in models is improving.'

Helen's face dimpled into a smile. 'That's very kind of you to say so.'

Sebastian felt an irrational spike of jealousy to see her responding to Sammy's gentle flirting. He was pleased that the kettle had recently boiled so they did not have to linger in the kitchen. He quickly loaded a tray, nabbing the biscuit tin from the top shelf. Sammy raised an eyebrow, but did not protest. There was a house rule that the tin was supposed to stay in the kitchen and not migrate to anyone's private rooms.

'Follow me.' Sebastian picked up the tray. 'Sammy, fend off the troll if you can.'

'I'll keep him down here.' Sammy nodded to their visitor. 'Goodbye, Miss Sandford. Nice meeting you, if but briefly.'

'And you,' she replied.

Behind her back, Sammy winked at Sebastian. 'I look forward to seeing the results.'

'Of what?' Her brow creased.

'The sketching.'

Her cheeks went pink. 'Oh, of course.'

Sebastian vowed to throttle Sammy later. He began the journey up the stairs. 'My studio is right at the top, I'm afraid.'

She trailed her fingers over the worn banister. 'You said. For the light.'

'Exactly. Would you mind going first to open the door for me?'

She brushed past him on the narrow landing, a touch of hip and arm against his side. 'Up here?'

'Yes.' He began to wonder if this was wise. He was already entertaining thoughts about her that he knew were quite unworthy. She was like a fire on a cold day, her sweetness drawing him closer. His family did not go in much for shows of affection; he longed to have someone whom he could claim the right to hold near. Not just someone: her. But she was not here for that; she expected him to keep an artist's objectivity.

He put the tray down on the little table by his easel and busied himself pouring the tea. 'Milk, sugar?'

'Just milk.' She was wandering the room, touching the objects he had collected for still-life studies – stones, driftwood, pottery. Pausing in front of a corkboard where he had pinned some recent work, she took note of each one. She lingered longest over the head of a girl.

'Who is this?'

He smiled down at the tray, pleased to hear a note of concern in her question. 'That's Jilly Glanville. I did it for my brother, Neil. He's besotted with her.'

She rewarded him with a vibrant smile. 'She's very pretty.'

'Yes. I thought I'd do a little oil for him, something he can take back with him after his next leave.'

'Serious then?'

'I think so. Hard to say with Neil; he sometimes

surprises me with his choices. Tea.'

She took the cup and saucer and looked around for a seat.

'If you wouldn't mind sitting on the sofa. It will put you in the best light.'

She sat down as directed. 'I'll definitely need that if you are to do anything so flattering to me.'

He took his place on the upright chair, already thinking through the poses he would prefer. He quite liked her as she was, tea held primly in her lap, eyes full of sparkle and none of the suspicion he had seen in them on their first few meetings. Did that mean she was coming to trust him? He hoped so. 'How would you like to see yourself then?'

Helen laughed. 'I'm here for you, not for my vanity.' She waved the teaspoon. 'Do your worst, sirrah.'

'I cannot lie on paper.'

She wrinkled her nose. 'Oh dear, I fear I will be crushed.'

He smiled and took up his pad, putting his own tea aside. 'Quite the opposite. I hope you'll see what I do by the time I've finished.'

She looked sceptical, but gamely finished her tea then placed it on the table. 'I'm ready. How would you like me to sit?'

'Place your elbow on the arm of the sofa, then angle yourself towards me, as if I've just called you and you're looking over your shoulder.' He tapped a pencil against his lips. 'Would you mind taking your jacket off?

Your blouse is a lovely cream colour against your complexion.'

She shrugged off the tweed jacket and shivered. 'March – ugh. I hate spring when it still feels like winter.'

He got up and lit the coals waiting in the grate. He did not normally have a fire during the day up here. 'I'll push the boat out then and make sure you don't get too cold.'

'You don't notice the temperature?'

'Not when I'm working. Yes, that's the pose.' But it wasn't quite perfect. 'Would you wear your hair loose for me?'

Her hands hovered uncertainly for a moment then took the pins from her hair, shaking out the plaits that she had wound round her head. He felt privileged to see her as only those in her close family would know her. 'You're turning me into a Pre-Raphaelite then?'

He laughed. 'Maybe. You have the hair for it.'

'I find their work very beautiful, but somehow not true.'

He picked his favourite pencil. 'You're very astute. Too much romanticism in an unromantic age. Perhaps that's why they did it – to compensate, I mean. The poets too.'

'*She saw the water lily bloom,*' Helen murmured.

'*She looked down to Camelot.*' Sebastian studied her carefully.

'So you remember it from school too?' She picked up the verse again.

'Out flew the web and floated wide,
The mirror crack'd from side to side.'

Helen twirled her hand to his looking-glass which reflected the pair of them sitting a few cautious feet from each other. 'That's the bit I like – the bursting of the bubble. Life invading and taking the Lady of Shalott to her death.'

'So you don't believe in the bubble?' He put his pencil to the paper, making the first stroke.

She shrugged. 'It's not that I don't believe in it; I don't trust it. The love is more often off balance, one person suffering while the other takes.'

'But perfect love drives out fear,' he murmured, already caught up in the drawing. He had found just the right curve for her cheek as it ran into her jaw. Sebastian frowned at his pencil mark, wondering if it were possible to overcome her wariness about love. If not, it did not bode well for his own hopes.

Helen thought a moment then recognized the quotation. 'The Bible now? My, we have travelled far from Tennyson.'

'I never could go very far with him; found he dabbled too much in the shallows for me. Though *In Memoriam* is very fine and heartfelt. I can forgive him much for writing that.' He sketched the bones of her neck, the delicate V at the base of her throat. 'A poet who stares straight at the cruelty of life. "*So careful of the type she seems,*

so careless of the single life – Nature, red in tooth and claw" –
brilliant. I think he was the first poet to grapple with
Darwin and what his theory means for us.'

'And what do you think it means?'

Sebastian looked down at what he had drawn, for a
moment seeing the bones as they would appear in a fossil,
human life extinct like so many other species before them.
Individual life seemed so fragile while Nature romped
on; yet his own feelings for Helen were growing into
something stronger – a protest against the cold calculation
that saw us as nothing but a step on the ladder of life. 'I
think it means we should value our existence as Nature
won't. Yes, that was the point of writing the poem.' As
he would value her if she would let him. He caressed the
line he had drawn, wishing he had the right to trace the
same path on the original.

'He also understands grief, I think. Not that I've ever
lost anyone close to me.'

Sebastian felt a shiver down his spine. In these days, it
was tempting fate to say such a thing. 'I hope we don't
learn how true he is to the experience.'

Sobered by the thought, Helen dropped her eyes to
her lap. 'Yes, you're right.'

They sat in silence for a long while. Sebastian knew the
sketch was going well. He felt each pencil mark now as a
touch of his fingers on her skin, a worshipping of her spirit
and unconscious beauty. It was very distracting – his heart
was racing far more than it should for a sketching assignment. 'So, do you have a favourite poet then?'

She shook her head slightly. 'Oh sorry, I moved.'

'No, it's not a problem. I'm almost finished.'

'Do you then, have a favourite?'

Screwing up his courage, he made her an offering of words that spoke of what he felt.

> *'I wonder, by my troth, what thou and I*
> *Did, till we loved?'*

'Oh yes, I love that one! John Donne, isn't it?'

He held her eyes. *Listen, Helen, listen to my heart.*

> *'And now good morrow to our waking souls,*
> *Which watch not one another out of fear.'*

She broke the gaze and looked down again.

Ah. She was listening.

> *'My face in thine eye, thine in mine appears*
> *And true plain hearts do in the faces rest.'*

He turned the page around, willing her eyes to meet his, for her to be caught in the same longing that he was. 'Here, have a look at yourself.'

Her eyes flicked up and her mouth opened in surprise. 'I'm . . . well, that isn't me, is it? I'm regal!'

He glanced down. She did look like the queen of heaven in her quiet dignity. 'I draw as I see.'

She rubbed her arms nervously which he took as a sign

that she was feeling the same tension, attraction wrestling with fear of rejection. 'I wish I felt as you see. Thank you: it's lovely.'

A little more confident, even hopeful that they might progress to more direct discussion of feelings, Sebastian checked his watch. He just needed time to wear down her resistance. 'If you're not bored rigid, would you mind posing for more?'

'I'm in your hands. I have my bribe to earn.'

'Tea at the Ritz demands more than one sketch. Now for something less formal. Would you recline on the sofa, propped up at this end, angled towards me?'

She kicked off her sensible shoes and wriggled her toes in her stockings. 'I feel silly.'

'You look lovely. As ever.'

A pretty rose-blush bloomed on her cheeks, but characteristically she undercut the compliment with a joke at her own expense. His Helen was not used to accepting praise. 'You've obviously not seen me at the hospital after a hard day on the wards.'

He smiled and shook his head.

Obediently, Helen took the pose he requested and he set back to work.

The Somme, forward medical station, 1 July 1916, 4 p.m.

It was getting dark and still the casualties kept coming. Helen took a quick break for tea and a sandwich, leaning against the wall in the nurses' tiny rest room. Mary

Henderson came in, weaving on her feet. Tall and thin like one of the French poplars that lined the roads of Flanders, Mary looked close to falling. Her glasses were misted with tiny specks of blood; she took them off and cleaned them frantically.

'I don't know if I can stand it, Helen,' she whispered. 'That's the third man in an hour to die on the table. What's the point of putting them through all this pain?' Her shoulders hunched. 'God, he was only sixteen, that last one. Too young.' She looked up, tears streaming down her cheeks. 'He thought I was his mother. Said something – I'm not sure what – and then was gone.'

Helen bit the inside of her cheek to stop her own sobs. 'He probably said he loved her. Most do. At the end.'

Mary managed a hoarse laugh. 'Actually, I think he said, "Don't wake me up so early, Mum."'

Helen brushed her hand across her eyes. 'It hurts, doesn't it?'

Mary pressed her hands to her breast. 'Like a rusty knife sawing at my ribs. I can't go back out there.'

Helen put down her cup and straightened her shoulders. 'Yes, you can. They are relying on you. There are those that will survive because of what you do here; and those that don't will bless you for trying.' She poured a cup of now very strong tea. 'Here, get this down you. Almost as good as a shot of rum, I've been told.'

Mary sipped and gave a trembling smile. 'Who told you that?'

'Sebastian. My . . . my friend.' Mary nodded; she knew

about her room-mate's soldier at the front. 'He's in the 1st Somersets. He wrote that tea is his second favourite drink these days, after the rum ration. Doesn't think the army would function without it.'

'My mother wrote to tell me that it's getting hard to find in London and very expensive.' They drank in silence for a moment, relieved to be contemplating something as normal as buying groceries in England. The noise and groans outside seemed to recede, leaving them in an island out of time and place. 'Do you think they know, back home, about all this?'

Helen closed her eyes. 'They can't understand, no matter what tales they hear, they can't. The men don't tell the truth, afraid to burden their families. Every soldier is "killed instantly", according to their commanding officer, or missing in action, rather than blown to bits.'

Grimacing, Mary bit into a slice of bread, tearing off the crust. 'That's a joke.'

'I think it's meant as a kindness.'

Mary nodded, swallowing with difficulty. It was hard to eat, but they made themselves do so. 'Yes, I think you're right. There are some things no one should know. And some are so badly hurt I wonder if we do them a favour patching them up. Better to give them a couple of those and let them drift off.' She gestured to the locked medicine store with its supply of morphine capsules.

Helen had felt that temptation herself when despair had taken her in its grip like an undertow in the sea of misery in which they swam. The nurses took it in turns to hold each other's heads out of the water. It was enough to know that one of them still believed in what they did to keep the others from drowning. This was her turn to find the right words. 'I know what you mean, but still I'd rather not be the one to decide. Who knows what someone will make of their life, even with terrible injuries to deal with? Sometimes they're better off than the ones whose wounds are inside.'

Mary put her cup down, relieved to hear the words she needed to patch up her shredded confidence. 'Are you sure you're twenty, Helen? You sound much older.'

Actually, she had just turned eighteen, but no one was to know that. 'I've grown up since being here.'

'You can say that again. I feel as if I've aged a decade. I thought I was coming out to mop fevered brows and carry the lamp through the wards like a latter-day Florence Nightingale, not that.' She gestured to the horrors beyond the door.

'So glamorous, our life, isn't it?' Helen straightened her scarf, ready for another bout. The cracks papered over again.

'Oh yes, a real "aba daba honeymoon",' said Mary wryly, quoting the popular song everyone was enjoying back home. 'Shall we?' She opened the door, the sounds kicking back in at full volume.

Before returning to theatre, Helen sought out the young soldier from Sebastian's regiment. He had got through his operation and was now lying on a pallet bed in one of the wards. Once a cowshed, even under the odour of disinfectant it was possible to smell the previous inhabitants. It didn't remind her of dirt; it recalled wholesome countryside, milkmaids and rambles on spring days. She knelt down at his side and took his hand.

'How are you, soldier?'

He squeezed her hand. The operation had taken his voice; she hoped he might get it back eventually.

'I see you're from the Somersets. Do you know Lieutenant Trewby?'

The soldier's eyes widened and he managed a nod.

She put a restraining hand on his shoulder. 'Don't move, please. I should leave you in peace.'

He pressed her knuckles, clearly not wanting her to go.

'It's just that I was wondering if he's all right.'

A flicker of a smile lit the boy's face and he squeezed her hand once firmly.

'Is that a "yes"?'

He repeated the gesture.

'Thank you. I think you've got your Blighty wound. It's home to family for you.' She checked his tag. 'You'll be put on a transport, then a train to one of the ports.' She made to rise, but he would not let go of her hand. He was staring at her face intently, waggling his eyebrows.

'Oh, me? I'm Nurse Sandford. Helen Sandford.'

He closed his eyes, content now he had her answer.

She got up to find the matron standing by her.

'Should you not be in theatre, nurse?' Sister Richards asked.

'I was just on my way, matron.'

She flicked through her list of patients. 'What were you and Miss Henderson doing in the nurses' room for so long?'

Stopping each other cracking under the strain. 'The doctors sent us for a break as we had worked through the lunch hour.'

'I see. You'd better get back then. I don't know how we're going to manage. You've worked two shifts already, I think?'

'Yes.'

'You must go off at six and get some sleep. If you work much longer, you'll start to make mistakes, or forget your duty.' *If you haven't already* seemed to be the implicit meaning of her statement.

'Yes, matron.' Helen hurried back to the operating theatre, feeling the chill of the matron's disapproval at her back. She rarely stepped out of line and it struck her as unfair to be caught where she should not be on the one occasion she let her worry for Sebastian lure her away. Still, there were far more important things to occupy her now than a slight infraction of the rules.

9

The Ritz Hotel, London, 20 March 1915, 4 p.m.

Tea at the Ritz. Helen could hardly contain herself contemplating the treat that awaited her behind the Palladian facade of the hotel. Admittedly it was showing somewhat less of its pre-war splendour, many of the clientele in khaki, no lights allowed to spill on to the street, but still the foyer was the finest place she had ever stepped inside. There was a crystalline glitter to the place – marble pillars wiped clean of any smudges, wall mirrors buffed to a state of perfect reflection, floor shining despite the dirt inevitably tracked in by the visitors.

The colours chosen for the drapery and walls in the Palm Court were light and airy like the golden sponge cake and scones topped with cream arranged on elegant stands. The tea services were all silver, the cups bone china. Since coming to the capital, Helen had come to realize that most of it was grubby and dog-eared; finally this was the London she had read about in the silver fork novels of the Victorians, the kind of place society would go to see and be seen. And Sebastian was taking it all completely in his stride, tipping the doorman smoothly, asking for a table without apology or hesitation. Grandson of an earl, indeed, and she the daughter of a solicitor's clerk – what was she thinking?

The waiter seated them near the string quartet, palm fronds separating them from everyone else in a little jungle clearing of their own. The dance floor was sprinkled with couples moving in dreamy harmony.

Sebastian ordered tea then sat back and smiled at her. 'I think you've earned your reward. I was really pleased with the sketches. I hope you were too.'

Helen's only criticism was that she feared he had flattered her too much. 'They were lovely. You're very talented.'

'Strange kind of skill to have in these days.' His eyes followed a captain in the Guards who was squiring his companion round the floor in a neat one-step.

It was not hard to guess where his thoughts had gone. Helen felt a twinge of alarm. This parasite war was sucking up more and more men, sending home the husk of their bodies. Many were finding their way to her hospital, gentle, ordinary men who had lived through terrors that left them with nightmares. The wards were changing, common diseases replaced by serious war-related injuries. There was no hiding the full cost of this conflict from the medical staff who had to pick up the pieces. She did not want Sebastian pushed into that horror. 'I hope that you don't feel ashamed of something you do so well.'

Sebastian rubbed the back of his neck. 'Not ashamed exactly. Irrelevant.'

'Beauty and art are never pointless.'

'Even when your country is at risk? Can I sit and let others defend it, like my brother and Des?'

She tweaked the light-brown material of her skirt straight, unsure what to say. The social pressure was building to a steamy heat and every man of military age must be feeling it; the jungle drums of newspapers, posters, even the sermons on Sunday, beat loudly and insistently, not letting them forget what was expected of them. She did not want to see Britain defeated any more than the next Englishwoman, but selfishly she wished it did not have to be done by those she knew.

Sebastian had taken her silence as agreement. 'You must think me an awful prevaricator.'

She looked up, startled. 'I think nothing of the sort.'

He gave a rueful laugh. 'Then I must be thinking it then. Let's not spoil our tea with my dilemma. It will resolve itself soon enough, I fear. Would you like to dance?'

Her gaze slid across the couples on the dance floor. 'I'm not very good.'

'Neither am I so that means we won't be disappointed in each other.' He stood and held out a hand. 'Come.'

She let him steer her into a gap at the edge of the floor then, like swimmers waiting their turn to dive into the lagoon, they plunged in. He was not as bad as he had led her to believe, confidently guiding her, even if he did not have the flair of a truly gifted dancer. She did not disgrace herself either, so was able to enjoy the sensation of being held. Her life was so empty of human touch that the demands of the dance – the warmth of his palm on her back and the strength of his hand holding hers – felt overwhelmingly intimate. She began to notice little details, like how her head came up to his chin. If she dared, she could move forward and lay her cheek against his heart. A mad impulse to seek out the steady pulse of life seized her – a move she was sure would embarrass them both. With difficulty, she crushed the urge.

He reversed direction to avoid another couple, helping Helen to put firmly behind her that odd moment. Existence was such a strange thing. Living alone, touching others only to nurse them, it was easy to forget that she was first a girl, one who needed to feel another person's warmth. And not just anyone; it was Sebastian she wanted.

But the middle of the dance floor at the Ritz was not the place to announce that, she admitted to herself with a frustrated sigh.

Too soon, the quartet came to the end of the piece and the dancers stopped to give them a polite round of applause. Sebastian glanced over to their table.

'Our tea has arrived.' He looped her hand round his elbow and led her back, stepping out of the shallows and into the refuge of their palm clearing. 'Thank you for putting up with me as a partner.'

Helen smiled, squeezing his arm. 'You were more than adequate – as I'm sure you know.'

'So my mother's lessons were not completely wasted?'

'I'd say not.' Helen sat down, aware that her heart was still beating faster than normal and her face was probably flushed. She could not blame the exercise; it was a mixture of nerves and excitement as she revelled in her situation. As a little girl, she had dreamed of her grown-up self in such a place: attending a tea dance with a handsome young man. She just wished she could be the fairy-tale character she had imagined for Sebastian rather than the prosaic girl dressed in brown and cream beset with random thoughts about the nature of life. Did he know, she wondered, that when he smiled, creases appeared either side of his mouth like happy brackets? His jaw was squarer than hers, neck much thicker. Why did men get that as they grew while women remained slighter, more rounded? Would life be easier facing it with a frame that could withstand a blow or two? Would she be as confident as he was if she had more angles to her, a chin that confronted the world with a blunt claim on its right to be there?

He nudged the cake stand towards her. 'What are you thinking about? You've got an odd look in your eye.'

Glad he had not heard her thoughts, Helen flushed, making a show of choosing a scone and jam from the top layer of the stand. 'I was just wondering what it would be like to draw you. Have you ever done a self-portrait?'

Sebastian tweaked his own chin. 'More times than I can count until I'm quite sick of this old phiz. I'm the only model I can rely on to be available at all hours.' Their eyes met through the frame made by the handle of the cake stand. 'If the experience wasn't too ghastly, would you be prepared to sit for me again?'

Yes, yes, please, she wanted to shout. Instead, she settled for a reply that did not expose her eagerness too embarrassingly. 'I enjoyed myself, so yes.'

'You must be busy at the hospital these days.'

'Not too busy to spare a few hours for a friend and encourage a talented artist.' She took a bite of scone, squashed a little cream on her nose and quickly dabbed it off. Why did that kind of thing always have to happen to her when she was trying to impress?

Though his gaze lingered on the place the cream had been, he kindly made no remark about her faux pas. 'Thank you. I think you help bring out the best in me.'

She was thrilled he thought that. Surely he must like her, more than just a little? 'I'm glad to be of assistance.'

They parted at the Underground, Helen going on the branch line to Highbury, Sebastian taking the train in the opposite direction down to Goodge Street. She had adamantly refused his escort home, saying she travelled around London on her own every day so did not need to change that now. He had not pushed. Instead, he spent the journey congratulating himself on managing his day with her fairly well. She had been a pleasure to sketch and she had enjoyed the Ritz, though it had daunted her at first. He had loved her shy embarrassment when she had cream on the end of her nose and had had to stop himself leaning over to kiss it away. And he had even thought up an excuse to see her again. Soon he would have to indicate that his interest in her was not just as an artist, but he sensed she would be slow to cotton on, too innocent of her own attraction.

Sebastian arrived back at his lodgings expecting to find that most of the others had gone out to their habitual Saturday haunts. Instead, he found Sammy waiting for him in the kitchen. He came out when he heard the key in the lock, hands dug deep in his trouser pockets. Even more unusual, the troglodyte's door was shut.

'Evening, Sammy.' Sebastian waved, eager to go back to his studio to study his day's work.

'Um, Seb old chap, I thought you ought to know – a telegram was delivered earlier. I put it under your door. Didn't want you to miss it.'

Sebastian's heart squeezed, turning into a tight nut of anguish in his chest. He could anticipate no good reason for a telegram. 'Thank you.' He changed direction to go to his bedroom.

'I'm here if you need anything,' Sammy said softly.

'Yes, thanks. Right.' Could he do this? Could he mount those stairs or should he turn round and go back out and try his entry again? If he did so, perhaps there would be no Sammy, no message waiting for him.

'Do you want me to come with you?' Sammy had not moved.

'No, no.' He cleared his throat. 'Probably nothing.' They both knew that was a lie. He climbed to the first floor and opened his bedroom door. It was to the rear of the house, with a nice view over a small city garden. He had always liked going in before.

The telegram. On the lino like a bitter pill he had to take. He picked it up and slid his finger under the flap.

Neil lost at sea. Come home. Pa

Helen did not go to Highbury as she had told Sebastian. Excited by her day, she gave in to the impulse to drop in on her sister at the theatre, thinking that she would be mightily unlucky to cross paths with her father on an unplanned visit like this. The doorman waved her in with a broad smile.

''Ow 'ave you been keepin', Miss Sandford?' he asked kindly.

'Very well, thank you, Mr Jones. And yourself?'

'All good, except for this blasted war. Too old to enlist myself, but my three boys 'ave gone. Proud of them, I am.'

'And rightly so. No trouble for my sister over the last few months?'

He shook his head. 'Your dad has been up once or twice, but he's always waited to be invited in, not like that first time.'

'Good. And I suppose you haven't seen him tonight?'

'Not this evenin', miss.'

Her mind set at rest, she ducked inside. The performance was about to begin and she had high hopes of seeing all her old friends in the dressing rooms, perhaps even helping out like she used to do. Her entry into the chorus girls' area was greeted with shrill exclamations of delight. Toots smudged lipstick on both her cheeks this time and a couple of others whisked off her hat and coat like magicians, making her relinquish them before she even thought to do so.

Sitting at her mirror, Flora waited for Helen to approach. She scooted round, knees together, her body draped in a fetching rose-pink silk dressing gown. 'Darling, lovely to see you. Is everything all right?' She dropped the last cosmetics back in her vanity case. She looked beautiful as always, if a little flushed, fuller around the face than Helen remembered. The other girls tactfully made space around them so the two sisters could catch up.

'Five minutes!' called the assistant stage manager outside.

'I haven't timed this very well, have I?' Helen kissed her sister on the cheek. 'And yes, everything's fine. I've just been to tea at the Ritz.'

Flora's squawk attracted the attention of the rest of the room. 'The Ritz! My little sister!'

'Oooh!' groaned Toots, dipping into the conversation over Flora's shoulder. 'I'm green with envy.' She fluttered an emerald spray of ostrich plumes at Helen. 'How was it?'

'Divine.' Helen hugged herself.

'And the company?' Flora arched an eyebrow. 'I take it a young gentleman took my sister there?'

'He wasn't half bad either.' Helen perched on a stool and nudged Flora's knee. 'You remember him, Flora, Des's friend?'

'Oh yes, Soulful Sebastian. Des is very close to his brother; they serve on the same ship.' She pressed Helen's fingers. 'Good for you!'

'I say,' giggled Toots. 'If he can afford to take you to the Ritz, he's worth a second glance. What does he do?'

'Art student,' Helen supplied.

Toots's face fell. 'Oh well.'

'From an American financier's family,' added Flora. 'My sister is not a fool, Toots.'

Toots looked at Helen with new appreciation. 'You don't say. Well, if he's handsome, rich and good company, are you sure you don't want to pass him on down the line to those less fortunate than yourself?' She adjusted the bodice of her costume, pushing her perky breasts up a little higher.

'If you don't mind, Toots, I'll keep him to myself just for the present, but I'll bear your request in mind,' Helen promised with mock solemnity. She had no intention of giving up Sebastian – not ever.

A tap at the door. 'Two minutes, ladies!' thundered the assistant stage manager.

Toots slipped off her wrapper with a sigh, revealing her costume in its full feathered glory. 'I hope you stay around, Sandy.'

'I think I might. What on earth are you doing tonight?'

'Some silly piece called "Birds of a feather",' explained

Flora, shimmying out of her dressing gown to expose her own outfit of blue. She resembled no bird Helen had ever studied. Grimacing at her sister's reaction, Flora placed a kiss on the top of Helen's head. 'I know – it's frightful. Do stay, Sandy. I've got something to tell you.' Moving off, she brushed her fingers affectionately over where she had kissed.

Catching sight of a flash, Helen grabbed her hand. 'Oh my.' Her sister was wearing a little diamond ring on her third finger. 'Des?'

'Who else? Are you pleased?'

'Oh, it's wonderful! I'm astonished . . . and delighted.'

Flora frowned slightly. 'Astonished? Why, didn't you think he would come up to scratch for a girl like me?'

Helen wondered how she had managed to offend her sister so easily. 'No, no, I didn't mean it like that. I'm surprised because I hadn't known that you'd had the time to get really serious with him.'

Flora shrugged. 'The war. It concentrates the mind.'

'I suppose it would.' The dressing room was now empty. 'Hadn't you better go?'

'Yes, I must. Don't leave – there's more I need to tell you.'

Helen passed the first number quietly going about her old duties, tidying up and straightening the dressing table. She allowed herself to imagine Flora's wedding – a beautiful dress from some pre-war chest in the attic, a country church, a happy family. Blanking out her own parents, she guessed that Des's own family would be tall blond Vikings like him. The children of such a marriage would be gorgeous – it all made perfect sense even if Flora was from a lower social bracket than her in-laws. They would no doubt fall in love with her when they met her just as their son had. Maybe they had been introduced already? She had seen so little of Flora of late that was entirely possible. The only drawback was that she might actually have to spend the day with her own parents, either that or miss her sister's wedding. Still, that was a problem for tomorrow, not one to dwell on and take the shine off this wonderful news.

For the second act, Helen watched from the side. It was then she noticed something odd about her sister. She was, well, to put it bluntly, spilling out of her costumes. Inches now sat on the bust and waist that had not been there when Helen last sewed for her. A suspicion began to form in Helen's mind what the additional news might be. It would explain a lot.

When the curtain fell, Helen helped Flora change. She had to pull strongly to release the hooks and eyes on the corset.

'Would you like me to let out your costumes for you?' she said quietly. 'I noticed that they didn't fit you well.'

Flora bit her lip then nodded. 'Thank you. I'd be grateful.' Checking no one was near, she held Helen's gaze, deep blue meeting frank brown. 'You know, don't you?'

'I . . . I guessed. When?'

Flora blushed. 'I think it will come in August. I'll have to give up work soon before it becomes too obvious.'

Helen folded up the costumes to take away for alteration. 'I can get these back to you by Monday morning. Will that do?' Her heart was pounding, but she managed to act as if the news were nothing too shattering.

Nodding, Flora slipped into her gown. 'I've written to Des. When he knows, I'm sure he'll make it right.'

That presented Helen with an unpalatable possibility. 'The ring – it really is from him?'

Flora looked annoyed now. 'Of course! What do you take me for? We made plans, promises, but it was to wait until he came back from the war. Mother Nature had other ideas. He'll be pleased.' She said the latter more as if to convince herself than Helen.

Dread settled on Helen like a cloud taking the warmth of the sun on a spring day. She could foresee so many possible problems, but that was not what her sister needed to hear now. 'Well, I'm delighted for you.' She squeezed Flora in a hug. 'Really thrilled. All will be made fine and dandy with a little visit to the vicar on Des's next leave and then you can enjoy the rest of it.' She felt like an actress mouthing lines she did not believe.

Flora let her forehead drop on Helen's shoulder for a second, before regaining the steel in her spine. 'Exactly. This is good news. Lord knows what I'll do with a screaming infant, but I'm sure, like millions of women before me, I'll find out soon enough.'

Helen could not imagine her beautiful butterfly sister with a baby either. She was made to flutter free of such nets. 'It will be easier to love when you hold it.'

'Let's hope so. Just at the moment I'm finding it damned inconvenient, if you must know.' The bitter undertone was unmistakable; she was making the best of it, but inside Flora was terrified. Helen wished she could do more to help, but this was one journey Flora would have to take on her own. At least she would have Des to help her.

They both put on their coats and said their farewells to the other girls.

'Come back soon, Sandy!' called Toots as she draped a fur stole round her shoulders. For all her teasing about suitors, it looked as if her own luck in that department had changed.

'If I can.'

'And only if your handsome, rich artist hasn't spirited you off to his bower of bliss.'

'I'll still try and fit you in between bliss and bedpans, don't you worry.'

Toots laughed. 'If I had a wealthy suitor on my line, I wouldn't be working my fingers to the bone in a hospital.'

'You're counting the chickens before they hatch, Toots. See you soon.'

'Make sure you get some rest tomorrow, Flora,' Toots added in a gentler tone. 'It's been a bit of a week for us.'

She knows, thought Helen.

'Yes, you too.' Flora proudly straightened her shoulders and left, trailing some of her usual confidence.

'Look after her,' Toots muttered as Helen passed. Helen nodded and closed the door.

IO

White Towers, near Taunton, 21 March 1915

Sebastian emerged from the family parlour, leaving the sobbing women behind for a moment while he caught his breath. He leaned forward, facing the wall, head hanging between his arms. His mother was inconsolable, his Aunt Hermione almost as bad. Mrs Glanville, their near neighbour and mother of Jilly, the girl Neil had loved so much and for so long, had not been much help. Coming over to show her support, she had rapidly succumbed to tears, mourning the loss of the match she had worked so hard to sponsor as well as the lost boy. The three women, all friends from the same generation of debutantes, perhaps found some solace in each other, but Sebastian was finding the display of their distress too much to witness. He did not disapprove of their way of grieving; he just struggled to be left on the outside. Men were supposed to be stern, keep their emotions locked down, but how to do that when his best friend of childhood, his big brother, had been snatched away?

The house was silent elsewhere, the staff going about

their business like ghosts. They tried to make up for the gaping hole left in the family by performing their duties with renewed diligence. The parquet floor was beeswaxed, the surfaces dust free, the stair carpet brushed to velvet smoothness. It was all so bloody pointless. Sebastian did not know what to do with the ugly emotions swirling inside him. His father had escaped to take a solitary walk on the Quantock Hills, his grief too deep for words or even company. Steven was at school and only expected home later that week for the memorial service; he had to be feeling wretched, but it might be better for him to be spared the first few raw days. As for himself, Sebastian wanted to howl and rage and smash things, but instead he found himself passing round tea and making absolutely stupid small talk that circled the same few facts. Neil's ship, the HMS *Irresistible*, had sunk in the Mediterranean two days ago while taking part in the Gallipoli expedition. It struck a mine near the narrows of the Dardanelles. The crew transferred to the *Ocean*, which then met the same fate. Between the mines and the shelling from a nearby Turkish fort, it was a miracle that most of the crew from the two ships had been rescued. Except, that was, for Neil and Des who had both perished in the first explosion. Their CO had sent a message that they died instantly – that was some comfort. Not much, but some.

A through breeze blew the door ajar.

'Why did it have to be my boy?' his mother asked for the hundredth time.

Yes, why him when others had been saved? But Sebastian knew war did not play favourites.

'It's too cruel, too cruel,' murmured Aunt Hermione.

The family's butler, Pennington, slipped out of the door leading to the servants' quarters, bearing yet another tray of tea. His usually lugubrious face had sagged into even graver lines. He had known and loved Sebastian and his brothers in his own way since they were born, having served Lady Mabel, their mother, all her life, first as an under butler at the family pile, Bewley House, then as butler at White Towers when she returned here from America. He stopped when he spotted Sebastian.

'Can I get you anything, sir?' he asked.

A day of oblivion would be welcome. 'No, thank you, Pennington.' Sebastian opened the front of the silver carriage clock that sat on the hallway table and stilled the little pendulum, not really sure why he was doing so except that the frantic ticking was driving him insane.

'I'll just take the tea to her ladyship then.'

'Yes, of course. Perhaps you could tell my mother that I will return in an hour. I'm just going out to the stables.'

'Very good, sir.'

In the refuge of the humble red-brick stable block hidden behind the arrogant honey stone frontage of the main house, Sebastian sank down in the stall that held the motorbike. It made a strange companion to the two carriage horses, brought back out of retirement since fuel was hard to obtain for their Packard – a beautiful limousine that his father had had shipped over from America in 1913. That was now mouldering under a tarpaulin, waiting for more favourable days. They had a few fuel cans in reserve for the bike so Des had given permission for it to be housed in Somerset for the year while he served in the Mediterranean, little thinking that he would not be coming personally to reclaim it. Sebastian wondered what he should do with it now. It was an open-frame Douglas drop-handlebar racing bike that was worth at least fifty pounds; Des's family would have to be asked. Perhaps he should go down to the memorial service for Des, see if the right moment arose to make enquiries. He could even ride it there. He would like to attend as Neil's representative.

My God, realized Sebastian, *does Flora even know?*

He could not bear to think of Helen's sister left in ignorance, to read about Des's demise in the newspapers. He would send a telegram to Helen; the news would be better coming from her than from a stranger. Kicking the bike off its stand, he started it up and roared out of the stable, straw flying from under the wheels.

At the telegraph desk in the post office in Taunton, Sebastian struggled to find the right words to put on the blank form he had been given. In the end he settled for *Bad news. Des gone down with Neil in Med.* Helen would know he intended her to tell her sister so there was no need to add that. He pushed it across the counter.

The clerk's eyes softened as he calculated the cost of the message by counting the words. 'That'll be sixpence, sir.'

Sebastian dropped the coins on top of the message and

turned to leave. He finally knew what he wanted to do: he was enlisting. The Germans and their allies had taken his brother; he was going to see what he could do to even the score.

The Somme, 1 July 1916, 4.30 p.m.

'I think Jerry's realized we're 'ere,' Cook said laconically as a shell exploded near their position in the dugout. It was followed by three more in rapid succession. The battery-powered light flickered as earth trickled from the ceiling.

They had only advanced a few hundred yards since the morning and already their new territory was being contested. The hope of the decisive break through the German lines was fast dissipating.

Cook passed Sebastian a tin cup of the petrol-smelling tea he had brewed from the supplies left behind by the last occupants. ''Ere you go, sir, *tray bone*, as the Frenchies say. 'Ow long do you reckon we're gonna be here?'

Sebastian picked a clod of earth out of his mug, too exhausted to feel revulsion, but God knows what that soil contained after so much fighting. 'We have to wait for the relief.'

Cook climbed the few steps to the entrance and stuck his head outside. Sebastian heard fragments of a conversation with the men on guard then Cook returned and sat on the bottom stair. 'No sign, sir. Can't say I'll be sorry to say goodbye-ee to our latest digs.'

Sebastian smiled grimly at the joke. What had happened to the wave upon wave of following troops they had been promised?

'But Jerry knows 'ow to make a decent place, doesn't 'e? Better than the one we were in this morning.' Cook approved of the neatly constructed den, patting the walls with admiration. 'This'll last unless one of them whizz-bangs lands a bullseye.'

Sebastian was uninterested in German carpentry skills. He pulled his notebook out from his leg wrappings and leafed through the pages. He wanted to draw Cook, capture the cockney's resilience even on this most hellish of days. Taking a stub of pencil from his top pocket, he made a quick sketch.

'Can I 'ave a butchers?' Cook asked, after a few minutes had passed.

Sebastian turned the page to face him.

'Stone the crows, that's amazin'!' Cook scratched his chin. 'I need a shave.'

'Don't we all.' Like the rest of the men, Sebastian dreamed of a bath, shave, fresh clothes with no lice or fleas. To take his mind off his discomfort, he leafed through the other faces in his notebook. Helen – there she was, her features filling at least half the pages. He paused at a copy of the one he had done that first time in his studio, then again on the riverbank and at a table somewhere. The Ritz? No, he hadn't had a pad with him then. It must have been later. He peered at the little note he had made, hard to read in the poor light. Bramley. Oh

God, yes. That ghastly time at Des's memorial service. No wonder Helen looked so sad in that picture. He turned back to the one of her smiling sleepily at him as she lay in the spring sunshine – that was his favourite.

Flipping a few more pages, he came across ones of his family. All done before the ship went down. Neil, hale and hearty in his cricket whites, prominent ears, bold face, eyes sparkling as he made some off-colour joke to Des and him; Steven, the family scholar, frowning as he read some thick tome, twiddling his hair as he did so; his mother, smiling coolly as she posed for his attention (she refused to be drawn unawares, insisted on choosing her own stance and wearing her pearl choker); his father, genial smile, thick greying tawny hair brushed back from his forehead, arms folded comfortably across his broad chest, amused by his wife and her airs. Sebastian gazed longest at Steven's picture. He wished he could stop the clock on his little brother's growing. Rising sixteen, it wouldn't be long before he would be facing the same pressure to join up as Sebastian had. Pray God he had the sense to delay it as long as possible. It would break their parents to lose another son and Sebastian knew his own chances of surviving the battle were touch and go.

The next thing Sebastian recalled was being flat on his back, unable to see anything, earth in his mouth and nose. Panic hit him like the bombshell he had not even heard. He was buried alive. Christ, he was going to die here by inches, the worst possible death.

Time stretched endlessly on the rack. He shifted his

head to one side, finding a pocket of air by his left cheek. The earth on top of him was loosely packed; the ceiling planks had caved in, but done some of the job of keeping him from being completely crushed. Then, miraculously, he felt a hand on his ankle. He kicked vigorously to show he was alive. The answering squeeze told him help was on its way. Trying to calm his racing heart, he took an inventory of his body. His left hand still held something – yes, the notebook. His right was wrapped round a pencil. He was bowed back in an awkward shape, head and feet lower than his middle, like St Peter being crucified upside down. The stool he had been sitting on must still be under him somewhere. No screaming pain, no numbness, he began to hope he had not been too badly injured. As long as he kept his head, he should survive. He began to count slowly to a hundred. He reached it and carried on going.

Rescue came at two thousand and arrived from overhead. Planks shifted, sprinkling yet more dirt in his eyes. He closed them so missed the moment when the afternoon sky appeared above. He was hauled by his jacket, thrown over a man's shoulder and carried clear of the remains of the dugout. Bentley checked him over briskly while Norton offered him a flask. Gasping, Sebastian took a swig and spat the earth from his mouth.

'All right, sir?' Norton asked anxiously.

Wiping his eyes, Sebastian saw quickly that he was fortunate among the casualties. Several men who had been just beyond the dugout had been obliterated, a crater left where they had stood on sentry duty. 'Not injured.

Bruised only.' He stuffed the notebook in his jacket pocket then gingerly felt his ribs. 'How many men?'

'Five, sir. Three in a direct hit; two beating back a German squad who rushed us, trying to get this bit of prime estate back. Privates Jones, Dalworth, Sugden in the blast; Hoxton and Lance-Corporal Taylor in the counter-attack.'

'The enemy?'

'All accounted for. They won't come calling again in a hurry.'

'Cook?'

'Bit worse off than you.' Bentley helped Sebastian regain his feet. 'Took a piece of shrapnel to the head and is swearing like a fishwife now he's regained his senses. We think his arm is broken.'

It was unlikely stretcher-bearers would come this far forward, not while the shelling carried on without pause. They would have to evacuate Cook themselves when their relief arrived. 'Make him comfortable. See if Fritz has left us a stretcher.'

'Already seen to, sir. Couple of planks and a bit of canvas – we've made him an A1 stretcher.' Bentley grinned. 'Not that the stubborn bugger appreciates it.'

Sebastian hobbled down the remains of the trench, having to climb over mounds of earth where the shell had destroyed the embankment. He still had enough men to guard the little stretch of territory they had claimed, but they were all shaken and tired. Now they knew the Germans had found the range of their trench, there was the ever-present threat of sudden annihilation from the skies. It was enough to wear even the bravest man's nerves thin. He reached the man at the end of their line, a mill-worker from Manchester called Joe Hadley. He looked spooked, his lips moving continually in some silent prayer or monologue as he guarded the bomb stop of barbed wire and timber frame that marked the end of their little kingdom.

'You're doing well, soldier,' Sebastian said firmly. 'Our reinforcements will be here soon.' Or so he hoped.

Hadley stood up straighter. 'Thank you, sir.' He then caught a good look at his commanding officer. 'Sir, what happened to you?'

Sebastian tugged at the collar of his shirt and felt the soil trickle down his back. 'I was in the dugout, but they pulled me out.'

'You look like a collier, if you don't mind me saying, sir.' Hadley smiled faintly.

'Better dirty than dead.'

'True enough, sir.' Sebastian was relieved to see that the man could still find humour in the situation. It meant he wouldn't crack up – not yet anyway. Those who could not take their mind off the shells were the ones to worry about.

He made his way back, finding his men were already clearing the trench of the debris. Cook lay a little further on in the middle of the narrow way, swearing a blue streak when anyone brushed against his arm, which they could not help if they wanted to get past.

Sebastian knelt at his head. 'How are you, Cook?' The man smelt strongly of spirits which suggested he had been doing his own doctoring.

The answer was vivid, but as it ended with a 'sir' Sebastian felt no need to reprimand him. 'Not long now. Think about those pretty nurses who'll be seeing to you tomorrow.'

'You're not going to be able to carry me back across that, sir.' Cook gestured to the pockmarked no man's land. 'I told Bentley not to bother with the stretcher. I'll walk out of 'ere. It's just my 'ead and arm. My legs are fine. Eyesight's a bit wonky, but if someone can prop me up, I'll make it.'

'Glad to hear it.' Sebastian didn't like the look of the deep wound across Cook's left ear. He would have to check on him regularly to make sure he did not drift off into unconsciousness. 'Gather your strength for now.'

He needed a distraction. His body was shaking now that the shock of escaping death had caught up with him. Walking away to the nearest fire step, Sebastian took over from the man on sentry duty, telling him to get something to eat and drink. Where was the relief? They had been going since dawn and they surely deserved replacements by now? The strain of keeping ever alert and combat ready was making him feel like an over-wound clock. He could imagine his inner workings springing out of his gut with a clunk and zing, rivets popping. *Keep calm. Carry on. Duty. Survey the enemy.*

He ducked under the steel helmet hood constructed

to camouflage the loophole at the top of the trench work. A little slot gave the barrel coverage of about two hundred yards of broken ground for about sixty degrees left to right. You had to be careful peering through these holes because the really crack shooters on the other side would sometimes take potshots just in case someone had their head in the way.

The view was lively, reminding him that their little pocket becalmed in the battle was not the whole story. The whizz-roar of falling shells and spewed earth plumes from the resulting explosion bizarrely recalled the fountain display at Versailles that he had once gone to admire on holiday before all this madness. His brain tried to find a pattern in it, identify which guns behind him were responsible for particular elevations of dirt. The answering German fire seemed to be lessening, their appetite for revenge satiated for the day. Once the allies' bombardment ended, perhaps there would be time enough to collect the dead and wounded, though some of the bodies stuck like washing on the barbed wire appeared to have been there for some weeks. Sebastian didn't want to look too closely in case he saw a comrade.

Someone tapped him on the shoulder. He ducked out of the helmet sniper vantage point, giving it back to the man on duty. 'All quiet; no sign of the enemy,' he said to the soldier as he held out his hand for the message waiting for his attention. Signals had not got a wire this far so HQ were sending runners up the line.

'Yes, sir. I've seen movement to the extreme right by that bit of gun carriage. Nothing else.'

'Might be another sniper team. Keep it under observation. Take a shot if you get a chance. Still quite a few more hours of light.'

'Sir.'

Sebastian opened the scrawled note from Captain Williams. 'Relief due under cover of dark. Hold your position.'

He stuffed the message in his pocket with his book. Was this day never going to end?

II

Bramley, Surrey, 28 March 1915

The little country church with its spring flowers nodding over the quiet graves was everything that Helen had imagined: achingly beautiful, England encapsulated. The ground was bare under the yew trees by the lychgate, the scent of fallen needles released as their feet disturbed the thick yellowing drift gathered at the edge of the path. Further on, the grass sprang with lush growth, dotted with primroses and daffodils, nature carrying on oblivious to the death that brought everyone here today.

Flora stopped suddenly, her fingers clawing at Helen's sleeve. 'I can't do this. Let's go home.'

Helen took a couple of deep breaths. Flora had been like this since she had broken the news of Des's loss to her, distraught, unfixed, spinning like a seaside windmill on the top of a sagging sandcastle as the tide came in. 'We'll go if you want to. Just take a moment.'

Even Flora's beauty seemed to have been dimmed by grief, her complexion taken on a greyish cast. She looked so frail in her severe black dress and hat, her blonde hair scraped back. The realization had dawned that her big sister, the one Helen had looked to for answers, was young too. Helen had taken Flora so much for granted. Whom did Flora have to lean on now if not her?

Flora bit her lip. 'No, you're right, I can do this.'

Helen had not said this, but that was hardly worth arguing. 'I know you can.'

'It's what Des would have wanted. He must have mentioned me in his letters by now. They'll be pleased that something of him has been left behind.'

A rook flapped by, heading for a nearby colony of nests at the top of a clump of elms. Harsh caws echoed like mocking shouts.

'Perhaps you'd best wait to see how the land lies,' Helen suggested tentatively.

The hollow *clip-clop* of heavy horses forewarned them of the arrival of the funeral cortège. With no body to bury, they were bringing only floral tributes and mourners to the church, but Helen did not want to get caught up in the close family group and have to explain their presence with Flora in this state.

'We'd best go in.' Helen tugged her sister's arm gently.

Flora nodded and followed her, eyes glassy like a sleepwalker. They joined a stream of locals who had all come to pay their respects, women in Sunday best, working men in ill-fitting jackets and ties, big hands awkwardly clutching the hymnals. A photograph of Des had been set before the altar, flanked by jonquils springing from a pair of blue vases.

'Oh God, I can't do this,' Flora whispered again, tears pouring down her cheeks.

'Yes, you can.' Helen's reply was fierce. Her sister would never forgive her if she let her give in at this point. 'No turning tail. Des would want you here.'

They took a place on the left-hand side of the church – bride's side, thought Helen miserably. They garnered a few interested looks from the locals, but soon their entry was superseded by that of the family. Heads in the congregation turned as Des's parents and a clutch of youngsters came into the nave, the funeral directors following with the wreaths. Helen saw the young man she had met only a few times in the jutting jaw of the father, the colouring of the mother. The vicar rushed over to greet them, his consoling words spoken in a low tone. Helen caught a few stray phrases – 'died a hero', 'great loss to the village', 'proud of his courage'. The parents took each sentence with stony public faces; two young women at their side wept. The sight of their tears was infectious; Helen felt an answering prickle in her own eyes. She dabbed it away with her handkerchief, reached over and squeezed Flora's wrist.

The low rumble of a motorbike cut off outside. The church door opened again and a man came into the church, leather bike coat flapping about his legs. It was Sebastian. Helen longed to go to him, knowing how cut up he was about the loss of Neil, but now was not the moment to leave Flora. On seeing the group in front of him, Sebastian made directly for the family. He was the one who had informed Helen of the time and place of the service so she was not surprised to see him there. He shook hands with Des's father and mother, their faces taking on more animation with a boy they clearly knew and liked, a fellow sufferer. Mr Packenham even put an arm round Sebastian's shoulders and patted him on the back, inviting him to sit with the family.

With a nod to the organist, the vicar announced the first hymn, 'Abide with me'. The congregation rose to their feet, singing as the family came down the aisle. Bending like a willow wand, Mrs Packenham placed a large anchor-shaped wreath by Des's picture, then one of the girls placed another in the shape of a heart. Curious about the choice of tribute, Helen studied her carefully. Dark-haired, round-faced, pretty, the girl did not look like a Packenham; she seemed very close to a blonde, large-framed young lady whom Helen had pegged as a sister. Why had she, rather than the sister, placed the wreath? Helen's eyes met Sebastian's. He gave her a nod of acknowledgement then looked away. The life had gone from his face, stamped out by his own sorrow. She wished she could go over and give him what comfort she could, but she had Flora to tend.

Fortunately, Flora gave no sign that she had noticed the oddity in the wreath-laying. She stood unmoving while the congregation struggled with the hymns. Helen tried to sing, but had no voice, her throat choked with emotion, the words too poignant in this setting. She would get through a couple of lines, then a hitch would appear and she would have to stop and breathe through the moment, swallowing hard. It was a relief when the vicar invited them to sit.

The service passed in a blur until the vicar got up to speak. The heartfelt address from the pulpit left her with a sense that Des had been very much a boy beloved by the entire parish, noted for his sporting prowess and high spirits. That all chimed with the man she had met. The vicar went on to mention anecdotes about Des teaching his sister to skate, driving his mother for the first time and ending up in a ditch, beating his father in a round of golf on his last leave. Affectionate rumbles of laughter and sniffs were heard from all quarters. Des's scruffiness was lightly celebrated, but then the vicar's next words shook Helen to the core.

'Desmond's sartorial reformation in uniform had been noted by all, but we all held out hopes that Miss Garnet would make the improvement permanent. We all said that he only needed a woman's touch to keep his wardrobe in check.' He looked pointedly at the dark-haired girl sitting next to Mrs Packenham, his eyes warm with sympathy. 'Alas, that was not to be. Another flower of our English manhood plucked from life before his time, but not in vain – let that be a comfort in this dark hour.'

Helen turned cold. Had he meant what she thought? Please, no. Her sister could barely withstand this blow; finding another had a claim to Des's heart might be the final straw. She glanced sideways. Flora was as pale as the whitewashed wall behind her, her teeth burrowing into her bottom lip. Helen could not be sure that she had even understood what had been said. She looked across to Sebastian; he had been waiting for her to meet his gaze because he shook his head slightly. Some kind of message, but what did it mean? That he had not known? That he did not believe the vicar's hint?

The service drew to a close. The vicar led Desmond's parents out first and Helen wondered if they were actually going to miss the chance to speak to them, which, considering what they had just heard, might not be a bad thing. The slow drain of the congregation from the church gave her some warning. She directed Flora to remain in her seat.

'I think Des's parents are greeting mourners at the door. Shall we wait for the crowds to pass?'

Flora gave a jerky nod. Her eyes were still fixed on the photograph, left hand pressed to her stomach.

Sebastian waited inside the door by the square Norman font, hoping to catch Helen and Flora before they ran the gauntlet of Des's family. He had been a bit of a mess for the last week and had tumbled directly into this service from the one for his brother two days ago. He had wept during the Nunc Dimittis even though the choir had been inept and fumbled the beautiful tune. He doubted that either Des or Neil had departed in peace. Fortunately he had been listening to the address or he might have missed the heavy hints about Des's girlfriend in Bramley. It was the first he had heard of such a thing, but knowing how his own mother plotted with her friends, he would not be surprised to find the relationship was more in the mind of the villagers than in Des's own thoughts on his future. Careless though he was in his attitude to life, Des would not string two girls along at the same time. At least Sebastian liked to think he would not. Sebastian could believe, however, that Des had not tied the ends off his relationships neatly: that would be one hundred per cent in character.

The Sandfords had not moved. He could still see their heads bent close to each other in the shadows down the front, the light from the stained-glass windows striking either side of their pew but missing them. Excusing himself from Des's sister, Maureen, he made his way through the tide of people leaving.

'Helen, Flora,' he said softly.

Helen turned to him, rose and reached out two gloved hands, taking him by his upper arms in a gesture that might have ended in a hug if they had not been in this public place. 'Oh, Sebastian, we're so sorry about Neil.'

He looked down at the polished wood of the pew seat. He still did not have the words to say when people offered him their condolences.

Helen rubbed his sleeves then let go. 'It must be so hard. If there is anything I can do?'

Fold him in her embrace – kiss him to take away the pain. 'I . . . no, there's nothing anyone can do, I'm afraid, but thank you for offering.' He cleared his throat. 'How is Flora?' He was concerned to see that she appeared not to be responding, gazing fixedly at the altar. She looked very much how he felt.

Helen gave a feeble shrug. 'She's devastated of course.' Turning back to her sister, she tapped her on the shoulder. 'Flora, Sebastian's here.'

Flora turned her gentian-blue eyes on him. Sebastian immediately felt guilty for all the times he had belittled her depth of emotion; he could tell she was shattered, her soul like a window spider-webbed by a stone, but still just hanging on in the frame. 'Oh, Sebastian. Helen told me about your brother. So . . . so sorry.'

He leaned past Helen and kissed Flora gently on the cheek. 'Thank you. I too, about Des. I know how he loved you.'

It was the best thing he could have said. Something of the old Flora floated back to the surface and she summoned up a brave smile. 'Yes, he did rather. I . . . I was lucky to have him while I could.' She stood up, pulling her gloves neatly over her fingers. 'I was letting myself get very down, I'm afraid, what with the family and that man's words.' So she had noticed. Sebastian had rather hoped she would remain oblivious to the conclusions everyone had been drawing from the vicar's sermon. 'I must go and speak to his parents. Tell them how much Des meant to me.'

Sebastian shot a warning look at Helen, but she took no notice. Rather, she fell in with her sister's wishes. 'Yes, Flora, it was what you came for after all.'

'Helen, is this wise?' he whispered as she stepped out

to allow her sister past. Sebastian did not think he could cope with another emotional scene – selfish perhaps, but he had hoped to keep this visit uncomplicated. In his mind, he had seen himself briefly attending the wake, making arrangements to leave the bike and then going back to London with Helen and Flora. He had business to conclude before he reported to his regiment. He had not imagined Flora actually wanting to meet Des's parents, people to whom she had not been introduced as far as he knew.

'It is necessary,' Helen replied. 'Please, Sebastian, there's more going on than you know. Flora was engaged to Des.'

What did that matter? Sebastian wanted to howl. The man was dead, ending any hope of marriage. Why stir up the family with news that they would not welcome? Either they would not believe Flora or they would be hurt that Des had not told them himself. However, he could do nothing to stop Flora making the announcement, short of tackling her to the ground: she had reached the end of the queue of mourners. Helen hurried to stand at her side, giving her support. With a sigh, Sebastian joined them.

'So kind of you to come,' murmured Mrs Packenham, working on her automatic setting. Sebastian knew how that felt; he had been like that at Neil's memorial. 'Do stay for some tea.' Mr Packenham was shaking everyone's hand and saying their name, as if that sufficed. The vicar hovered anxiously. Mrs Packenham turned to Flora. 'So kind of you to come. Do stay for some tea.'

Flora did not move on as the others had done. 'Mrs Packenham?'

The woman's eyes rose to her face and frowned, trying to place her. 'Sorry, I'm not sure we've met. Are you a friend of Des's?'

Flora met her gaze boldly. 'Yes, ma'am, from London.'

'Oh, you've come so far. Do stay for tea if you have time.' Her maternal instincts alert, Mrs Packenham showed every sign of wanting to usher Flora along and out of sight. Her eyes shifted to the space behind her, eager to get on with the ritual.

'I'm sorry for your loss – for our loss.' Flora stood her ground. 'I'm Flora Sandford. Did Des have time to tell you about me, before he left, I mean?'

'Flora Sandford,' the poor woman repeated. 'No, no, I don't think so.'

Sebastian would have thought that Flora was quite composed if he had not noticed that her hands quivered. The few people left in the church porch fell silent, sensing something momentous was happening at the door. The girl the vicar had named as Miss Garnet was staring at Flora with intense dislike. She for one had begun to suspect what was coming. 'That is a shame,' continued Flora. 'You see, Mrs Packenham, Des and I became engaged in December. We were to be married when he came back, but . . . anyway, I think you should know that I am carrying his child.' She tossed it down like a challenge.

Mrs Packenham reeled, reaching out to clutch the vicar's arm; her husband flushed an alarming shade of red, speech strangled in his throat. Sebastian could not help himself – his gaze dropped to Flora's waist, much like everyone else in earshot. It was hard to tell with the loose folds of her coat disguising her form, but he knew she would not lie about such a thing. To risk disgrace for a matter that time would prove true or false was not in her best interests and, if he understood Flora even the least bit, she had a keen sense of what was good for her. He had to admit, Flora was magnificent standing in a church of all places and declaring that she was going to be an unmarried mother. Des had a lot to answer for, leaving her in this predicament.

'I apologize for springing this on you, but really there is very little time left and I wanted you to know.'

The vicar came forward, cheeks pink with embarrassment. 'Young lady, this is hardly the time or the place.'

Flora ignored him and gestured to Sebastian, knowing the battle for her child's place in Des's family was with the ones in front of her. 'Mr Trewby here can vouch for me – he joined us on occasion when I went out with Des. As did my sister.' She fumbled with the catch of her handbag, more desperate than Sebastian had realized. 'We met at the theatre where I work. I have letters too – they will tell you everything.'

Mrs Packenham clutched her hands to her breast, refusing to touch the proffered envelopes. 'I . . . I don't know what to say. George?'

Her husband hitched his trousers up by the belt, unfurling like a man preparing to join a bar fight. 'This is all nonsense – fakes, forgeries. Sebastian, what have you to say about this . . . this woman?'

Sebastian had a vision of a quiet room, a sofa, Helen's hand in his, peace. 'Flora was a very good friend to Des; I saw them about London during the winter whenever he could get leave. They were a devoted couple.' He could give Flora that much, even if he had no grounds on which to support her claim to be engaged.

Maureen Packenham had moved to her friend's side. On hearing Sebastian's statement, she gave a strained laugh. 'I'm sure what Seb said is true, Father, but you have to remember that Des enjoyed going out with girls. Lord, he escorted most of my friends to the hunt ball or to the theatre at one time or another. He falls . . . fell in and out of love as regularly as I change my hat. Tori here was the only girl he showed any constancy towards; we all knew it would be her he would settle down with, in the end.' She scowled at Flora, marking her out as a passing fancy.

Sebastian had to admit that also sounded like Des, but before he could think of a riposte, Helen got there first. 'That's all very well, Miss Packenham, but I doubt your brother got any of your friends with child.' Though her face was scarlet with humiliation, Helen forged on. 'I apologize for my plain speaking, but I cannot remain silent while I see my sister being treated in this shabby manner. Your son, God rest his soul, loved her and intended to marry her. Tragically,' her voice hitched up a notch, 'that is no longer possible, but he left behind part of himself, a child. You seem to be overlooking that fact.'

The remaining parishioners were getting quite a show. The vicar had heard enough to know that any other details Flora chose to share were not going to be of the morally edifying sort. 'Please, my dear people, let us take this discussion from the church to a more private place. We came together to remember Desmond; we do his memory no honour by quarrelling.'

Mr Packenham pointed a shaking finger at Flora. 'She . . . that Jezebel is not stepping foot over the threshold of my house. I will give her five minutes in the graveyard, no more. Fiona, Maureen, you go on home. I'll deal with this.'

Sebastian winced at Mr Packenham's melodramatic declaration; they all seemed to be behaving like actors in a bad play. Couldn't they just be allowed to grieve with dignity?

Mrs Packenham had had time to gather her thoughts. 'George, a grandchild, a baby.' She at least had reached the essential truth: this was nature giving back when war had so cruelly taken a child away. 'Should we not at least talk this through? We could invite the young woman home after the wake – discuss what's to be done.'

Her husband folded his arms. 'There's nothing to be done. We have no proof that it's Desmond's baby. A girl like her – could be anybody's and she is trying to palm it off on us!'

Flora gasped. 'How dare you!' Spinning on her heel,

she began to walk away. Helen started after her, but Mr Packenham was too fast. He caught Flora's elbow and dragged her to a halt.

'*You* came here, miss; *you* were the one to bring this to our doorstep, disgracing my son's memory in front of his family and neighbours! You will face the consequences!'

'I am already *facing the consequences*!' Flora spat back. 'In August I'll have living, breathing consequences, so don't you speak to me like that! I loved your son, and it is only the feelings I had for him stopping me now telling you exactly what I think of you, you pompous old . . . !' She cut herself off and wrenched her arm free.

Mr Packenham dug in his breast pocket and drew out his wallet. 'How much do you want?'

'What!' Flora backed away, aghast, placing a lopsided gravestone between them. 'I don't want anything from you. I thought you might want this child as much as I do – might love it for being part of Des, the only part we have left. I don't want your money.' She stuck her left hand out, brandishing the ring in his face. 'Des gave me this – that was all I wanted from him, all I'd accept from his family.'

Mr Packenham's rage had grown to such an extent, Sebastian feared he no longer knew what he was saying or cared for the damage he was doing. 'I know your sort – all fine words, but at the bottom you were trying to catch a wealthy boy who'd lift you out of the gutter. Who are your people? Who are you?' he sneered. 'A gold-digger. Not a decent girl, I'm sure of that. My boy sowed his wild oats, I know that; he had a man's taste for a pretty bit of fluff now and again. I'm not ashamed of him for doing so. Boys will be boys. But I promise you, he would have come to his senses before you could drag him to the altar.'

Helen slid between the two combatants, turning her back scornfully to Mr Packenham. 'Let's go, Flora. You don't have to listen to this. You did your duty to Des.'

Deflated by her sister's gentle touch on her arm, Flora rested her head on Helen's shoulder. 'Why's he saying these things to me, Sandy?' she sobbed. 'Why?'

'Forget him. He's upset. We have to leave.'

Shaken, perhaps sensing he was allowing the tide of sympathy to turn Flora's way through his very public response, Mr Packenham faced his family who had not left when he had ordered. 'Back to the house!' he barked like an army officer on the parade ground. 'That's enough of this nonsense!'

The two groups began to move apart, Helen and her sister towards the station, the Packenhams to their large house on the far side of the churchyard. Sebastian wished he knew what to do, but both sides had argued themselves into entrenched positions and would now only lob abuse at each other if they continued. He ran to Mr Packenham. 'I'll be along later, sir,' he said. 'I have to see the Miss Sandfords to their train.'

'I hold you partly to blame for this.' Des's father wiped his brow with a shaking hand. 'I take it they are here because you told them about the service?'

Sebastian had no intention of denying a truth. 'I thought she had a right to be here. Blame me if it makes you feel better, but, sir, I do believe it is Des's child.' Planting that thought and hoping it would mature, he reversed direction and caught up with Helen and Flora. Helen was practically having to hold her sister up; the blast of anger that had given steel to Flora's spine had passed, leaving her prey to her feelings of hopelessness and grief.

'It will be all right – I'll make it all right,' Helen was intoning. 'We'll move in together – do this together.'

Sebastian slipped his arm round Flora, taking over the job of offering support. 'Please don't take what he said to heart. He's driven mad with grief; Des was his only son. Mrs Packenham doesn't feel the same. Did you hear her? Let her work on him.'

Flora stumbled. Only Sebastian's grip kept her from falling.

'How long till your train?' he asked Helen.

'An hour. We've just missed one.' Helen looked about her, at a loss to know what to do.

'Let's take her to the tea shop by the station. If I remember rightly, it has lots of little rooms. Perhaps we can find one to give us a bit of privacy.' Word about the confrontation at the church must be spreading fast; he did not want Flora to be exposed to any more abuse. A village like this would not treat an unmarried mother well once they learnt she had shamed their favourite son at his memorial. It had been a foolish way of breaking the news even if Flora's judgement had been clouded by desperation and grief. 'Has she eaten?'

Helen shook her head. 'I've tried but she's been so listless.'

'Flora, you've got to eat.' He gave her a little shake. 'For the baby, for Des. I know that you just want to give up – I feel that way about my brother – but please, he'd want you to keep strong.'

'I'm not giving up,' Flora said quietly. 'I just want this over.'

The tea room was in a slant-floored Tudor cottage and smelt of fresh-baked scones, heartening after the chilly damp of the churchyard. The waitress gave them a measuring look as they entered, but found them a quiet spot in a room upstairs, walls covered with polished brass and copper warming pans like some domestic armoury. She took their order for plain scones and jam before disappearing down to her kitchen. Flora rested on the window seat, half-turned so she did not have to look at either of them.

'They treated me like a prostitute,' she said in a low voice.

'They were taken by surprise. It's a terrible day for them.' Sebastian wondered what he could say to soften the blow. 'I'm trying to imagine how I might have reacted had I been in their shoes. I probably would have made a muck of it too.'

'But you would never have been unkind. You don't have that instinct to go for the kill,' Helen said, defending him against his own self-criticism. 'Flora, you have to forget them. What matters is the baby – and you. We'll make plans, find somewhere nice to live together.'

Flora shook her head. 'Will we, Helen? You on a nurse's meagre salary, me no longer able to work: what exactly is going to keep the wolf from the door?'

Helen rearranged the sugar and condiments. 'You could go home. Mum will help.'

Flora gave a ghastly laugh. 'Oh yes, I can see that, can't you? I'd be putting myself in a cage for the rest of my life. No, that's the last thing I'll do. It would be the death of me and ruin this child.'

'I'll get a new job – a better-paid one.'

'Helen, you're sixteen with next to no skills.' Flora's voice rose in pitch, strung out with tension and barely contained hysteria. 'No employer in their right mind will pay you enough to support me and the baby. Forget it. This is not your problem. I apologize that I've let grief blind me to the situation.' She got up, gathering her handbag in front of her like a shield. 'Stay here. I'll be back before the train.'

Helen rose. 'Where are you going? I'll come with you.'

Flora's eyes sparked with annoyance. 'Sit down. I'm going alone. Sebastian, keep her here. On your honour, do not follow me.'

Sebastian nodded. With a flash of insight, he thought he could guess her intent and could understand why she did not want anyone to witness further humiliation. 'We'll come looking for you if you're not back in an hour.'

'Oh, I don't think it will take that long, do you?' She gave him a hard smile, revealing the character that had allowed her successfully to make her own way in London. 'Now I understand how the land lies, I think my attack will be more successful this time.'

She walked out, held together by a bitter determination to survive.

12

The Somme, forward medical station, 1 July 1916, 6.30 p.m.

Ordered off duty, Helen lay fully clothed on top of her narrow bed and tried to snatch some sleep. It was so hard to do so when she could hear the unending stream of casualties being brought from the regimental aid posts, but she had been ordered to rest and be back on duty at midnight. There were so many on stretchers that they were being left in the open with only hastily rigged shelter from the sun. The groans of the sufferers reached her; in the end she put the pillow over her head to try to muffle them. The promised evacuation trains had not arrived and the station's resources were hopelessly swamped. Helen had worked on exhausted, her nerves stretched like barbed wire between posts of duty and compassion, until she had finally been sent away. The sister-in-charge warned her that, if she collapsed, she would be another burden, not a help.

Tossing and turning, Helen buried her head further under her pillow and resolutely closed her eyes. Images from the hours in theatre flickered past her closed eyelids. Forcing her mind to find pleasanter subjects to dwell on, she recalled the happier days she had spent in London with Sebastian a year ago. Though the time was marred by loss and Flora's desperate situation, there had been sweet mixed with the bitter, for herself at least. Having taken the decision to sign up with his local regiment in Somerset, Sebastian had returned to see out his term at the Slade while waiting for his application for a commission to be considered. He had been prepared to go into the ranks, but his mother had insisted he try this route first. Lady Mabel was horrified that any of her sons would consider enlisting as a Tommy if they could get into the officers' mess. Those two months between the end of March and end of May had been the real beginning to Sebastian and Helen's relationship after the false start of the October before. Helen had enjoyed each steady step they had taken together, moving from two individuals to being a couple who wanted to share everything, every thought, mood and moment. She had never known anything like that closeness, not even with Flora.

Her mind dwelt on the hours in his studio, Sebastian sketching or painting while she read or did a little embroidery. She liked to stitch designs of the wildflowers she collected and pressed for her diaries. They had spoken about everything – art, poetry, books, music, travel. Over time, she had even confessed to her botanical enthusiasms and been met with interest rather than the scorn she had feared, knowing she only dabbled and was no professional at what she did.

She had been impressed that Sebastian had toured through many of the European capitals before the war –

Paris, Vienna, Rome. He seemed so sophisticated compared to her. She had only ever travelled to the Norfolk coast on holiday and once to the Isle of Wight. She had made Sebastian laugh when she claimed this counted as 'abroad'. His laughter was a precious thing, lighting up his face; it reminded her of how the sea glittered when the sun came out unexpectedly, turning from sad grey to a flashing silver. She was pleased she had been able to amuse him in the dark days when he had to live through the sharpest grief for his brother.

Sleep stole up on her, bringing with it dreams of her sister. They were children together, sitting in the walnut tree in the garden of the family home, and yet Flora was also grown up in the bizarre way of dreams, holding a baby upside down as she swung backwards on the branch.

Should you be doing that? Helen asked anxiously, dropping to the ground so as to catch the child should it fall from its husk of blankets.

> '*I had a little nut tree and nothing would it bear*
> *But a silver nutmeg and a golden pear,*'

sang Flora. Then she sprouted blue-feathered wings and flew off.

The Somme, 1 July 1916, 7.30 p.m.

'Here, sir, look at this!' Bentley beckoned Sebastian over. He shook off his lethargy and stepped over Cook, glad to see the man was still alert as he smoked a Woodbine.

'What is it, private?'

'Jerry's up out of his trench and holding a white board – there's a red cross on it. I think they want a chance to get the wounded off the battlefield.'

A good, compassionate idea, but Sebastian did not consider he had the seniority to offer a truce. 'Take word to Captain Williams.'

Bentley hurried off at a run for the last known position of the captain. Sebastian took over the watch of the German standing in plain view. It was possible that this was a ruse to get them to show their heads above the parapet; he had not forgotten the suspected sniper team by the gun carriage. Anyone who went to discuss a truce would be senior, so a superior bag for the marksmen. Still, it would be fiendish of the Hun to abuse the Red Cross in that way; he was inclined to think the offer genuine.

Bentley came back a few minutes later. 'Sorry, sir, but Captain Williams has gone. So have most of his men. Direct hit from a shell. Bloody shambles. Corporal Wilmot is doing his best, but there are wounded to evacuate.'

Sebastian swore. Aside from the pang of grief, that left him the commanding officer in his little stretch. He grabbed a grubby handkerchief from his pocket and tied it to the end of a thin metal stake used for fixing barbed wire. 'I'm going to see what Jerry has to say for himself.'

'Right you are, sir.' Bentley moved away from the fire

step to make room. 'He looks pretty keen; been out there exposing himself to our guns. He didn't have to do that.'

'That's what I'm relying on.'

'How's your German, sir?'

'Same as yours, I would guess.' Sebastian heaved himself up and slithered over the top, waving the flag of truce. He couldn't help but hunch forward slightly, anticipating the bullet as he stepped across the no man's land between the German rear trench and the one they had occupied. Behind him, he could feel the eyes of his men on his back, alert for any treachery. He hoped they all kept their heads. One wrong move and this situation could rapidly spin back into hostilities. Thank goodness the artillery had faded into silence having pounded the ground all day with their missiles.

The German stepped forward smartly, weaving his way through the tangles of wire.

'*Guten Abend!*' he called – absurd for it was a greeting more suited to a social occasion than the field of slaughter.

'Hello,' replied Sebastian, deciding he had come far enough.

'I am doctor, yes? We stop for one hour to help our *Kameraden*?'

Sebastian had to admire the man's pluck. He made an impressive character with his trim beard and blood-spattered uniform. The problem was that Sebastian had no way of getting a message back to the gun crews behind the old lines to halt their shelling. Signals had not caught up with them and he now doubted he would get access to a telephone cable that day. He gestured behind him. 'They will not stop.' He could not be answerable for what the men in the gunners' observation post would decide was a legitimate target.

The doctor pointed to Sebastian's men, then to his. 'But we stop, yes?'

A groan from one of the wounded rose from a shell hole beyond Sebastian's view. He realized that the movement by the gun carriage he had spotted was not a sniper team, but some poor soldier who had been lying there all day. God Almighty, he hated the war. 'Yes, my men will not fire on you if you remove your casualties. One hour.'

The doctor nodded. 'And we will not shoot if you take your men back.' He pointed to the exposed spread of land between their position and the trench they had left that morning. With no communication tunnel yet dug, they would be easy to pick off by a good marksman as they carried stretchers that way.

'Fair enough. Good evening.' Sebastian saluted the brave doctor and hurried back to his trench. He dropped down the side. 'Get the wounded ready. We have an hour to evacuate them to safety.'

Bentley touched his cap. 'Yes, sir. Didn't think Jerry had a merciful streak. Have to say, speaks well of them.'

Sebastian rubbed his chest, his heart hurting. 'If the captain's remains can be buried, do that too. And any of the lads, if there's time.'

'Sir.' Bentley strode off to fulfil his orders, leaving Sebastian to monitor the German stretcher party. The thought came to Sebastian that he was watching a scene as old as the hills: those left behind scouring the battlefield for survivors, pronouncing this one beyond help, that one worth moving. A lump formed in his throat as he watched the doctor pull his revolver and dispatch a horse twitching behind the gun carriage. The truncated body of a man was heaved on to a stretcher and carried off. Perhaps it would have been kinder to put a bullet in the driver of the gun carriage too.

Cook was carried past, supported by two soldiers.

'Permission to retire, lieutenant,' Cook asked, the spark of his normal cheek still flickering.

'Permission granted. Look after yourself, Cook.'

'And you, sir.'

The light was beginning to fade. Dusk was approaching and he had hardly any men left in the trench for the evening stand-to. Even so, he had to keep to the army's routine; it would be more distressing for the infantry if he neglected to do so.

'Men, at your positions!' he shouted. 'Stand-to.' The soldiers, who had been waiting at ease, moved wearily to attention. He walked the line, taking note of the missing. From the expression in their eyes, he could tell they were thinking the same as he was: it should have taken him longer to make the inspection. Four were away with the wounded which left him only seven. The horrid arithmetic meant that he, in his small section, had lost over half the troops since daybreak. Fifteen men, individuals with their own sense of humour, hopes, families, absurdities, either injured or killed in twelve hours. God knew what that meant for the rest of the army fighting on the Somme; Sebastian did not even want to think about that, his own loss enough to bear at that moment.

'Stand down.' He stared out across the darkening field. A swift cut across the skies, catching its evening meal. Inside he was weeping.

Whitechapel, London, 15 April 1915

Juggling her parcels, Helen knocked on the door of Mrs Glock's boarding house. Her former landlady answered, greeting her with a fond smile, the hair straggling from her loose bun, face flushed with the exertion of cleaning the stove. 'Hello, love, how have you been keeping?'

'Well enough, thank you. How's my sister? I went to the theatre first, but they said she hadn't come in.'

'No, poor lamb, she's not been up to it.' Mrs Glock stood back to let Helen enter. 'I hope they hold her position for her.'

Helen did not think that likely. Toots was gloomy on the subject. The management took the view that Flora was by no means the only girl to lose a loved one to the war and they could not indulge her low spirits as it would set a poor example to the rest. She was expected to buck up and carry on. 'There's not much anyone can do. If she can't perform, then that's that. Where is she?'

'In her room. I've not seen her down in the kitchen since this morning. Took her a cuppa at one, but she's kept to herself for the rest of the day.' Helen frowned. 'But she's all right; I've heard her moving about, opening drawers and such like. She's keeping active. Probably catching up on her housework, the mending and so on.'

Mending? Unlikely. Flora had always passed that particular chore on to Helen. 'I've brought her a few treats from Fortnum and Mason.' Actually, Sebastian had bought them for Helen, but she had not felt like eating them alone. 'I doubt even Flora's spirits will remain so depressed after eating some of their fruit cake and a bar of Fry's milk chocolate.' She aimed for a bright tone, but it sounded tarnished even to her.

Mrs Glock clucked her tongue. 'Now, that's a kind thought. You go on up.'

Helen took the stairs then knocked before entering her old room.

'Who is it?' called Flora.

'It's me.'

Silence, then – 'Oh. I suppose you'd better come in.'

Not the warmest of welcomes. Helen turned the handle. 'I come bearing gifts. I know how much you like –' She halted on the threshold. The room was in chaos, two suitcases already piled with clothes, a third half-packed. 'You're going somewhere?'

Flora stood by the window, a coat hugged to her chest. 'As you can see.'

With that amount of luggage, this was no weekend away. 'For how long?'

Flora folded the garment and put it in the valise then picked up a pile of blouses and tucked them alongside.

'Flora, how long?'

'For good, I expect. Isn't that a funny phrase: "for good"? It can hardly be "for bad" as it is so horrid here.' She swept her cosmetics into a case. 'Don't you think that London's such a small-minded place, so confining? And now the Zeppelins are trying to rain death on us from the skies, I'll be pleased to put it behind me.'

'Does Mrs Glock know?'

'Don't worry, I'll settle my rent with her. I'm quite flush, don't you know?' She glared at her handbag that sat like a fat cat dozing on the bed.

Helen leaned against the jamb. 'No, I didn't know. Are you moving to the country then?'

Flora gave a harsh laugh. 'I'm moving *country*, darling. Booked passage on the *Lusitania* leaving from Liverpool on Sunday.'

'Where are you going?' Helen's voice rose.

'America. New York.'

'But how . . . ? What are you going to do there?' Helen came in and shut the door so Mrs Glock would not overhear this conversation.

'Well, thanks to the Packenhams' hush money, I have enough to establish myself as a respectable widow.' Flora's lip curled with distaste. 'I won't have to work for a year at least, not till I've had the baby. Then I'll see what's what.'

'On your own?' Helen dumped the packages on the bed next to the suitcases. She was trying not to feel hurt, but Flora had arranged all this without telling her a thing. Had she intended to leave without saying goodbye?

'No, I'm carrying my own company, remember?' Flora's manner was brittle and falsely cheerful.

'I . . . I could come too, if you want. It wouldn't take me long to pack and there's nothing really to keep me here.'

'Nothing?' Flora closed the lid of the suitcase. 'What about your training?'

'I could pick it up again in America – at least I expect so.' Helen felt sore inside, like when she had skinned her knees in the playground as a child, bits of grit – regrets, complications – sticking to her offer to go.

'And Sebastian? I suppose you'll just drop him too?'

Why did Flora sound so angry with her? This wasn't her fault. 'I . . . I don't know. He's half American, remember? He might even join us eventually.'

Irritated, Flora threw a scarlet silk scarf into the air and snatched it away. 'Oh yes? Listen to yourself, Helen: building dreams with matchsticks when the deck is burning around you. They don't come back – he won't come back to you. They don't marry our sort so don't raise your hopes too high and don't, whatever you do, go to bed with him. One stupid Sandford girl is quite enough in our family.'

'You're not stupid.'

'Oh, I beg to differ. The proof is before you. But then again, Baby bought us our ticket, so maybe I'm not such a fool after all.'

'Stop it, Flora! Don't talk about yourself like that.'

'You don't understand me, Helen: I'm not as nice as you'd like to think. I landed myself in this ridiculous position and I'm getting myself out of it the best way I can. America will be a new start – no ties, no reputation dragging behind me.'

'No ties? Does that include me then?'

Flora's face softened for a second before she forced herself to stick to her decision. 'Yes, I'm afraid it does. I . . . I can't be doing with the Sandfords any more. I'll take a new name, be the person I want to be, not what others tell me I am.' Her eyes fell on a honeycomb Chinese box on her dressing table. Folding it flat with a snap, squeezing the tigers away, she held it out. 'Here, have this. I need my jewellery, you understand, but perhaps one day this will be a pleasant memento of the happy times at the Palace.'

Helen took it automatically, twisting it in her fingers. 'Can I write to you?'

'I'll wire to let you know I've arrived safely.'

That wasn't an answer. 'Flora?'

She sighed, then moved to put her arms round Helen, resting her cheek on the top of her head. 'I'm sorry, Sandy, you deserve a better sister. I just don't have enough in me to carry all this . . . with me. I've got to start afresh. Forgive me – if you can. I won't hold it against you if you bear a grudge.'

'A letter now and again wouldn't hurt, would it?'

'I suppose not. A letter. Now and again. I can cope with that.'

'I wanted to be there, help you through this.'

'I know, but you'll be helping me best by letting me go without making me cry. I've wept buckets these last few weeks; it's got to stop.'

Helen brushed her wrist across her own wet cheeks. She tried to be strong for Flora. 'I see – really, I do. You go. I love you, you do know that, don't you?'

'I know – and I'm proud of you. You'll do well, if you don't make the same mistakes as me and keep away from our father.' Flora grimaced. 'I won't be sorry not to see him again: he stifles the life out of me. I'll let them know I've gone. Don't worry about you having to do that.' She dragged the closed case on to the floor. 'I think that's everything. I've a taxi coming to take me to the night train.'

Helen drifted to the window, feeling bereft already. She tweaked the curtain back to look out on the outhouse roof that had proved her salvation in December. It was a grim view of brick houses and small backyards; men's shirts flapped their surrender from swaying clotheslines. New York had to be better than this. 'Have you decided on a name?'

Flora paused in putting on her lightweight fawn-coloured coat. 'Desmond for a boy, and I thought perhaps Helen for a girl.'

Helen's eyes watered again despite her resolution not to be weak. 'That sounds lovely. I hope you'll be happy.'

Flora picked up her hat and pinned it to her hair. 'I'm counting on it.'

'Goodbye then.'

'Goodbye. You'll be all right, Helen; you'll see.'

On the way back to her own lodgings, Helen found the unopened bar of chocolate in her pocket when she reached for her keys. She held it in her lap and gave in to her sobs.

13

'This was a good idea of yours to suggest we came out here.' Helen rummaged in the picnic basket, looking for the paper bag of sandwiches she had made as her contribution to the feast. 'I don't think I realized how tired of the city I had become.'

'You deserve a holiday. I've barely seen you smile since Flora left. You told me how much you love the country-side.' Sebastian stretched out on the long grass of the riverbank, propped up on one elbow. Having come to visit his brother Steven, they were in the fields of Eton College just across the Thames from Windsor Castle so he had a good view of the battlements and the barrage balloon bobbing behind it. The round tower was the kind of castle a child would draw — a fairy-tale palace for a beautiful princess, not so suited to the bluff, bearded King George V who currently occupied the premises. Sebastian tossed a cricket ball thoughtfully in his hand, worn leather settling with a satisfying slap in his palm with each throw. A nugget. A little red sun. He had some news, but he was not sure how she would take it so soon after losing her sister to America.

'And your brother is very sweet.' Helen brushed a money spider from her sleeve, twirling it three times round his head for good luck before casting it away.

Sebastian raised a brow at this. 'Steven, sweet?' He gestured across to his brother and two friends who were playing a game roughly based on rugby with Sebastian's hat. If it came back wearable, he would be astonished.

'Yes, he is. Very sweet.' Helen smoothed back a strand that had dropped over her face from the loose knot of hair at her nape. She turned back to the basket. 'He knows all about chemistry. I think he must be very clever.'

Sebastian sat up. 'When did you get a chance to discuss chemistry?'

Helen gave a little hum of pleasure when she located the squashed bag she sought. He took absurd delight in learning her mannerisms – this was a new one for him. 'While you were talking to his house master. I take it Steven is coping? It must be so hard to lose someone and not have anyone around him to share it with.'

'Sadly, he's not the only one to be mourning a brother.' Sebastian plucked a blade of grass and twiddled it between his fingers. 'Not that it helps. The masters at Eton aren't very good at talking about feelings with the lads.'

Helen huffed. 'Men. You behave as if you are all machines. The poor boy.'

What about me? Sebastian wanted to ask. If she was lavishing sympathy on a Trewby, he wanted it to be him. 'I'll talk to him later if his friends give us a moment.'

Helen beamed at him. This had apparently been what she had been hoping, getting the promise from him in this roundabout manner. 'I'll distract them for you.'

Sebastian wasn't sure he wanted his girl 'distracting' two lively Etonians – it would be akin to putting a fresh meat pie in front of two hungry puppies and expecting them to behave. They would be flirting outrageously before his back was turned. 'Only if you talk chemistry with them too; better yet, arithmetic.'

She shook her head and laughed. 'I left school at fourteen, Sebastian. What I know about mathematics can be written on the back of a very small postage stamp.'

'Perfect chance for them to enlighten you then.'

Shaking her head, she handed him the paper bag. 'Here, take yours before I call the boys over. I'm afraid it's only cheese. I couldn't see any decent-looking ham at the butcher's.'

Sebastian wasn't feeling very hungry, not for sandwiches at any rate. 'Leave it for the moment, Helen. Let's just lie back and enjoy the sunshine.' He patted the blanket beside him. 'That's what holidays are for in my view.'

With a sigh, she complied, one hand on her waist, the other shading her face. She looked quite lovely lying there in her pale blue Sunday skirt and white blouse. 'Have you noticed that if you stare at the sky for long enough,' she said, 'you can also see a pattern on the surface of your eyes – veins, I suppose, or something.'

Sebastian smiled at the sky. His girl was not known for her romantic sweet nothings. 'No, I hadn't noticed. Talking anatomy now?'

'Don't you find it fascinating?'

He rolled over towards her, tickling her chin with the blade of grass. 'Absolutely fascinating.' He dipped down, replacing the seed head with his lips for a light kiss. 'You look like Botticelli's spring goddess lying there. Don't move.'

But she had shifted her hand to touch her lips, tracing the ghost mark of the kiss. 'Why did you do that?'

He gently pushed her hand away and gave her a firmer kiss so there could be no doubt about it. 'Because you are beautiful, full of the promise of the new season, and a spring goddess has to be kissed or the mortal perishes.' He dug his notebook out of his jacket pocket. 'Stay still. This is going to be a masterpiece.' He quickly sketched her and made a little note underneath for himself. *First kiss*.

He had crossed a bridge he had been contemplating for some days. Now she had to know that he was interested in far more than friendship with her. They had clung together the last few weeks, both abandoned by loved ones in their different ways, Neil lost to death, Flora to distance, and he had been anxious that Helen thought he only sought her out for comfort. Nothing could be further from the truth. The comfortable choice would have been to separate himself from everyone, make no more emotional ties in anticipation of more loss to come, but he had been unable to help himself. She had become as essential to him as his art for she was the only one who allowed him to express his true self. He never had to hide what he was from her for fear that he would be thought unmanly or foolish.

If only they could carry on as they were.

'Helen, I have something to tell you.' He tucked the notebook away in his breast pocket, folding the memory close to his heart.

She looked up at him warily. 'Nothing bad, I hope?'

'Depends how you look at these things.' *Cut the prevaricating*, he told himself. 'My commission has come through: Second Lieutenant, 1st Somerset Infantry. I'm leaving tomorrow for training camp.'

She sat up, happiness fading from her face. Her hair swung down, a fallen halo. 'Oh. We knew it was coming.' She tried a smile, but her eyes were sorrowful. 'I'm pleased that you got a commission.'

He shredded the seeds from the stalk and scattered them to the wind. By the time they sprouted he'd be in France. 'Yes, they are getting harder to come by. In some ways, it's good that I decided to sign up when I did. The men coming on behind will have to go into the ranks, I expect, unless they have experience.'

'But you don't.'

He gave a self-mocking laugh. 'I don't. I expect my mother pulled strings, or got my grandfather to do so. I'm anticipating being the most useless officer the Somersets have ever known. I hope they can knock me into shape before I have to do the real business in the field.'

Helen rubbed her arms. 'I think you'll be very good. You're steady under pressure – considerate. Look how you handled Flora and Mr Packenham that day and how good you are with your brother and his friends. The men will respect you and follow your lead, you'll see.'

'Oh, I can marshal order among fourteen-year-olds, but give me a squad of battle-hardened men all older than me, all more experienced, and I imagine you would not be so easily impressed.'

She got to her knees and rested her hands on his so they were face to face. 'I believe in you, Sebastian. You are your own worst enemy.'

He gave a wry smile. 'I thought that was supposed to be Germany.'

'Exactly. Save the attacks for the Kaiser's army; spare yourself.' She leaned just a little closer and kissed him, blushing at her own daring. 'There. Remember that.'

'The kiss?' he asked, smiling.

'That I believe in you.'

He pushed the stray hair away from her cheeks, framing her face with his hands. 'I will.'

The Somme, 1 July 1916, 10 p.m.

The messenger arrived with the darkness. Sebastian opened the note, reading it with the faint light from a torch one of the men had salvaged from the abandoned possessions. At long last they were relieved and could fall back. This pitiful stretch of trench was now someone else's problem. Shortly after the message, a group of sombre but as yet uninjured khaki-clad men dropped down the western side of the passageway. Sebastian knew his troops looked like the walking dead, with their bloodied and muddied uniforms and wild-eyed faces – no reassurance for the men taking over their positions. He saluted the captain who was leading them. He could tell from the new arrivals' expressions that they now had a fair idea of what they faced from the carnage they had had to cross to get here.

'You are relieved, lieutenant,' said the captain, who had introduced himself as Johnson, from the South Midlands Division.

'Yes, sir.' Sebastian could see his men already filing away, retreating down a German sap tunnel before emerging out in the open.

'Report to HQ. They want to know what the hell happened out here.' Sebastian's face must have shown his distaste for the task because the captain patted him on the shoulder. 'No need to be anxious. They think you've done well to get this far and hold it. The others haven't done as much. Whole day has been a complete disaster. Probably a medal in it for you.'

That was the very last thing on Sebastian's mind at that moment. He wanted something hot to eat and drink, then a bath. 'Good luck, sir.'

'Thank you. I think we'll need it.'

Sebastian turned to follow his men. Only Bentley and Norton had waited for him. No need for words, they made the exhausting journey down the sap tunnel, stepping on the bodies of dead friends and foe, too exhausted to be shocked by the necessity. Sebastian felt hardly human – a scarecrow man stumbling back, lurching from plank to plank.

'We have to go up here.' Norton gestured to the wooden rungs in the wall of the sap where the tunnel petered out.

Sebastian nodded, the weight of the pack cutting into his shoulders, so heavy that it made each step up feel like the dead hands of the casualties were clinging to his ankles. He fantasized that he could just slip it from his back, throw away his rifle and float up into the sky like a barrage balloon. Instead, bent over like a snail, he slithered out of the sap on to the cursed ground they had crossed that morning.

He looked for familiar landmarks, but there was none. No lights to mark the British trenches as this would be a beacon attracting artillery fire, only the occasional burst of a shell high overhead or Very flare to light up what had become in a matter of hours an unimaginable killing ground. Bodies had been left where they had fallen, with arms flung out or folded to one side as if the soldiers had just decided to lie down and have a kip. Some had been so battered by shell and sniper that they were barely recognizable as human, just lumps of meat no butcher would touch.

'Lord have mercy,' muttered Bentley.

They staggered forward, boots catching on wire and debris. It was like being caught in some devil's maze, a perverted fairground amusement for the damned. The white tape that marked the passage through the churned wire lied more often than it led to safety, a new shell burst having destroyed what had briefly been a way through.

'This is insane,' remarked Norton, catching Bentley's arm as he was about to slide down into a deep shell hole. No one wanted to join the bodies heaped at the bottom, pits that would now be their graves.

'Tot of rum, a smoke and bacon,' chanted Bentley, giving them all something to look forward to when they got back. 'Tot of rum, a smoke and bacon.'

They picked up their pace, walking in time to that little bit of doggerel, until Sebastian stumbled over what he thought had to be a bit of British wire. He fell on his hands and knees. A burst of machine-gun fire. Only when the pain caught up with him did he realize he had been hit.

Norton gave a gurgling cry and crumpled over him, pushing his face down on the tangle of wire.

'Jesus Christ, you stupid bastards, we're English!' yelled Bentley, screaming again as a bullet ripped through his pack.

The gunfire stopped. Sebastian lay crushed against the ground, cheek burning as if red-hot pincers were pushing into flesh, hand mangled, leg throbbing. It took him a moment to realize that he had survived the first day of the Somme only to be mown down by an overzealous sentry on his own side.

Then darkness swept him away.

I4

We don't want to lose you, but we think you ought to go . . .
Hold on, sir.

'How long do you think you'll be gone?'

'There's training camp to survive first. They're cutting back the time we spend in that, sending us off to France to Etaples or maybe Le Havre.'

'Then to the front.'

'Yes. That is the point after all.'

'Sebastian, I really don't want this – don't want to lose you.'

'I know, darling. I don't want to go either. If it weren't for Neil, for everything, I'd say "hang it all" and go draw South Sea Islanders.'

'On your own?'

'What fun would Tahiti be without you? I can just imagine you in a hammock under a palm tree, flowers in your hair, dressed in a grass skirt.'

'Stop teasing!'

'Ouch! I'm joking – well, sort of. It's very tempting.'

'If you come back safely, I'll consider it.'

'Well now: there's a reason for a chap to live if ever I heard one!'

Bring him over here. Sorry, no stretchers left. Grab that sheet of corrugated iron – it'll have to do. Lay him on that.

How's my pal, sir?

Sorry, soldier: he's gone.

What do we have here? He's lost a lot of blood: it'll be touch and go. *So careful of the type she seems, so careless of the single life* . . . Nurse Henderson, put this man on the next train if he lives that long. The doctors on-board can deal with him. The next one now. God's sake, men, lift him carefully!

Voulez-vous de l'eau, monsieur?

So hot, so hot.

Si, monsieur, je le sais. Le train arrive.

'You promise you'll write from France?'

'Of course. Every day if I can.'

'When will you get leave?'

'I don't know, darling. I have to wait my turn. It won't be for months.'

'Oh, Sebastian, I . . . please, please keep yourself safe.'

'I told you that you shouldn't have come to see me off. I knew you'd get more upset.'

'I'm sorry. I promised myself I wouldn't. I'll buck up. Stiff upper lip and all that.'

'That's foolishness, as well you know, and I like your lips just as they are – not all stiff like a colonel. There – that's to remember me by.'

'That's the whistle. Oh God. Did I tell you that I think you look very dashing in your uniform?'

'My brave girl. No, but I'm pleased. I had it made by a tailor.'

'You didn't! Why, Mr Trewby, you are quite the knut!'

'Where did you learn that phrase?'

'From Steven. He says it means a dandified officer.'

'Well, knut or not, army-issue stuff is perfectly ghastly and never fits.'

'The whistle again. This is it, isn't it?'

'Yes, my darling Helen. For the present.'

'I love you.'

'I love you too. You'd better let go of my hand. The train's moving.'

'I can't. I'll run. To the end . . . of the platform.'

'Helen, write to me.'

'I will. I'm going to . . . apply . . . overseas service.'

'No! Stay in London.'

'Can't . . . keep . . . up. Love . . . you!'

Dearest Helen, you can't be serious about accepting the position with the army medical service. You are doing good work in London! I forbid you to take such a risk in the hope of being near me. You are right: it is brutal out here and I can only bear it knowing that you and my family are safe . . .

You don't understand: I have to do this. I accepted the position today. Is a woman's contribution to the war effort any less than a man's?

Darling, please don't write such rot! War is vile, not suited for men, let alone women and boys. Some of the lads have lied about their age (remind you of someone?). I swear there are fifteen-year-olds seeing sights that make veterans sick. Stay in London. If you love me, stay in London.

This one – yes, that's right. His medical notes are attached. Possibly a bullet still left in the wound – make sure they understand that.

1st Somerset Light Infantry. Second Lieutenant Sebastian Trewby. His battalion will have sent a telegram to his family by now. God, what a mess.

PART THREE

Letters

15

Green Park, London, 23 May 1915

'I think this might be our last outing before I go to the West Country to begin training,' Sebastian said, spreading out the rug on the grass.

Helen did not want that news to cast a cloud over the glorious spring day. They could not change things, but they could ignore them. 'Let's not think about that now. I want to make the most of this sunshine.'

'Very wise.' He sat down on the rug and patted the space beside him. 'Plenty of room.'

'I should hope so.' She thought he looked so handsome sitting there smiling up at her. His hair curled back from his forehead in what the barber called a cowlick, forming a natural little wave, leaving his forehead and dark eyebrows clear. His jaw was nicely square, just a little shadowed from his early-morning shave. Her fingers itched to trace it, but they were in a public place so she had to behave and content herself with looking. He had not grown a moustache yet as so many men did and she was rather pleased by that fact. The army would probably make him have one as it seemed to be the fashion these

201

days, something to mark the British officer out from his foreign counterparts.

He started to laugh. 'What are you looking at?'

'You.' She tugged her skirts to one side so she could sit down without getting caught up in the fabric.

He waggled his eyebrows. 'Do I pass muster?'

'You do.'

'For that answer, you get one of these.' He took up her hand and kissed the back. He then placed her palm against his cheek, fulfilling one of her wishes to explore his face. 'I don't want to leave you.'

'Don't tell me: "But you think you have to go."'

'I hate that song.'

'So do I.'

He placed a thrilling kiss on her palm. She could feel the brush of his lips all the way to her toes. 'Helen Sandford, you are worth fighting for.'

Their sweet moment was interrupted by two women in elegant walking dresses, one in rose-pink trimmed with grey, the other in blue and yellow – a chaffinch and a blue tit flapping to the garden feeder in a billow of skirts. They approached the blanket with a purposeful step. Sebastian dropped Helen's hand to his side, but did not let go.

'Ladies, can we help you?' he asked politely when it became clear they had something they wanted to say.

The older of the ladies, white-haired and determined, studied him with distaste. Helen wondered if their behaviour had been somehow shocking, but they had only been holding hands.

'Young man, you are not in uniform I see.' Her voice was as clipped as a box hedge.

Sebastian's sunny smile dimmed. 'No, not yet.'

The lady looked to her companion as if gathering courage, her tone becoming shrill. 'My sons are all serving in France. It is a disgrace that able-bodied boys like you are sitting enjoying the sunshine while they risk their lives to keep you safe.' She held out a white feather that she had already in her hand. It quivered in the breeze, a little exclamation mark of fluff. The badge of a coward.

Something horrid squirmed in the pit of Helen's stomach. She realized it was anger.

'How dare you!' she exclaimed, rising to her feet.

The woman looked shocked to receive such a reception. 'I beg your pardon.'

'It is his pardon you should beg.'

'Helen.' Sebastian tugged at the hem of her skirt, his voice weary.

Helen ignored him. 'You march up to strangers you know nothing about and demand they go and get themselves killed for you. If you are so keen, why don't you sign up yourself?'

'Don't be preposterous!'

The woman's companion muttered something about disgraceful chits.

'No, I'm perfectly serious.' She plucked the white feather from the woman's hand and thrust it at her. 'There. I'm in medical service, nursing wounded men.

What are you doing for the war effort? Your country needs you too.'

'Helen, it's all right. I don't need you to defend me.' Sebastian got up and buttoned his jacket. 'I have just received my commission, madam, so I will soon be in uniform. You should have asked more before making your assumption that I was shirking my duty.'

The woman flushed. 'You should have said at once.'

Helen let go of the feather. They all watched it twirl to the ground then tumble away in the direction of the pond, running away in disgust to have been so used.

'Why should he tell you anything? What business is it of yours?' Helen couldn't get a grip on her temper. All her rage at the poor boys dying by inches in the beds at her hospital now irrationally seemed this woman's fault.

'The women of this country must encourage our men to do their duty,' the lady replied, reaching for the argument that had been repeated too many times like a stamp when the ink wears off.

Helen linked her arm through Sebastian's. 'He is not yours, he's mine. Now go away and take your poisonous words with you.'

The women turned, backs stiff, and walked quickly off towards St James's Park.

'Oh, I could slap the pair of them!' fumed Helen.

Sebastian pressed her to him and hugged her. 'Calm down, darling. They've gone.' He paused, stroking along the line of her spine, then added, 'I've never seen you like this. You have a temper.'

'Yes. Sorry.' She let out her tension with a huff. 'I behaved badly, didn't I?'

'I don't know. Maybe a little. They didn't mean it personally.'

'I can't bear these whippers-in for the government, self-appointed judges over those who have to decide for themselves if they're going to fight or not!'

'Somehow I could tell they weren't your favourite people in the world.'

'Were you embarrassed?'

'No!'

Helen tapped his chest, demanding the truth.

'Well, yes. I can fight my own battles, you know.'

'Strangely I feel the need to defend you.'

He caressed her nape. 'So it would seem. As long as I'm allowed to return the compliment. Now, where were we?'

'I can't remember; the moment has quite passed.'

'I refuse to let two harpies spoil our day. We were sitting on the blanket.' He eased her down. 'You were about to tell me what a splendid chap I am.'

'I was?' A smile tugged at the corner of her mouth.

'Or words to that effect. I was about to stretch out beside you in a decadent manner, enjoying my last few hours of true freedom.' He matched his actions to his words. Helen ran her fingers through his hair. He snuggled closer, laying his head on her lap to allow her to sift through the strands. 'There, does that feel more like it? Has the moment returned?'

She traced the whorl of his ear, the stiff hair of his neat sideburn. 'It's perfect.'

He turned his head to kiss her fingers. 'And so are you.'

'Even with a foul temper?'

'*Especially* with a foul temper.'

The Somme, forward medical station, 17 September 1916

'What on earth are they?' Tugging on the reins, Helen pulled over to the verge. She had just made a supply run into Albert with Lance-Corporal Cook in the pony trap, but had been forced off the road by an enormous . . . well, *something*.

'That, me darlin', is what they're calling a tank.' Cook got down from the seat to steady the jittery pony. Solid under fire, the little creature was spooked by the armoured vehicles rumbling down the track towards them. 'Hush now, it'll be gone soon.' The pony threw its head up in alarm as the growling grew louder. 'There now, nuffin' to worry about.'

Helen felt her sympathies on the issue lay entirely with the pony. The tanks looked like something from *The War of the Worlds*, an invasion from Mars of outlandish spacecraft. A long, fat, cigar-shaped vehicle with two wide belts rather than wheels, it churned up the already pitted road, crushing anything foolish enough to remain in its way. A discarded tin got caught up by the nearest one, travelled round the belt, squashed flat like the flowers Helen used to press in the family bible. Her alarm was only lessened by the crew walking alongside, taking the air and leaving the steering to the driver. One gave her a wolf whistle. She did not take it personally: any female in the combat zone was regarded as worthy of male attention as the competition was so sparse.

'I wouldn't like to be the Germans when that lot come calling,' Cook said cheerfully.

'I hope it makes a difference,' Helen said wearily. The recent rain had wetted down the summer's dust; the tank only carved the road into new ruts like a huge pastry cutter running round the rim of a pie. Extraordinary. Sebastian would have been fascinated by these new war-beasts. His attention was always caught by anything new, particularly machines.

'You and me both, love. I want this blinking business over before I'm pronounced fit.' He patted the pony's neck and whispered secrets into her ear to calm her.

Helen prayed that it would be so. Cook had washed up in the medical station, overlooked during the evacuation of the most injured on the first day of the Somme. He had managed to bag himself a comfortable berth in one of the overflow tents and slept for a week. When he revived, he was on the mend and so decided to put in for light duty around the station, exploiting the few areas not so tightly caught up in military discipline: the uncertain ground of convalescence. The doctors were happy to have the man around as he proved an inimitable fixer, able to get hold of supplies others swore were not available. Dr Cameron carried on signing him fit only for 'light duty'. Seeing the state he had been when he first arrived — head bloodied, arm broken, concussion — the consensus was he deserved the rest.

Helen felt a special bond with Cook when he disclosed his connection to Sebastian. He had been with him during that first day on the Somme, though not at the end. *I'd've bleedin' well made sure 'e wasn't shot by our own side if I'd been there — pardon my French,* he had assured her. He went on to tell her all about Sebastian's bravery, his steadiness, the trust he engendered in the men. She suspected he might have elaborated a little to please his audience, but that was fine by her.

The tanks rumbled over the ridge and out of sight. Helen picked up the reins as Cook jumped up to the seat, rocking the old cart.

'The way I see it,' Cook continued, fired up by his subject, 'is we all have our turn then we should be allowed to go 'ome and let some other chap or —' he glanced at her, his square, hollow-cheeked face dimpling into a smile — 'chap-ess risk their neck.'

'And you've done your share?'

'I think so. Eighteen months is a long enough stretch at the front; blooming miracle I survived. I now deserve a nice cushy number at a desk or guarding the supply train or somefink. I get fed up with seeing the red tabs come out here and tell us what a wonderful job we're doing. "If it's so wonderful, why don't you get out of your staff car and swap?" I want to ask 'em.'

'I can see how you might think that.' Helen nudged

the pony round the rim of a shell hole. They had taken the trap because it was the only vehicle small enough to negotiate the pitted road.

'Then I sees a little lady like you being braver than half the soldiers in France and I think I should really get back to my regiment.' He puffed out smoke to one side so it did not bother her. 'But some'ow, I just don't 'ave the balls for it any more. I think they've gone and rationed courage and I've spent all me stamps.'

Helen swallowed against the lump in her throat. It was rare to hear one of the fighting men actually admit to such a thing, though many of them felt it: you could see it in their eyes. There lurked a fear of disgracing themselves in front of their companions. Sometimes the only thing that made them take the risks they did was the shame of being called a coward. 'You haven't lost your courage, Cookie. It takes an uncommon amount to admit that you're afraid.'

The cockney turned away again, but not before she glimpsed that he had – no, surely not – *tears* in his eyes. 'I 'ave this reputation, you see, darling. Cheeky chap, the fixer, good in a tight spot. But what 'appens when that cheeky soldier goes on his hols and leaves plain old Reginald Cook behind, eh? I'm not much good to anyone then. Not a fighter, me. If I 'ad me way, we'd get Fritz to the table and sort this business out like a couple of market boys haggling over a job lot of veg.'

Helen chuckled as she knew he wanted. Tears were not to be acknowledged. They were too terrible – like a fatal wound. 'I wish you were in charge. You'd soon sort this out.'

'That I would. But I'm not sure I can face the trenches again. Not knowing what I know.'

If only she had the power to give him a medical discharge, send him home to his large family and his beloved East End. 'You're a survivor, Cookie. That's what's left when Reginald remains.' The pony tossed its head as if agreeing.

'My wife calls me Reg. No one out 'ere does.'

She understood that to be an invitation to step behind the scenery and meet the real man. 'Well, Reg, let's hope those tanks are as good as they look then.'

Later, as Helen changed dressings on the newest influx of casualties to the medical station, she thought about what Cook had said. He was a brave man whatever his fears to the contrary. Sebastian had always said so in his letters. But had they both done to Cook what everyone else did: seen only the surface and not wondered what was going on behind those shrewd grey eyes of his? She feared she might have been yet another to underestimate him.

'Nurse, nurse, I can't see!' whispered the boy in the bed before her.

'It's the bandages, soldier. You were gassed, remember?' She patted his hand.

'It's so dark. I can't see!' The patient had been muttering this ever since he had been brought in.

'We don't know that yet. It may be only temporary. Have faith, private. We're doing our best for you.'

'Nurse, nurse, I can't see!' His lost, confused voice broke her heart. His mind was unable to take in her words of comfort.

'There now. Sleep if you can.' She sat holding his hand, hoping this would work where speech did not.

He subsided, his head tossing for a few more minutes before he dipped back into merciful unconsciousness.

Helen released his hand, nodded to the sister-on-duty that she had succeeded in quieting the patient and then continued her work. The men and women in the hospital rarely spoke about the serious things that surrounded them, or told each other what price they were having to pay for enduring it. The confession Cook had made to her had probably taken him as much by surprise as it had Helen. She sensed he rarely spoke to anyone about what was really going on in his head. It had been an honour that he had picked her. Soldiers often felt able to unburden themselves to the nurses as they were outside the ordinary military apparatus, reminders of the families back home, wives, daughters, mothers. The fact remained that she could do no more than listen. She could not stop the commanders sending men to the front, could not argue that this one had had enough and should be allowed home. Her voice was no more than a spark whirling up from the bonfire of the Somme.

Had Sebastian felt like this, she wondered? Cook thought him a hero, but she suspected that fighting had come no more naturally to him than it had to the cockney. How she would love to be sitting beside

Sebastian right now, letting him rest his head in her lap like he once had, sifting her fingers through his hair and allowing him to tell her what he had really felt about killing men and putting himself in danger for king and country.

Your country needs you. The slogan had driven many men into the teeth of battle and she had played her part in sending them there by expecting to be defended. But what did the soldiers now need from their country if they were so lucky as to survive? Ordinary men turned into killers – that would take its toll on their generation. How could you go from that back to being a bank clerk, a student, a farmer – or an artist?

She tucked the sheet round the boy, thinking of Sebastian and how he must have looked when he passed through hospital, though she had not seen him. An hour ago, just before she had parted company from Cook to go on duty, he had asked her if she had news of her 'young man'. Cook was devoted to Sebastian as his commander and the one who had recommended Reg for promotion to Lance-Corporal. It was a comfort to Helen to be able to speak of Sebastian with someone who knew him.

'Yesterday. He managed to write the letter himself. He's getting better he says,' she had replied. 'Thinks he should get himself back on active duty as soon as possible.'

Cook's response was emphatic and heartbreakingly familiar in the soldiers she nursed.

'If you love him, tell him to keep well away. He's done his bit.'

White Towers, near Taunton, 17 September 1916

Pencil lax in his fingers, Sebastian gazed out over the striped lawn from the terrace, watching the shadow-clouds race across the surface, turning patches of grass from dark emerald to muddy green then back again in one of nature's conjuring tricks. The wind whipped the tops of the trees of the copse at the end of the garden, shaking them with the vigour of his dog playing with a blanket. Sun glittered on the glass of the Orangery, in which he sat, splinters of light like frozen shell bursts.

So utterly strange. Part of him was still dangling by his fingertips over the blast furnace of the Somme slaughter while somehow at the same time idling in the English countryside in a scene of almost mocking beauty. His soul was disorientated as if it were a passenger that had slept through his station and woken up somewhere completely unexpected. No one here really could understand what was happening across the Channel. If they did, would they not run screaming in the streets, beat down the doors of Downing Street and demand an end to the madness?

'My dear, do you want more tea?' His mother came in from the house and pressed her hand comfortingly on his shoulder. Charlie, his chocolate Labrador, trotted in on her heels and slumped at Sebastian's side, exhausted. That dog needed more exercise or fewer biscuits.

'No thank you.' He touched her hand, signalling that she should remove it. 'Has the post come?'

His mother swallowed her exasperation at his often-repeated question. Being a convalescent at home had revealed new sides to his mother's character. Normally a waspish woman keen to have her way, he would have laid bets that Lady Mabel would make a terrible nursemaid, but she had been so relieved to get Sebastian back that she was more than happy to put up with his foibles while he recovered. Never having been comfortable with showing affection before, she now took every chance to touch him, reassuring herself he was still with her. Sebastian found the change sad because its cause was so terrible. She had already lost Neil and had so nearly been deprived of Sebastian; that realization had brought barriers tumbling down. Well, half down at any rate; his mother was not yet of the overly demonstrative school of love. A casual touch from her meant as much as a hug from another.

She squeezed his shoulder. 'No post so far. I'll bring it when it comes as I always do.' She bore his devotion to a girl she had never met with resignation. He suspected Helen was not quite real to her.

'What about the newspapers? Any more word of what's happening on the Somme?'

'Your father has them. I'll go and see.' She retreated with a steady *tick-tick* of her heels on the tiled floor.

He was being an annoying patient, Sebastian knew that, not suffering in stoic silence as a chap was supposed to do. The problem was that, while he fretted about his slow climb to regain mobility, he had little to occupy him but worry about Helen stuck a few miles from the front line. He couldn't even sketch – his lines seeming pitiful chicken scratches when lives were being lost every second in France. The grinding campaign on the Somme had continued all summer; more lives thrown into the war machine in the hope of the decisive breakthrough, but emerging only as minced meat. He knew how vulnerable even the forward medical stations were to shelling or aerial attack. He could be sitting here wrapped in a blanket while Helen lay dying somewhere; how was he to know? Only her letters had kept him sane.

He touched the pile of envelopes that he slipped down the side of the armchair in which he spent all day. In their exchange of notes, they had worked out that he must have passed through her hospital without realizing it, but she had been so busy during those awful days, and he barely conscious, that it was perhaps no surprise that they had not met. The confusion had meant that only the most urgent cases or most vocal patients had come to her attention – he had been neither.

As soon as she had heard of his injuries, she had written that she wanted to come to see him, but her duties had kept her in France so far. With casualties piling up every day, a nurse could not abandon her post, not when she was most needed. They had both known they would have to be patient, but the separation was at least as painful as his wounds. Sebastian wondered if in some way it was harder for him as he was the one condemned to do nothing but worry whereas at least she had her work to sustain her. He could now sympathize with the lives of the women left behind while their menfolk went off to fight. Waiting for news was the worst.

Footsteps returned at a rapid beat. 'Here, darling, I've got *The Times*. Your father says it's good news for once. It seems they've invented some new kind of armoured car that can roll over the wire.' His mother placed the paper on the table beside him. 'Ready for more tea?'

Sebastian fumbled with the large pages, finding the broadsheet awkward to manage while stuck in his chair. 'Really, Mother, no thank you.' She was right: there did seem to be some positive news at long last from the front. He felt his own uselessness more than ever. 'I'll read this properly later. I think I'll take a walk.'

Charlie looked up at that hopeful word.

His mother was less keen. She rubbed her palms together. 'In that case, I'll fetch your father.'

The last thing Sebastian wanted was company to witness his weakness. 'On my own. I have my sticks. I'm only going as far as the terrace wall.' Ten yards away. The distance was as difficult for him to cross as a patch of no man's land.

'Then let me help you up.' Without waiting for an

answer, she removed the paper, blanket and letters from his lap. 'Don't tire yourself. The doctor said you must take it slowly. Not expect miracles.'

'The doctors also said I'd lose the leg, but see, it's still with me.'

She placed her arm round his shoulder and heaved as he pushed. 'I know, darling. We are all proud of the way you've bounced back.'

He gritted his teeth against the agony. Sweat beaded on his forehead; his skin felt clammy. 'Not so much of a bounce – more a trickle back.' He grasped a stick firmly with his right hand, wrapping his left cautiously round the second. One bullet had deprived him of his little finger, but the hand had healed much quicker than his leg and he had lost very little dexterity, thank God. He had also come home with a scar across the left side of his face. It caught the corner of his eyelid, making it droop slightly. Steven had claimed he now looked like a pirate; Sebastian thought it just made him look perpetually tired, like a basset hound.

'I'll wait here, shall I? It really is a lovely spot you've chosen.' His mother plumped the cushions on the chair, gathering up the letters that had slid down the side.

'Please don't. I'll be fine. I'd like to do this on my own. I'll send Charlie if I need help.'

His mother snorted. 'That dog is the worst-trained animal in England. I doubt he'd come for anything but a treat.'

'If I really needed help, he'd dig deep and overcome his innate laziness.'

Reluctantly, she retreated. Sebastian knew full well she would send other messengers to check on him – Pennington most likely – but he could count on privacy for a few precious moments. Taking a breath, he put one foot in front of the other, Charlie keeping pace. The grinding pain was familiar, perhaps less than the week before. Creeping like an old man, he made his way across the tiles, over the step – pause for a breather – then continued until he reached the thigh-high grey wall. He sat on it, feeling like a castaway finally making the shore. He had made it – his first goal. Recovery was no longer a dream.

Charlie looked up at him in disgust as if to say, 'Is that it?' before settling down in this new patch of sunshine.

'Sorry, old chap. That was a marathon for me.' The only thing now was getting back without falling flat on his face. Maybe he would wait for Pennington to sail by and signal him to come save him.

16

Sebastian was feeling pleased with himself. He had managed to walk to the wall and back to his seat without collapsing. He had even allowed his father to witness the small victory, a sure sign he was regaining his confidence.

'I think you're making splendid progress,' Theo Trewby acknowledged as his son sat down with a relieved thump, a glance askance like a batsman checking with the umpire he really had hit a six. Elbows resting on the arms of the garden seat, Theo arched his long-fingered hands and tapped his mouth, certain about his verdict.

Sebastian revelled in the congratulations. 'Thanks. I didn't think I'd make it.'

'We had every faith in you.' Theo had a poise that reminded Sebastian a little of a large wading bird, an egret perhaps, stepping carefully through the muddy waters of English society. He smiled to himself – Helen would like that or maybe she would correct his naturalist's observation. Ever since they had been together he had taken more notice of the wildlife around him, almost as if she had lent him her eyes in exchange for his heart.

'We're very pleased that you're on the road to a full recovery.'

Ah. Sebastian knew his father well enough to sense the hollowness to those words. 'You'd prefer that I stayed wrapped up in a blanket for the rest of the war?'

Theo shifted uncomfortably, his big frame making the chair creak as he crossed his legs. He shared with Sebastian a long, lean stature that made normal furniture inadequately sized to meet his needs. 'The thought does have its attractions. Will you rejoin your regiment?'

That prospect seemed very distant to Sebastian. 'I suppose I should. When I'm fit.'

'I could ask your grandfather if there's something in Whitehall or army HQ for you.' An American democrat, Sebastian's father hated using his wife's aristocratic connections for favours, but for his son he would sacrifice such principles in the blink of an eye.

The offer reminded Sebastian of the special dislike the men reserved for the red tabs from headquarters when they toured the front. 'I'm not sure I could face myself in the mirror if I became one of the paper-pushers.'

'You need paper-pushers to make any business work.' His father said it in a self-mocking tone as he classed himself as one of these drones.

'Yes, but I don't have to be one myself.' From the evidence of other conversations, other moments shared like this in the late-afternoon sunshine, he knew that his father had a shrewd idea what the front was really like. Theo's imagination had always been more vivid than his wife's, perhaps because his was a generation that had been born in the long shadow of the American Civil War. If anyone could understand, it would be Theo Trewby. 'I don't want to go back to the trenches if I can think of something honourable to do with myself.'

His father poured them both a glass of brandy. The sun was dipping behind the copper beech on the western boundary of the garden so the indulgence was permitted. This father-son moment over the brandy had the sanctity of the confessional; Sebastian could be absolutely sure he would not share anything he said with anyone else in the family.

'It's not that I lack the guts for fighting, Pa. I just can't bear to return to the filth, the stupidity of the whole thing. If we're going to win this thing, I can't see it happening on the ground. It will be other factors.'

Theo nodded. 'Britain needs us.'

'You mean America? Is that likely?' His father had an uncanny knack for knowing which way politicians would go; it was an instinct on which he had built his fortune.

'Almost certain I'd say. It will take a while though. You don't mobilize so many men at the drop of a hat.'

The spring of tension inside Sebastian uncurled a little. If his father was right, then the war could be won. He had not realized that he had lost faith in that prospect, imagining the struggle going on for endless years, France turned into a wasteland, the youth of all countries spent like small change on useless purchases of land that were lost the following week. It was hard to believe in a world without the war now.

'I was wondering, Seb, if you'd thought of trying for the Royal Flying Corps? It would mean you were based back from the front line. Not an easy ride by anyone's estimation – plenty of risk involved – but at least you'd be out of the trenches.'

Sebastian laughed, having a brief image of himself looping the loop, unable to control the joystick. 'What makes you think I have the skills necessary to fly a plane?'

'Actually, I was thinking of you being the navigator, the man in the second seat. They need photographers, people who can interpret maps and whatnot. I thought your artistic training might set you up for this.' He turned to inspect the horizon. 'A mite safer than being the one in the cockpit.'

Sebastian was not sure what he thought about the proposition. He had always imagined that the men in the aircraft were somehow a breed apart. No one he knew had gone in that direction; all his friends had been funnelled into either the navy or the army. The airmen had a reputation of being a bit eccentric.

Then again, he had a taste for eccentric after the ghastly ordinariness of the trenches where individual sacrifice meant so little. At least in a plane you were someone special; your fall – if it came – would be noticed. Better to die like Icarus than a worm cut in half by the plough.

'I'll think about it. It's a good idea, but there's my old regiment to consider.' And that meant loyalties that he could not abandon lightly. Would they think it a defection?

Theo rumbled deep in his throat, a satisfied sound. He knew his seed of an idea had not fallen on rocky ground. 'Good, good. Your mother and I would be happier, I think. If you have to go back, I'd prefer to know you were spending your nights far back, out of range of a stray shell.'

Female voices in the house gave the men warning that they would soon have company. Theo tossed down the last of his brandy.

'Theo, Sebastian, look who's dropped in!' his mother called, waving from the orangery doors.

Sebastian had left strict orders with his mother that he did not want to see anyone other than immediate family. It was amazing that she had managed to keep to them for so long. He cast a panicked look at his father, delaying the moment when he would have to face the visitor.

Theo met his eyes sympathetically, understanding that his son did not like anyone to see his scars. 'It's all right, Seb; it's only Jilly Glanville.'

'Is Jack with her?'

Theo shook his head then turned on his company manners. 'Ah, Jilly, lovely to see you. You're looking mighty fine, if you don't mind this old man telling you so.'

'Mr Trewby, you are a born flatterer.' Jilly's voice was soft, suited to the company of an invalid. Sebastian could feel her at his shoulder – hovering – concerned. He was going to stand up if it killed him; a gentleman did not sit in the presence of a lady. Reaching for the arms of the chair, he pushed himself to his feet. 'Oh, please, Sebastian, don't get up for me.' He felt her fingers gently touch his elbow. 'There's no need.'

There was every need. His pride and self-respect demanded it of him. He stood, ignoring the fact that his leg was shaking like a jelly under him. He shifted his weight on to his good side. 'Jilly, how are you?' He looked down at her feet, not wanting to reveal his scarred face to her. *Come on, Sebastian, you can't avoid her forever.* Her black shoes had a shine his captain would commend.

'I am well, thank you. But how are you? You're looking much better than I expected.'

He managed a gruff laugh. 'Am I? What were you expecting then?' He raised his face to meet her gaze, challenging her to take in his ruined face.

'Oh, your poor eye!' Without thinking, she reached towards him. He got out of range by sitting down.

'Forgive me. I tire if I stand for a long time.' He had been right: his scar was worse to those who hadn't seen many battlefield injuries, more disfiguring than his parents and Steven had admitted. 'Please, do sit down.'

'Yes, of course. We must keep you off your feet.' Jilly looked around for a seat, settling finally on the wall where Theo was now perched, having given his own chair to his wife. She was flustered by her own reaction. She knew she had failed a test by not brushing off the injury.

Funny, it was the least of what had happened to Sebastian, but because it had marred the face that he had to use to present himself to the world, it had come to matter more than the other wounds.

'You haven't changed,' Sebastian said, not sure that he meant it as a compliment. Jilly had kept the air of youthful elegance that had marked her out among their set, neat clothes tailored from light-coloured fabrics, a dainty necklace of pearls, honey-blonde hair swept back in a chignon under a little blue hat that matched her coat and gloves. Neil had been drawn to her as she was the antithesis of his own slapdash ways; he had told Sebastian he had looked forward to corrupting her to mischief after marriage. She had probably harboured the opposite ambition, but all that was nothing now.

'Do stay for some tea.' His mother rang the bell on the table. 'Cook has made a cake. I smelt it as I came in from walking Sebastian's lazy specimen of a dog.'

'Oh, your Labrador! I'm always happy to walk him for you if it's too much,' Jilly offered, rushing to help as ever. Ask for a volunteer and her hand was always the first to go up.

Sebastian would have much preferred to walk his own dog, thank you.

His mother shook her head. 'That's kind of you, but I quite enjoy my rambles with Charlie. He's the best type of male company, quiet and usually obedient.'

Theo knew this was a dig at him, his wife's attempt to lighten the mood. 'Steady on, old girl!'

Jilly laughed. 'Mother sends her love. Jack is in Le Havre. Has a position at the base camp there, something to do with bayonet training.' Pennington brought a tray and set it down between them. Jilly smoothed her hair behind her ear nervously, taking the cup when it was offered to her, but then seeming unsure what to do with it while the tea was still too hot to sip. Once she and Sebastian had been good friends, brought together by her affection for Neil. Their relationship had been the teasing one of brother and sister. Now that dial seemed to have been reset to strangers. Actually, Sebastian realized, he was the odd one out: the others hadn't changed while he felt he was an impostor sitting in the chair that a younger Sebastian should be in. He pulled his attention back to the matter at hand. Jilly was still chattering. 'Mother and Jack have both been so worried. They'll want to know how you are. I hope you don't mind me asking, but is your sight affected?'

Annoyed by the sympathy in her blue eyes, he decided to blast her with the full facts of his infirmities. 'No, I can see, Jilly; I'm just scarred. My leg's out of action still due to a bullet taking its merry time to find an exit from my thigh. Apparently, I'm lucky to have it. Unlike my little finger.' He held up his mangled left hand.

Her pretty lips rounded in surprise. 'So many wounds! Mother told me you'd been shot, but I hadn't realized.'

'I was lucky to come away with only these injuries.'

'Lucky. Yes.' She looked down at her hands. The nails were manicured, even white crescents topping each finger. 'We're so relieved you survived. Our cousin didn't. Remember him? Ferdie? Died ten days after you were injured.'

Her gentle tone reprimanded Sebastian for his bad temper. She had suffered, was still suffering, even if she had not been in danger's path herself. There was nothing wrong with her or her attitude: she was a kind, ordinary sort of girl; it was he who was the brooding presence in the sunny landscape. 'I'm sorry, Jilly. To be honest, I'm more surprised when I hear someone survived the battle than to get news of another death. So many good men are losing their lives.' He buried his bad hand in his pocket so she didn't have to look at it.

'And you seem well on the way to mending. The scar makes you look quite dashing, don't you know?' Jilly had rallied, her initial, more honest, shock giving way to politeness.

'So Steven tells me. Says I have a great future as a pirate.'

She smiled, eyes gleaming with affection for the youngest Trewby. 'No, no, you mustn't listen to him. It's not as drastic as that. It's already fading, no need for a rascally eye patch and parrot. You must come to the hunt ball and let all us girls make a fuss of you.'

'The hunt ball? That old thing still going ahead?'

'Of course. We have to show the Boche they won't drag down our morale. It's not like it used to be, not with so many men away, but we make the best of it, girls dancing with each other and so on. I'll make sure you have a good seat near the action so you can watch us make fools of ourselves.'

Sebastian had a sudden recollection of dancing at the Ritz with Helen. They had muddled their way round the floor, neither of them expert at the one-step, but it had been the most magical dance of his life. She would enjoy the ball. Was there any chance she might get leave? 'When is it?'

'End of October. Plenty of time for you to prepare yourself.'

'For what?' If she thought he would be dancing by then, she would be disappointed.

'For being the centre of attention naturally. Our local hero.' Jilly stood up. 'Thank you for the tea, Lady Mabel. I must be off. I'm helping with Red Cross parcels today.'

'Of course, dear. Send our love to your mother.'

With a little wave, Jilly was off, guided by the ever-present Pennington out through the front door.

'Lovely girl that,' his mother said, placing her empty cup on the tray.

'Mabel,' murmured Theo in warning.

'I'm only speaking the truth. The Glanvilles have been good friends to this family. It would do nobody any harm if she and Sebastian revived their old friendship – good for both of them.'

'We are friends, mother.' Sebastian tapped his knee in frustration. 'But no more if that's what you're hoping.'

'He's got his girl – that brave little thing in France.' Theo got out his pipe and stuffed the bowl with a tiny pinch of tobacco from his pouch. 'Don't go meddling.'

His mother acted all surprised. 'It's you two who are jumping to conclusions. I only meant they were the only ones left behind of their old crowd what with the other boys being away or . . . or . . .' She cleared her throat then set off again. 'The young need each other's company. It must be tedious for Sebastian stuck with us day in, day out.'

'Please, mother, I know what you're doing even if you won't admit it. Don't throw Jilly at me or get her hopes up. I've seen it happen with other chaps and it's not pretty.' With a shudder, he remembered that churchyard in Bramley; that was not going to be repeated here.

His mother got up. 'I meant nothing of the sort, Sebastian. And it's unfair of you to accuse me of meddling, Theodore.'

Oh, now his father was in trouble. When he was called a full 'Theodore' rather than just 'Theo', he was in the doghouse.

His father took it with a shrug. He was well aware his wife had the quirk of blaming others when she was at fault. 'Then we don't have to worry about you stirring up the hornets' nest, do we?' He smiled at his wife.

'Oh, you two!' She stalked off to bark a few orders at the servants to relieve her feelings.

Theo sucked at the stem of his pipe. 'She means well.'

The Somme, forward medical station, 18 October 1916

Helen collected her dinner from the cookhouse and carried it over to the benches that served as the nurses' mess. Food at the hospital was not too bad: plenty of vegetables and meat, usually all thrown together in some kind of stew, but she had got used to that. From what Sebastian had told her about England, she suspected that the medical staff were better fed than many people back home.

Reg joined her at the table.

'Not eating?' Helen asked.

He shook his head and rolled a cigarette between his fingers.

'You need to keep your strength up.'

He huffed and lit up.

'Something the matter?' They had come to an unspoken agreement over the last weeks that he didn't have to pretend with her.

'Doctors 'ave cleared me for active duty. I'm being sent back.'

Helen put down her knife and fork. 'Oh, Reg.'

'Yeah, I've 'ad a good run 'ere. It 'as to come to an end I s'pose.'

'Are you returning to your regiment?'

He took an impatient puff on his cigarette. 'Yup.'

'I . . . I'll be sorry to see you go.'

'Not as sorry as me.'

'No, not as sorry as you.'

He patted her wrist. 'Eat up. I didn't want to spoil your dinner.'

She had lost all desire for her meal. 'Is there anything I can do?'

He nodded. 'Look, if I go west, will you write to my missus for me? Give her a word or two of comfort. You're good at that. Tell 'er 'ow I found friends out 'ere.'

'Of course I will. But I'm counting on you to come through, you know.'

'We'll see. I don't feel too 'opeful myself.'

'Then I'll be hopeful for you. When are you off?'

'Tomorrow.'

'I'll be there to say goodbye. Come back and visit if you can. You'll be much missed around here.'

He scratched at his throat, the noose of the next day already choking him. 'Yeah, I'll do that. If I can. Don't worry about me; I've got a plan. I won't be caught again without a way out.'

Helen puzzled over what he meant. 'You've got a chance of another position? We'd keep you here if your commanders allowed.'

He gave a mirthless laugh. 'And I'd take the offer like a shot. No, nothink like that, lovey. Just don't worry about me, all right? Worry about yourself; keep out of 'arm's way.'

His words did not reassure her. For hours after he had

left her, she fretted over what he had meant like a snag in a pair of stockings. The run of worry grew larger despite her efforts to stop it.

Reg walked off the next morning with a cheery wave, his public cheeky chap image firmly in place along with his newly brushed uniform. His unit was only a few miles away, a short walk that separated their limbo from the hell over the ridge.

'We'll miss him, won't we?' said Mary Henderson, linking her arm with Helen. 'He certainly knew the secret of raising morale around here.'

'And I imagine we'll notice his absence most when we run out of biscuits or tea,' sighed Dr Cameron. 'That man is a genius when it comes to finding things. He's wasted at the front.' He patted his pocket and drew out his cigarette case. 'And I owe him five shillings for our last card game; he never bothered to collect.'

'He's a good man,' Helen stated quietly. 'He hated leaving us.'

Dr Cameron drew out a cigarette. 'Perhaps I could have a word with his CO. I was wondering about running first-aid courses here for the men due to go up to the front.'

'When? In your spare time?' Mary looked sceptical. None of them could remember a quiet day since the Somme offensive began in July.

'Well, it does matter. Those first few minutes after a man's hit – we can't be there, but their mates can. We might save more lives this way.' Dr Cameron tapped the cigarette on the case, twirling it in his fingers.

'Don't they get training already?' Mary gestured in the general direction of England. 'Before they come out, I mean.'

'Yes, but I imagine it's all the more memorable on the eve of having to use it. Some of these boys are straight out of school – never seen a bullet wound or a shrapnel injury – don't have the foggiest idea what to do when they meet it for real.'

'What's this to do with Lance-Corporal Cook?' asked Helen.

'I'd need a man to run the scheme for me – work it out with the regimental HQs and so on. He'd be good at that.'

'Yes, he would. Did you mention it to him?'

Dr Cameron shook his head. 'I didn't want to raise his hopes. I'll put in the request now. See if we can sort this out in the next week or two.'

Helen prayed that Reg would survive that long unscathed.

17

The morning was dragging to its close when all the nurses were summoned to an urgent meeting in the matron's office. Helen had been in bed, having stayed up after her shift to say farewell to Reg. Their section leader, Sister Richards, stood at the window of her office with her back to them, waiting for the last to arrive. Helen counted those present: fifteen. That was the whole contingent. Only something truly extraordinary could have made matron pull everyone off the wards. Her feeling of unease grew.

Sister Richards turned round when the door closed behind Mary Henderson and Miss Kelly. 'Thank you all for coming. I'm sorry to summon those of you who are off duty from your rest period, but I have an announcement to make. Once you've heard what I have to say, I am sure you will understand how serious the matter is.'

The nurses exchanged nervous glances. Was this news that they had to retreat? Had the Germans broken through? Urgent though the meeting was, it didn't seem quite as desperate in tone as that. Helen tried to rein in her wilder imaginings.

'Last night, the medical supply cabinet was broken into. I checked the inventory and twenty morphine pills have been taken.'

In other words, enough to kill a man several times over.

'First I need to ask if anyone took the tablets and failed to write it down on the sheet.'

No one spoke.

'I did not think so. None of you applied to me for the key. The cupboard was forced with a screwdriver. That leaves a more worrying possibility: someone stole the medicine for their personal gain.'

There was a black market in the pills. Only officers were issued them to give out in extremis to treat battlefield injuries, but the common soldiers were keen to get their hands on some to use at their own discretion. An officer wasn't always on hand when a painkiller was needed.

'Who was on duty last night between two and five in the morning?'

Helen raised her hand, as did two other nurses. The matron must have known this, but she was making a point.

'Did any of you see anything untoward?'

Helen thought back to the previous night's work. She did not remember even going near the nurses' room, let alone the medicine cupboard. Night duties all blurred into each other after a while. She shook her head. The other two nurses did likewise.

'So none of you saw anything? Or anyone? Nurse Sandford?'

'Nothing out of the ordinary,' Helen replied. She didn't like Sister Richards' expression; the section leader was looking at her as if she were desperately disappointed. But what could she have done to prevent a theft? She had been nursing the injured, not standing guard over the medicine.

'You three remain behind. The rest of you can go.' Sister Richards turned back to her window.

Mary gave Helen a sympathetic look as the other nurses filed out. Helen and her two colleagues stood awkwardly in silence, wondering what more could be asked of them when none of them knew anything.

Then it dawned on Helen that she could guess who had taken the morphine. *Oh, Reg, was this your way out?* She had no proof, but it fitted. He was familiar with the hospital, had been driven to his wits' end. He would have seen the theft of a few pills as a small matter in the greater scheme of things. She doubted he realized the problems he had left behind for others. How could she even mention it as it would scupper any chance he had of coming back as Dr Cameron's first-aid man?

I have no evidence, just a hunch, Helen told herself. *I don't have to say anything.*

Doctors Cameron and Barnett entered without knocking. Both looked very sombre. They took seats behind Sister Richards' desk, Barnett in the middle. Matron took the third seat at his right hand. Suddenly the meeting had turned into a trial.

'Nurses, we have to get to the bottom of this,' Barnett

announced irritably. He had also been on duty last night and was probably desperate to get to his bed. 'Sister Richards here requested an opportunity to ask one of you to confess before we got involved, but I understand that has not happened. We are extremely disappointed.'

Dr Cameron cleared his throat and fiddled with the pile of letters on the desk in front of him.

Helen had a horrid recollection of a time when she was seven of being summoned before her primary-school headmistress to be blamed for a broken window when she had not even been among those throwing stones. The mistake had been straightened out quickly, but for a few minutes she had felt the awfulness of being a scapegoat. It was happening again.

One of the other nurses, a Miss Kite from Liverpool whom Helen hardly knew, raised her hand.

'Yes, nurse?'

'I would like to say that Miss Hunt and I were on duty together the whole time as I had been ordered to show her our routines as she's new to the unit.'

Miss Hunt, her face pinched and pale, nodded eagerly. 'That's the truth, sir.'

'So you can vouch for each other, for every minute? No one took a break, went outside under any pretext?' Dr Barnett pressed.

'No, sir. We had a break at four, but we stayed on the ward as a man was . . . well, he was breathing his last and we held his hand as he passed.' Miss Kite folded her hands in front of her, head hung, as if the admission of offering comfort were a shameful secret. 'Isn't that right, Sally?'

'Yes, yes, that's true. Neither of us stepped into the nurses' room, not even for a tea break.'

'Nurse Sandford?' Dr Barnett turned to her. 'Can you account for your movements last night?'

'Not to the same degree, sir. I remember it as a normal night. I remember seeing Miss Kite and Miss Hunt holding vigil with the corporal who died. Lung collapse and pneumonia.'

'Did you go into the nurses' room?'

'I think I did. I usually have some tea around three to keep me going.'

'Did you notice if the door was unlocked or if the cabinet had been tampered with?'

'No, I remember unlocking the door as usual. The room appeared undisturbed, but then I wasn't looking for any sign of a break-in so I may have missed it.'

'We're not looking for a person who broke into the room. The door was unlocked and locked behind the perpetrator. It was only the cupboard that was forced. We fear it has to be one of the medical staff.' Barnett drummed his fingers on the desk. 'Miss Sandford, you can see that you've left us in a difficult position.'

How had she done that? By acting as normal? 'Sir?'

'You are the only one to have admitted being in or near the room when the theft took place. I will ask Sister Richards to conduct a search of your quarters. Until then, you will stay here.'

Helen found the suggestion that her private things should be picked through on a flimsy suspicion immensely offensive. 'You won't find anything, I assure you.'

'Why?' Barnett glared at her. 'Because you've already handed the black market pills off to your contacts?'

'No!' Helen was truly shocked that he could entertain such a low opinion of her. 'I meant there was nothing to find because I didn't steal anything.'

Barnett flicked his fingers in the direction of the other two nurses who were standing close to each other in a mortified huddle. 'You two can go.'

They left but not before they had given Helen an accusing look as if it were her fault they were caught up in this ugly scene.

'Miss Sandford, Helen,' rumbled Dr Cameron, 'try and help us prove you innocent here. Can you think of anyone who might have had the opportunity to rob the cupboard last night? Whoever it was did not take much. My deduction was that it was either for personal use or because they hoped no one would notice. Only Sister Richards' admirable inventory and the scratches around the cupboard lock alerted us to the theft so soon.' Dr Cameron's balding crown no longer seemed a comforting beacon, more a rock on which Helen was about to be wrecked.

'People are coming and going all the time, sir. I really couldn't say. I was with my patients.' Helen's shock was thawing to fear and anger, a poisonous brew swirling in her stomach. How could she prove her innocence? She could fling accusations at Reg, but one, he was gone and they might say that she was doing it on purpose, choosing someone not there to defend himself; and two, she did not want to get a friend in trouble and take away his chance of getting his safe job. She would have to stick to her position of ignorance.

Dr Cameron frowned. 'What aren't you telling us, Miss Sandford? Your face is quite expressive, you know; you're not sharing all your thoughts with us.'

'I was trying to puzzle out how someone could have gone in behind my back,' she replied, hoping her voice was steady.

'Yes, that is a mystery,' agreed Dr Barnett snidely.

'I would never – have never – taken anything without permission from that cupboard. I know how dangerous those medicines can be in the wrong hands.'

The two doctors exchanged a glance. Helen rubbed her upper arms, trying to bring warmth to her chilled skin. The gulf between the male doctors and the female nurses had always been there, but now it felt as wide as the Grand Canyon. They were clubbing together, even nice Dr Cameron, assuming the fault lay with the nurses; why were they not questioning themselves? The doctors had ample opportunity to help themselves to the medicine store; why did it have to be her rather than one of them? She sensed they had entered the room with a pattern in their head of who would be guilty; she fitted that description so was condemned out of hand.

'This isn't fair, Dr Cameron; you know it isn't. What have I ever done to make you suspect me of this crime?'

He coughed and rolled a pen in his fingers. 'I do not suspect you of trying to sell medicine on the black market, Nurse Sandford –' she felt a wave of relief – 'no, my suspicion is that you have been prevailed upon to slip a soldier a few pills because they worked on your generous heart.'

Helen's jaw dropped. How could he think such a thing? She had trusted him, liked him, and all the time he thought her capable of such a betrayal – through weakness!

Dr Cameron was not looking at her so did not notice her expression. 'Quite wrong-headed, of course. Furnishing another with the means to commit suicide is no mercy. Our profession vows to do no harm, and this clearly breaks that.'

'You are wrong on all counts,' Helen stated firmly. Her knees were shaking, muscles spasming, but no one offered her a seat. Angry beyond words, she sat down on an unoccupied chair. Better that than collapse.

Silence fell in the room. Outside the noise of the hospital went on as usual, the growl of arriving ambulances, the calls of the injured. They sounded like the mewing cry of seagulls, hardly human. *What a waste of everyone's time*, she thought. *We should be out there – helping*.

Sister Richards returned bearing a sheaf of letters. She placed them on the table in front of Dr Barnett with care. He frowned, uncertain what they meant. Helen recognized them as her personal correspondence, most from Sebastian, a few from Flora, one from her mother that had been forwarded by Toots at Christmas – old stuff, nothing that could have any bearing on last night.

'Did you find any pills?' Dr Barnett asked.

'No, sir.' Sister Richards waited.

'Then why did you bring these?' He flipped the top envelope. 'I hardly think we should stoop to reading the girl's love letters.'

'I wanted you to confirm my suspicion. Please take a closer look at the letter at the top.'

Dr Barnett pulled it out of the pile and slipped it from the envelope. 'Good God, it's in German! Can you read this?' He thrust it at Dr Cameron.

The Scotsman picked it up gingerly and scanned it. 'I understand the gist – nothing but family news and Christmas wishes.'

Helen felt like a mountaineer as the slope she climbed began to crumble beneath her boots. 'Of course there's nothing else in it. It's from my mother.'

'You're German?' Barnett's question came out as an accusation.

'My mother is German. My father is English. She never learnt to write well in English so has always written to my sister and me in her native tongue.'

Barnett stood up. 'Sister Richards, did you know Miss Sandford was German?'

'No, sir. Never suspected it.'

Dr Cameron placed the letter back in the envelope.

'One moment, Dr Barnett, don't go leaping to conclusions. Miss Sandford here is only half German – no cause to question her loyalty to her English side.'

'So did you know then?' Dr Barnett's voice had risen a notch, indignation pouring from him like blood from an arterial wound. The more he let his mood splash and spill in the room, the less Helen felt like defending herself. It was so pointless. She was half German; she hadn't made it known because she feared a reaction like this; that was enough to condemn her, particularly when she had already been found guilty of the other matter without evidence to support it.

'I don't know what to say to you. Yes, my mother is German. No, that does not change how I feel about my job here as a nurse or my loyalty to my country, though I regret the war of course.'

Dr Barnett snorted.

'I did not take the pills and did not see anyone else do so. If you decide I am guilty of theft, you are doing so without a scrap of evidence; if you condemn me for my heritage, well, I can't do anything about that.' She shrugged, but the movement was mere bitter bravado.

'We are more worried that you hid your heritage from us,' said Dr Cameron.

'I did not hide it. I was never asked and it didn't seem relevant. I don't know who your parents are, Dr Cameron, or yours, Dr Barnett. For all I know they could be Japanese.'

'Don't be ridiculous. How could it not be relevant?

You must have loyalties to your mother's country – you might even be aiding Germany for all we know!' Barnett shook the Christmas letter at her as if this were a top-secret document.

Dr Cameron put a hand on his forearm. 'Steady on. We mustn't leap to conclusions.'

But that was just what they had done.

'I can't change what I am. I can't prove my innocence when you have already decided I am guilty.' Helen felt light-headed, almost reckless. 'Strange, I thought English justice was based on the idea that someone is presumed innocent until guilt is proven.'

'Miss Sandford, you had the opportunity. No one else did,' said Sister Richards.

'Clearly that is not true because I am not the thief.' She hugged her arms round her waist, fearing she would break apart.

'Helen, you have to see how it looks to us.' Dr Cameron squeezed his hands together, hating the whole business he had been dragged into.

No, she didn't have to see, because if he were her friend, as he had appeared to be for the last few months, he wouldn't do this to her. Her colleagues should at least give her the benefit of the doubt after her weeks of faithful service, wading without complaint through the blood of the casualties, but here they were, all too ready to believe the worst of her even before her German half had been revealed. With that put on the scales against her, she could see they would not shift from their view that she had to be responsible for the crime as a German girl would naturally be working against them.

'I am innocent,' she whispered. 'Why won't you believe me?' She bit the inside of her mouth to stop tears forming. No more – she would give them no more of herself.

'I'm afraid, Miss Sandford, the circumstances suggest otherwise. You are relieved of your duties and must be confined to your quarters until we decide what to do with you.' Dr Barnett made a note on a piece of paper in front of him. 'I'm not sure what steps need to be taken now, not having had a nurse do such a thing before. I suppose you should be court-martialled – the hospital functions under military discipline.' Dr Barnett straightened his cuffs.

'It's only a few pills,' pleaded Dr Cameron. 'I would have thought we could be satisfied with Miss Sandford's resignation.'

'What about her German affiliation? We can't let a dangerous person roam the front.'

'She is only half German and I've never seen any evidence that she had looked for information beyond what pertained to her duties. Don't throw such accusations about. The penalties are too grave for us to make a mistake.'

Helen stared at the wall, feeling detached as they discussed whether or not she had passed secrets to the Kaiser. They could get her shot if they carried on spinning such insubstantial stuff into formal charges. Her desire to do her duty, to risk the same as a man, had not even been mentioned. Her sacrifices all for nothing. She had never felt German, never considered for one second that she might side with the enemy. They were cutting her open with their accusations.

'Helen?' Dr Cameron was talking to her, but she didn't want to answer. 'Miss Sandford?'

She dipped her chin.

'Dr Barnett has been persuaded that it is enough if you resign and return to England at the earliest opportunity. Do you agree to do so?'

Her fingers clenched the coarse material of her skirt. 'I can't be a nurse any longer?'

'I'm afraid not.'

'Even though I've done nothing wrong?'

'We have to agree to differ on that.'

'You're giving me no choice.'

Dr Barnett spluttered. 'You have a choice between prison and freedom, Miss Sandford. I think we are being more than generous. I don't think you realize just what the repercussions of your behaviour are going to be. We're giving you a chance to leave before the news of your outrageous abuse of a position of trust becomes widely known.'

'You could stay and bring your case to a court martial, but I would not advise it,' Dr Cameron said. 'The penalties would be severe.'

'Again you assume I'd be found guilty.'

'You'd be held in custody until the military court convened.'

Helen was engulfed in a wave of fear and loneliness, suddenly aware how young and isolated she was with no family or friends around to advise her. Should she stand her ground and sit in a military cell until her case was heard? But so much about her was founded on lies if they asked – her age, her background. Doubtless, they'd turn what had been innocent stretching of the truth or omission of certain details about her family into a fiendish plot to undermine the British military. Already her reputation was to be shredded by the newspapers back home, it seemed, with no recourse to justice for her. She was being made a pariah. Really she had no option.

She gave a tiny shrug. 'Then I resign.'

Dr Cameron allowed himself a relieved smile. 'Go home, Helen. Put this behind you. You're not a bad girl though you may have made mistakes here. You can start again.'

But she didn't have a home and no one would take her in if her name were bandied about as a suspected traitor. All she had was Sebastian. Oh God, what would he say when he heard of her disgrace? Would he believe her or would he also turn out to be a man of straw when she went to him for help, much as Dr Cameron had? She couldn't bear it if he did. No, he wouldn't. Not Sebastian.

'Go to your room and pack your things, Miss Sandford,' Sister Richards said. 'The next medical transport leaves for Le Havre at three. Make sure you are on it.'

Leaving with no thanks, no reference. They truly were intent on destroying her.

Helen stood up, gathering her dignity to herself like a cloak. 'You are wrong, you know, about all of it. And I can't find it in myself to forgive any of you.' She walked out, leaving the door open behind her.

18

Helen sat in the corner seat of the carriage carrying her own quarantine with her. The nurses and doctors on duty had little time to spare to wonder about her presence, and had merely been told to ensure she went directly to Le Havre without alighting or talking to anyone en route. She had even been forbidden from making herself useful though she could see several injured servicemen in her vicinity who would benefit from fresh dressings and more liquids. Shock had dulled her feelings, otherwise she would have got up and dealt with the need in front of her rather than accept it. Instead, she was reduced to staring out of the dirty window, watching the fields flick by, crops scraped off mud so only stubble remained, bullet-like grain bundled to a miserable harvest home after a wet summer.

It was strange how quickly her life had been rolled up and stuffed in her valise. Mary Henderson had helped her — against orders — decrying the verdict passed so entirely without evidence. In fact, she had done most of the packing as Helen had been unable to do more than stand in the middle of the room hugging her diaries to her chest. Helen suspected from a few things Mary said that she too had reasoned that Reg might have been behind the theft. It would be well within his character to acquire what he needed. The doctors had applauded this very trait in him. Mary must also have decided that flinging accusations would not change the outcome, not now Helen's parentage had been dragged out and paraded before the entire camp. Even if found innocent of theft, Helen was irreparably tarred and feathered in their minds for collaborating with her German blood.

Mary had carried Helen's bag to the train and hugged her before putting her on-board.

'You'll be all right,' Mary whispered. 'Don't let them beat you down.' She gave Helen one of her particularly stern librarian looks which under normal circumstances would have succeeded in bolstering her spirits.

Helen had clung on to her colleague for a weak moment, then stood up straight. 'Thank you, Mary. I appreciate what you've done for me.' Her words lined up like tin soldiers vulnerable to being knocked over at the first careless swipe.

'I so wish I could bang heads together – do something to reverse this appalling travesty of justice!'

Helen picked up her suitcase. 'It helps – that you believe me, I mean.'

'You, steal anything? The suggestion is preposterous!' Mary's eyes shone with angry tears. The injustice was not to be borne, but what could they do?

'Thank you.'

Helen clutched Mary's words to her through the flat countryside of France, a little nugget of warmth in the chill afternoon. They left the rolling river valley of the Somme behind and entered the flatter ground of Normandy. The train bisected a long road lined by sentinel poplars, an elderly cyclist in a battered black hat waiting by the level crossing for the engine to carry its load of young casualties to the coast. He saluted those passengers well enough to be propped up by the windows, a gesture that Helen found profoundly touching as it recalled to her that her suffering was only one tiny droplet in a vast ocean. She needed to bob to the surface of her depression, but could not quite manage it. Not yet.

There was something about that road that was familiar. It may not have been that very one, but she remembered a golden afternoon in spring when Sebastian had managed to get leave and came to see her in Le Havre – the first time they had managed to meet since she had waved him off at Victoria the year before. He had somehow acquired a motorbike (she now suspected the hand of Reg Cook behind that) and lured her out on her afternoon off. They had driven along roads very like the one the track had just crossed, enjoying a rare few hours of unfettered freedom. Funny how that time had firmed up her resolve to be nearer him, and that had set her on the path that had brought her to sit on the train heading back to England in disgrace. Men talked of a Blighty wound – the lucky injury that was not too serious, but meant being sent home; the false accusation had proved to be hers.

Le Havre countryside, 7 May 1916

Waiting outside the little cafe near her hospital camp, Helen admired the approach of the dark green motorbike with its mud-splattered wheels, a mechanical warhorse just off the field of Agincourt with her own leather-coated knight in the saddle.

'Sebastian Trewby: where did you get the petrol?' She folded her arms in mock reproof as the engine died.

'Ways and means, dear girl, ways and means.' Sebastian lifted his goggles from his face, leaving white marks around his eyes, a reverse panda. He made a quick swipe across his cheeks with the end of his white silk scarf then swung off the bike. 'Darling!'

She ran into his open arms, not caring if her dress would bear the marks for the rest of the day. 'I am so, so pleased to see you!' She linked her arms under the flaps of the coat round his waist, enveloped in the musky smell of leather, motor oil and Sebastian himself.

He lifted her up and swung her in a circle. 'It's been too long. How many months?'

'Ten. Three hundred and fifteen days.' Her anxiety that somehow, over the months of forced separation, his love for her would have cooled, evaporated like morning mist; she was left with the clear sight of him still proud to claim her as his girl. She felt so proud, so happy, she wanted to fly up like a skylark and sing.

'I take it you're pleased to see me?' he asked, not letting go. He needed to re-establish closeness just as much as she did.

She nodded against his chest, letting the action speak for her.

'Sadly, I only have four hours before I have to return the bike. Let's not waste it. What do you say: we buy some lunch and go for a ride?'

'Good idea.' She pulled back, but he insisted on keeping hold of her hand, having removed one gauntlet so they could touch skin to skin. He was grinning at her like a man who had just learnt he had been left a huge inheritance by some obscure relative. Helen was delighted to be that stroke of good fortune for him, even if she could not quite believe anyone could see her that way.

The cafe where they had met was a popular spot: a terrace covered with a clownish striped awning, window boxes full of orange-red geraniums, merry gatherings of green tables and chairs. Sebastian towed her through the crowds of service personnel sitting at a Sunday morning breakfast of coffee and fresh bread.

'Monsieur, some bread, cheese, ham and wine, please?'

The Frenchman gave a surly nod, his rosy cheeks bearing false witness to a cheerful disposition; in truth, he was famous in the town for treating his patrons with outrageous contempt. Instead of turning customers away, it perversely encouraged them to come back and bait him in one of his moods (and his wine was excellent so a little pain was worth enduring). He scraped together the requirements for a portable lunch, banging about in the kitchen with much dark muttering as if Sebastian were tearing the last crust out of the mouths of his infants. He proceeded to charge them an exorbitant price for the admittedly fine picnic.

'*Voilà, monsieur, et merci!*' Sebastian exclaimed, throwing the coins on the counter with a flourish. He would pay any price to be alone with Helen and did not even think to challenge the sum charged. His lack of complaint disappointed the proprietor, depriving him of a chance to defend his prices. 'Come on, darling: the open road awaits!'

On the pavement outside the cafe, Helen realized that his scheme had a hitch. 'I don't have the right kind of clothes for motorcycling. Aren't ladies supposed to wear special trouser-skirts?'

Sebastian whistled between his teeth. 'By George, you're right. I fear this is going to be very risqué!' The prospect quite delighted him. He shrugged out of his long coat. 'Here, this is designed for riding, divided at the back but long side flaps to protect legs and hide any . . . um . . . *unfortunate* glimpse of calf and ankle.' He wiggled his eyebrows at her in a theatrical manner like the villain in the melodrama about to tie the maiden to the railway track.

She batted his arm. 'You're enjoying this, aren't you?'

'Every moment. Now, no more excuses. Once we're

out of town, we needn't worry who will get a look at the legs of the most beautiful nurse in France.' He got on the bike, kicked it off its stand and waited for Helen to settle herself behind him, arranging the flaps of the coat as he had suggested. They were attracting quite a few remarks from the men at their breakfasts, most suggesting Sebastian was a lucky dog to have both a bike and a female companion with which to enjoy the sunshine. With a smile to herself, Helen wondered which they hankered after most; she suspected the motorbike.

The vehicle shuddered into life, sending vibrations from her seat to the top of her head. Even her teeth felt like they were rattling.

'Gracious!' she shouted in Sebastian's ear, clinging to his waist. 'I didn't know it was like this!'

'Hold on tight!' he called back. 'Now comes the good bit!' He revved and released the clutch. The bike began to pick up speed, the wind catching on clothes and trying to remove Helen's violet gauze headscarf which was securing her hat in place. Using one hand to tug the brim back, another to keep a grip on Sebastian, she could do nothing to stop the flaps of the coat doing just that: flapping. A cheer from the terrace told her that she had revealed more leg than was seemly.

'You didn't warn me!' She hid her blushes against his shoulder blades.

He laughed. 'I told you it was the good bit. Poor boys – out here risking life and limb for their country; don't you think it only fair to brighten their day?'

'Oh, you!' Helen kept her face concealed until they had escaped the town, hoping she wasn't spotted by anyone she knew.

Sebastian had no plan, being content to let the road lead them where it would. They passed quickly down the long roads, the shadows of poplar trunks painlessly strafing them. He turned the bike north and eventually they reached the cliffs on the coast above Le Havre where he slowed down.

'Here?'

'Yes.'

He parked by a gate and helped Helen clamber over. Hampered by the coat, she paused on the top bar, slid out of it and handed it back.

'You look like a butterfly emerging from her cocoon!' Sebastian laughed.

'I've always thought myself more of a moth. But I've already flown – on the back of the bike. We're getting this all in the wrong order.'

'Then we'll have to fly to the cliff edge.' He vaulted the gate, slung the net bag that contained their picnic across his back, took her hand and began to run. Holding her hat with one hand, she tried to keep up, blushingly aware that she was not sufficiently corseted for such strenuous activity. Sheep scattered in front of them, dirty white tails jiggling as they dashed to a gap in the hedge to escape the two humans.

Sebastian slowed as they came to the fence preventing the livestock getting too close to the edge. Not as high as the white ones on the other side of the Channel, the cliffs still made a pleasant vantage point from which to survey the shipping passing across the blue-grey waters. A little further along, the brown concrete block of an army lookout post stuck to the precipice, binoculars trained on the surface of the sea, seeking the sleek, silver shark U-boats coming among the shoals of hospital ships. The breeze smelt fresh and salty, carrying the faintest tang of the ranker shore smells below of seaweed and fish.

'Perfect!' Sebastian declared, gathering Helen to his side so they could admire the view together. 'If we put our backs to the lookout post, we can pretend the war isn't even happening.'

'Except you're in khaki.'

'Well, we can't help that.' He unbuttoned his jacket, showing the top of his high-waisted trousers, held up by braces over a dark green shirt, standard issue for an officer. 'I'm rather disappointed you aren't in your nurse's uniform.' He tapped her nose in reproof. 'I don't think I've ever seen you dressed for duty.'

'I'd look silly going around with my white scarf and apron for a picnic.'

'No, you'd look like an angel.'

'The men call us that sometimes.'

'Good job they don't know about your temper then.'

'Oh, you!' She scowled at him. 'You'll never let me forget how I told those two harpies off for trying to give you a white feather.'

'No, I won't. It's one of my fondest memories.'

The breeze played in his hair, making it fall over one eye. She brushed it back. 'I think this day is going to be one of mine.'

He moved forward and kissed her, his fingertips tracing the line of her jaw and neck, playing havoc with her tingling nerves when he found the sensitive spot just below her ear. 'Mine too.' He held her close to his chest so she could hear his steady heartbeat under the coarse cotton of his shirt. 'Do you know what we've got here, darling?'

'What do you mean?' She traced the fastenings down the centre of his chest, fingers doing a teasing walk from button to button until he made her stop by the simple expedient of covering her hand with his.

'I haven't been very clear with you, have I? Never told you exactly how I feel.'

'I . . . I think it's hard to put these things into words without sounding like you're in a bad play.'

He kissed the top of her head. 'Agreed, but I'll risk it anyway. I love you. You are everything good and beautiful to me, everything worth fighting for. I knew I had to tell you – I've been too close to death to waste another moment.'

Helen was lost for words, almost scared of being so much to him when she knew she was really not a beauty, not even very nice if anyone lifted the lid on her secret thoughts.

'And I want you,' he continued, 'to say if you agree that we have an understanding. I don't want to rush you – we've not had the luxury of much time together – so I'm not pushing for an engagement or anything like that . . .'

No, he should not tie himself to her, not when she feared she was essentially unlovable once people came to know her well. Her father had taught her that. 'I see, not an engagement but an *understanding*. What are we understanding exactly?'

He laughed. 'I'm making a hash of this, aren't I? We are understanding that I'm for you and you are for me: we're going to stand against this mad, sad world together.'

'I'd like that. Yes, we have an understanding, Mr Trewby.'

'Thank you, Miss Sandford.' He pulled her to sit beside him on the tough, broad-bladed grass that kept the earth from sliding down to the beach below. It was dotted with yellow and purple flowers, prickly gorse and common mallow. A black and orange beetle hung bobbing from one stem.

Helen looked towards England, thinking of all the problems she had left behind there, the broken state of relations with her parents, her lack of roots. Few people would even notice if she disappeared. Only Sebastian offered any hope of her life actually holding on to an anchor, but she did not want to cling on to him for the wrong reasons. She regretted the fact that he was independently wealthy; perhaps it would have been easier to meet as impoverished equals.

'What are you thinking, darling?' He flicked at the

beetle, helping it on its way. It tumbled happily into a new tussock.

'That I wish we were more equal; you have so much and I so little.'

He looped his arm over her shoulders. 'It's true that I'm blessed with a family who have more money than we know what to do with, but that only means I want to share it with you. You mustn't see it as a drawback. I want to make up for all that life has withheld from you. It's a pleasure for me. Besides, you have so much to give me.' He pulled her back so they lay looking at the sky together, her head resting on his arm.

'Like what?'

'I only ask for love – because that contains everything else I need. I am complete with you – more of an artist, more of a person.'

Fine speeches were all very well . . . 'But I worry it won't last – that you'll discover I'm not enough, that I'm not this . . . this *muse* you seem to think I am.'

'Poor darling.' He turned to face her. 'Your father's really knocked the confidence out of you, hasn't he? Please, start to see yourself through my eyes, not his.'

She closed hers for a second. 'I'll try. But have you ever wondered what happens after the "They all lived happily ever after"? What if the prince decides Cinderella is embarrassingly low-born or the princess thinks the frog was much more fun than the man he turned into?'

He chuckled. 'You have the most extraordinary mind.'

'Don't dodge my question – I'm serious!'

'In that case, I'll tell you that I don't see either of us as a fairy-tale character. We are certainly not living in a fairy-tale world. "Happy ever after" is a work in progress, not an end point to our story.'

'I'm sorry, I'm spoiling our day.' Helen felt angry with herself for marring with her doubts the moment when he declared his love.

'Don't, darling. You're right to ask. I've seen enough horror in the trenches to ask the same questions myself. So far, I've always come through thinking that, despite the insanity, love does survive. My family – you – are more important, not less so, when the bullets start flying.'

His words comforted. They made sense: if everything were stripped from her, the last thing Helen would want to let go was her love for others, for him. It was time she admitted this to him; war meant that such things should not be delayed.

'I love you, Lieutenant Trewby.'

He turned his head to hold her gaze, eyes glistening. 'And I love you too, Nurse Sandford. I can't believe how lucky I am to have found you.'

'Oh, Sebastian.' She blinked her own tears away. 'Thank you.'

He tapped the corner of her mouth, reminding her to smile. 'Now, enough serious stuff! I have the most expensive picnic in Christendom in my bag, a sunny day, a beautiful girl with whom I have an understanding –' they shared a look – 'and I'm going to enjoy all of them for the next two hours and forget the Kaiser and his armies for a while.'

'Yes, let's do that. There are only us two in the world. Everything else has disappeared.'

A sheep bleated loudly from behind the hedge.

'*Almost* everything else has gone,' Sebastian teased.

'Us and the sheep then. Perfect picnic companions.'

19

Bewley House, near Taunton, 21 October 1916

Sebastian had been avoiding his mother's family since his accident, but the hunt ball was to be held as usual in his grandfather's home so that self-imposed isolation would have to end. Bewley House sat on a rise at the foot of the Quantock Hills commanding a view of a wooded valley, a secret place where the traditions of previous generations could hang on in defiance of the railway world that whizzed by with new ways and ideas down on the Somerset Levels. No one would dare speak the blasphemy of women's suffrage near the earl, or whisper the name of a trade union. The house itself was the epitome of a stately pile: crumbling grey walls held up by ivy and a moss-covered slate roof that should have been replaced fifty years ago, but was ignored. Buckets in the attic had served the Earl of Bessick's father so damned if they wouldn't work for him too. The best part of the estate was the gardens, but since the war had taken away most of the hands needed to keep such a vast area in check, this too was becoming a wilderness. It reminded Sebastian of an illustration from a book of fairy tales: Beast's castle disappearing under rampant rose bushes. He had always thought his grandfather something of an old monster, so the image was apt.

'Damn my eyes, if it isn't little Sebastian!' crowed the earl as the family got down from the carriage. Once six foot, now stooping a few inches lower, the earl made an impressive figure with the full sideburns and flowing locks of the fashion of his youth, white now rather than the ginger he had once been. 'A tad bashed up, but still a fine figure of a Bessick! Old Jerry didn't get you, eh? Good boy! Good boy!' The last exclamation was accompanied by a hard slap on the back, quite ignoring the obvious fact that Sebastian used a cane to keep balance. Theo Trewby kept a firm grip on his son's elbow to stop him falling, muttering maledictions against his father-in-law.

Sebastian's mother slid in between her father and son. 'Father, Sebastian is still recovering. You must go gently with him.'

'Rubbish, the boy looks in top-notch condition! Bessicks don't take as long as mere mortals to get over a brush with a bullet. I didn't – emerged from the Crimea without even a scratch. Now that was a fight, I tell you. Not like this modern tactic of hiding in the ground and not facing each other like real men. Give me command of the army and I'd have it sorted out in a week!'

Theo rolled his eyes.

'I think you'll find, Father, that Sebastian has done more than his fair share of combat,' Lady Mabel said firmly. 'He did not get his injury hiding from the enemy.'

'Of course not! He's our blood, isn't he, Mabel? Theo.' The earl nodded at Sebastian's father. 'Good to see you. How are my shares, eh?'

'Doing somewhat better since you gave them to me to look after,' Theo replied. He and his father-in-law, after years of bitter family warfare (no American was good enough for an earl's daughter), had finally come to a peaceful coexistence.

'Tolly's running up fearful bills in the Guards; could do with some funds.' The earl frowned slightly at the thought of his wastrel of an heir. He had had to wait for a son, having first a string of 'damned useless' girls like Mabel and her sisters. Tolly was only thirty and still unmarried, living a bachelor's life to the full in London in the fashionable Horse Guards regiment.

'The idea, sir, is to allow the shares to mature, not to pluck the fruit prematurely,' Theo cautioned.

'Hmm, I suppose you're right. I'll have to see what I can get for the Rembrandt then. Gloomy thing – can't say I'll be sorry to see the back of it.'

Sebastian grimaced at this sacrilege. The artwork was a beautiful Dutch still life, one he had enjoyed studying and sketching as a child before he even knew it was famous.

'Had hoped to leave it to your boy here, but there you are.' The earl cruelly dangled grapes in front of Sebastian then whisked them away again.

'Perhaps I could buy it off you,' Theo suggested.

The earl waved away the matter. 'Speak to my agent. Would be good to keep it in the family, even in a cadet branch.' Sebastian suspected that his grandfather had been angling for such an outcome even before he had broached the subject. He was a wily old fox, keeping his world together by strength of will. 'Come along then. Let's go in and see the women.'

That rather ungracious description meant his wife and the unmarried daughters who were unfortunate enough still to live at home, Lady Gertrude and Lady Clara. Sebastian could not bear the elder, Lady Gertrude, who had inherited her father's manner, but he cherished a soft spot for Aunt Clara who was a happy soul in her late thirties. It was a tragedy that her beau had died in the Boer War; she had never found love again and been condemned to spend her spinsterhood in the unforgiving company of Gertrude. She really should be allowed out for good behaviour, Sebastian thought.

The women were waiting for them in the countess's drawing room. Sebastian's grandmother, a bird-like lady with bright eyes and iron-grey hair fastened back in a gauze snood, glided forward and reached up to kiss her grandson. The jet beads on her purple gown glittered in the candlelight (Grandfather resisted conversion to gas, let alone new-fangled electricity). 'You are a naughty boy, not letting any of us visit. We are so pleased to see you well again.'

'Grandmother.' He felt a rush of warmth towards the

old lady. He would not have minded her visiting, but that would have been a breach in the dam letting in the earl and Aunt Gertrude.

Clara joined her mother. 'Dear, dear Sebastian, we have been so worried about you! And, thank the Lord, you came through with only a scratch or two considering the danger you were in!'

'It's nice of you to make light of my appearance.' He kissed the slender Clara on the cheek, noting that her auburn hair had picked up a few white streaks of late. He hoped he was not the cause.

Her intelligent brown eyes twinkled. 'Fiddlesticks, Sebastian, you look very fine. A few knocks make a man more interesting to us ladies.'

A deep cough sounded behind her. Aunt Gertrude was waiting for Sebastian to pay his respects as was her due. He bowed. 'My lady, I hope I find you well?'

'Tolerably so. This autumn weather is playing havoc with my lungs.'

'Fie, Gertie, you're as strong as a horse!' teased Clara. Compared to the elfin Clara, Gertrude was something of an Amazon, broad-shouldered and stately. She would have made an admirable eldest son had fortune fallen differently, a vast improvement on the frivolous Tolly.

'Is Uncle Bartholomew going to be here tonight?' Sebastian asked his grandmother.

'Tolly? Heaven knows! We are the last ones to whom he confides his plans.' His grandmother moved on to greet her daughter and son-in-law, her thoughts skipping over her son like a flat stone on a pond. He had given her too many sleepless nights for her to worry any longer.

The earl stood before the hearth and kicked the cast-iron fire dogs. 'I hope you've got a good appetite. We've asked cook to prepare a special dinner before the ball. Thank the Lord for our home farm else we'd be eating corned beef if the government had its way. Can't bear that foreign muck.'

Sebastian thought fleetingly of all the navy men who risked their lives to escort the flotillas of ships across the Atlantic to keep Britain from starving. His grandfather had never been known for his gratitude to others, but expected inordinate praise whenever he did something.

'I'm sure that will be very welcome, sir,' Theo said calmly, refusing to rise to the jibe against foreigners and their food.

'Sebastian, you can sit by me,' the earl declared, 'tell me all about the war. I know a few people in the House still who have the ear of the men who count; now's your chance to put them straight on a few things. First order I'd give if I were in charge would be to turf them all out of their headquarters and put them where our boys are fighting – that'd soon wake them up!'

Sebastian made a mental list of all the subjects he would prefer to discuss: art, music, family, Helen – not that he would want to broach any of these with his grandfather. The war was the last matter he wanted to dissect over dinner. 'I'm not sure I know very much, sir. I only saw my little corner of the front.'

A gong sounded in the hall. 'Ah, time to go to the table.' The earl rocked on his heels, knees clicking. 'Don't put yourself down, my boy. A Bessick always sees more than another man. I'm sure you know a great deal more than those idiots in Whitehall.'

Theo gave Sebastian a sympathetic look, but the fact that he did not step in to demand a reorganization of the seating arrangements was proof that he considered his son recovered enough for the ordeal. Sebastian supposed that was good news.

Clara took Sebastian's arm as he was to lead her into the dining room. She patted his damaged left hand. 'Don't worry, dear, I'll sit beside you and head Father off as much as I can.'

He raised her hand for a light kiss of gratitude. 'Thank you, Aunt. I fear I may need your cavalry charge before dessert.'

Helen stepped off the train at Norton Fitzwarren, the station closest to White Towers. A little branch line, few others alighted there, only a couple who hurried away to a nearby house before she could ask for directions, and a well-dressed man from first class. The guard unloaded a stack of London newspapers then got back on the train. She didn't want to look too closely at the bundle; she lived in fear that her story had become public. It was only a matter of time.

Dusk was gathering, the world fading. A few beacons of colour resisted the darkness: a bank of evening primroses bloomed against a south-facing wall, teetering on the brink of destruction, yellow trumpet flowers fanfaring the night; a scattering of late white roses rambled over the gate that led to the road below. As the train puffed out of the station, the man paused on the platform to light a cigarette, the flash of the match illuminating his narrow features and military coat. Moths mobbed the light over the closed ticket hall, wings a wicker of protest. Helen looked around her, wondering how she was going to get to White Towers. Sebastian had never said how far it was from the railway station. She supposed she could walk; there seemed no other option available at this sleepy place, not even a porter. Steeling herself, she realized she would have to ask the military gentleman for advice.

'Excuse me, sir?' She stopped a few yards from him, not liking the necessity of approaching a stranger on a darkened, lonely platform. The shadowy elms rustled nearby competing with the sound of the retreating train; a union march of rooks circled, scraping the sky with their raucous protests before settling back to their nests.

'Yes, miss, how can I be of assistance?' He gave her the easy smile of a man about town, amused by her nervousness. Helen felt he had rapidly assessed everything about her from her parentage to her purse, working out if she were the sort of girl who was up for a night's companionship.

She assumed her primmest manner. 'I wondered if you had heard of a house in the area called White Towers?'

Interest flared in the man's eyes. 'Indeed. Why, may I ask, is a lady like yourself asking for the Towers?'

'My . . . my friend lives there.'

'Oh yes?' His gaze ran over her modest coat and dull shoes. 'And who are you exactly, my dear?'

She was not prepared to hand out her name to a stranger, not with scandal chasing her. 'I've just returned from medical service in France, sir. I wish to visit my friend; he's been injured.'

'Ah.' His manner warmed a little. 'So you do know Seb then. Met him in France I expect?' He was fishing for details; why, she could not fathom.

'No, we met in London, but we also saw each other in France too. But is this relevant, Mister . . . ?'

The man threw away his cigarette and held out his hand. 'Bartholomew Bewley, Viscount Fitzwarren. Your Sebastian is my little nephew.'

'Oh, er, sorry.' Helen shook the hand and dipped an awkward curtsey, feeling quite unprepared for the niceties of English high society on a country station.

'Not at all, dear girl, not at all. Now, you want to know where White Towers is?'

She nodded.

'Well, I'm not going to tell you.'

'Oh.'

He grinned at her crestfallen expression. 'I'm going to do better than that: I'm going to take you to your Sebastian. Seeing you will cheer the poor chap up after the beating he's taken. What say you to that?'

'That would be very kind of you – if it's not too much trouble.'

He waved her remark away. 'No trouble at all. Innsworth will be along in half a tick with the carriage and I can take you right to him.'

'If you're sure it's not out of your way.'

'Not in the slightest. You see, my dear, Seb is at our house tonight – I can deliver you right into his waiting arms. How does that sound?'

Helen was trying to put what she knew about Sebastian's family together with what the viscount was telling her. Weren't they frightfully high class, far above her touch? 'I wouldn't want to interrupt a private occasion.'

'Nonsense, dear girl, nonsense. Half the county is at Bewley House tonight. One more lady won't make any difference.' He turned to the lane. 'Ah, I can hear the carriage approaching. Are you coming?'

Helen decided that his offer was the best she could hope for, surely preferable to walking the country roads only to find Sebastian not at home. 'Thank you. I am much obliged to you.'

The viscount took her arm and steered her down the dark steps to the lane below the station platform. 'No trouble, Miss . . . ?'

'Helen Sandford.'

'Miss Sandford. I look forward to seeing the expression on my nephew's face. You make me feel like Father Christmas delivering an early present.' He swayed a little too close, wafting brandy-breath over her.

Moving discreetly out of range, Helen did not say anything to disabuse him of this pleasant idea, but she was acutely aware she was bringing a whole parcel of problems. She was still whirling from her hurried expulsion from France, desperate to see Sebastian, but afraid that even he would distance himself from her when he heard the story. Exhausted, Helen just wanted to lay her head on his shoulder and weep, but would he let her?

20

One good result of sitting next to the earl for dinner was that Sebastian was looking forward to the ball like a prisoner his release by the time he reached the port-and-cigars part of the meal. The girls who made up the committee organizing the event were already in occupation of the ballroom, directing the last-minute preparations. The room was filled with autumn flowers – chrysanthemums, roses, sprays of greenery and strings of small pumpkins – and looked splendid. Knowing it had to be faced, he made himself brave an audience as he went forward to congratulate Jilly.

'You've all done a marvellous job!' he declared with forced jollity.

'Sebastian! I'm so glad you like it!' Jilly took his arm proprietarily. 'You remember Gladys and Wilhelmina Jones?'

He nodded, greeting the sisters who were busy distributing the music to the orchestra.

'Belinda Forbes, Minnie Bennet . . .'

Sebastian held out his hand to Minnie who was closest

to him. 'Miss Bennet, how are you?' He had not seen her for years. She had grown up from a freckled little know-it-all into . . . well, a freckled larger know-it-all if her combative expression meant anything.

'Mr Trewby. We are delighted you could come this year, though we regret the cause that brought you home,' Miss Bennet replied neatly.

'Thank you. And Miss Forbes. How is Michael?' Her brother had been his senior by a few years; their paths had crossed a few times in the village cricket team.

Belinda Forbes, a pale, fair-headed girl with an uncertain air to her like a faint sketch on ageing parchment, squeezed her hands together. 'I'm afraid he's . . .'

'He's missing, Mr Trewby,' Minnie said stoutly, sparing her friend from having to make the admission. 'In France. We are all praying for his safe return.'

Missing. Sebastian knew what that meant. Unless Forbes had the extraordinary good fortune of being made a prisoner, it indicated that there hadn't been enough left of him to make an identification. He closed his eyes, swaying on the spot as a snatch of battle-memory shook him in its teeth. 'I'm sorry; I hadn't heard.'

'Old news now,' Belinda Forbes said quietly. 'He's been missing a year. That's probably why no one thought to tell you.'

There had been so many losses in the intervening months that one man's fate could get overlooked.

'I'm sorry,' Sebastian repeated. 'I . . . pray . . .' No, he couldn't pray, not any longer. God – if He existed – had stopped listening to prayers from the battlefield. 'I hope he turns up soon. He could be in Germany.' He cursed himself for offering such false comfort when the chances were so slight.

'Yes, that is what we hope too, but . . .' Belinda gave a shrug, gesturing to a year of waiting and praying, a fruitless vigil.

Sebastian's thoughts went back to the village cricket team – the boys of his generation – and realized that none of them, not a single one, would be playing next season. So many gaps, the rest away, the entire side had been bowled out.

'Do you need to sit down, Sebastian? You're looking a bit peaky.' Jilly took his elbow and steered him to a chair by the window where he would have a good view of the dance floor, but enough air to breathe. He felt stifled by her overly solicitous manner, but it was easier not to protest.

'Thank you, yes, I will. I hope Miss Forbes didn't mind my clumsy words.'

'You weren't to know. No one blames you. I should have briefed you properly before you came in here. If it's anyone's fault, it's mine.'

'Don't be ridiculous.'

She smiled, gently brushing a petal off his arm. 'If I am exonerated, then it is equally foolish to blame yourself. Just tread carefully tonight; there are many families who have lost someone.'

Sebastian pushed the door to the garden open with the

end of his stick, letting in a draught of cooler air. The air smelt fresh, clean. 'I don't think I'll be making that mistake again.'

'Don't worry, I promised we'd look after you. One of us will be on hand to make sure you know all you need to know to have a lovely evening. I'll see if the newspapers have arrived yet – give you something to amuse yourself when we're dancing.'

'Thank you.' Sebastian had fallen into the habit of scanning the papers daily, fearing to read news about something happening to Helen's hospital or his old comrades.

'Can you put it behind you now, Sebastian?'

Struck by the odd note of Jilly assuming the position of caring for him in his own family home, Sebastian caught her gaze, her blue eyes ringed with a darker rim; she was looking at him with a warmth he hoped not to see. He adopted a brisk tone to deter her from getting any wrong-headed ideas about where their relationship was going. 'That's what this is about, isn't it? Putting the war behind us for a night?'

'Yes, one in the eye for the Kaiser,' she agreed, looking a little confused by Sebastian's response to her attentions. 'Us British . . .'

'And Americans,' he inserted, in honour of his father who had just entered the room.

'. . . and Americans can still enjoy ourselves despite everything.'

He chuckled weakly, beckoning his father over to

defend him against the local maidens. Somehow he knew that more would have to be said to clear things up with Jilly, but he would leave that just now. No need to create more sadness on a night designed to be a respite from it. 'Amen to that. Jilly, had you better not get the ball started?'

Helen had been unable to prevent Innsworth collecting the London papers when he met the viscount at the station. She tried to tell herself she was worrying unnecessarily; her dismissal might still only be known to a few people in France. However, she couldn't shake off the impression that the bundle behind her was a ticking time bomb. That was not her only problem. The carriage ride to Bewley House had given Helen time to realize that she was not dressed appropriately for an evening's entertainment, particularly not a ball of the sort the viscount had described. She really should not have come. Who was she doing this for? Not for Sebastian – he would be embarrassed by her arriving in a shambles, unannounced. She had not thought this through at all.

'Would it be possible,' Helen asked as the carriage turned into the long, curling drive leading to the house, 'for a message to be sent to Sebastian so I can meet him privately?'

'Why would you deprive me of my reward?' the viscount pouted.

'Well, for one, I'm dressed for travel, not a dance.'

'You look perfectly acceptable. I doubt Sebastian will

notice what you are wearing once he glimpses your face.'

Maybe. But everyone else would.

'And when you have greeted him, I'll have a word with my sister and see if we can sort out something for you in the way of glad rags.'

'You like arranging scenes, don't you?' The viscount was nothing like his nephew who would not play games with such cavalier disregard for the consequences. Her remark came out with an unintended hint of disapproval, but he laughed it off.

'Of course, dear girl. Not much else to my life if truth be told. I'm the singularly most useless man in creation according to my father.'

Helen wondered why a man of thirty was still fretting over his father's opinion of him. But then the aristocracy were different, all bound up by blood and breeding. 'I really would rather wait outside. If this goes wrong, allow me to blame you.'

'Absolutely, dear heart. My shoulders are well used to bearing the shame of failure.' Conversation lapsed for a moment as the carriage rounded a bend revealing the house lit up for the evening. No blackout restrictions here. For a moment it looked like the house was on fire, every window ablaze with lights.

'Father never does things by half, I'll have to say that for the old coot,' the viscount said genially.

The carriage rolled to a stop by the main entrance and an elderly footman unfolded the step. The viscount jumped out and turned to help Helen himself, pre-empting the servant. The butler came forward when he saw who had arrived.

'Lord Fitzwarren, welcome home.'

'Good evening, Masters. Is all the family here?'

'Yes, sir. The ball . . .'

'I know, I know, that's why I've torn myself away from London. This is Miss Sandford. She's a guest of my nephew, but I doubt she'll be staying here. Ring White Towers to let them know they should prepare a room for her.'

Helen gulped. The viscount seemed so sure she would be welcomed to the family; then again, he seemed the sort of person who would make himself at home in any circumstances, demanding his due from a hostile Amazon tribe if his canoe got beached by their village, his supreme assurance enough to repel any poisoned dart.

A door further into the house opened, releasing a gust of music and laughter. Innsworth placed the newspapers on the hall table. Helen glanced over at them, wondering if she could accidentally-on-purpose set fire to them with one of the many candlesticks illuminating the foyer.

'Miss, may I take your coat?' Masters asked, having already relieved the viscount of his.

Helen unbuttoned her plain grey coat and shrugged out of the narrow sleeves with the butler's help. Masters made no remark, but she knew her unadorned white blouse and dark blue skirt were not up to scratch. A footman passed through the foyer and took the top

newspaper on a silver salver and headed into the ballroom.

Helen's sense of panic went up a further notch. She
had thought to rush the no man's land until she reached
Sebastian and then hold her position until he had given
her a hearing. Somehow she suspected that the mess of
a real social encounter in the ballroom, the newspaper
already lobbed into the battleground, would not allow
her tactics to unfold as she had hoped. 'I really think we
should wait. Tomorrow, I can see him tomorrow.'

'Poppycock, dear girl. Deprive Sebastian of a whole
night's happiness? Never.' Taking her firmly by the arm,
the viscount guided her in the direction of the ballroom.
The other guests must have come in by some other
entrance for they only met servants hurrying to and fro
with refreshments on the path he took. Reaching a pair
of double doors, he pushed them open and strode in.
Helen barely had time to take in the crowd. Girls were
whirling in a kaleidoscope of beautiful dresses to the tune
played by a string orchestra. Some darker figures revolved
with them on the dance floor, older men spared military
service, but many pairs were female, making up for the
lack of partners. Older women and those who did not
care to dance were seated along the walls, gossiping and
watching the waltz with tepid interest. The viscount's
arrival proved to be of much more curiosity and Helen
sensed that most eyes, even some on the dance floor, had
turned to them.

'Mother, Father!' The viscount greeted an elderly

couple seated along the centre of the wall facing the bank of windows that led to the garden.

The countess rose and kissed her son with absent-minded affection. 'So you came.'

'Of course. Not much happening in London but a few Zeppelin raids so I decided to rusticate for the weekend.'

'Dear boy. You can help by partnering some of these lovely girls.'

'That was my intention, I assure you.' He shook his father's hand.

'About those bills, Tolly . . .' the earl rumbled threateningly.

'Later, sir, please. I have someone to deliver first.' The viscount tugged Helen forward.

The countess raised her lorgnette to her eyes by its ornate handle and inspected the new arrival through the lens. 'Who is she, Tolly?'

'A nurse I scandalously kidnapped off the train.'

The countess raised her eyebrows.

'A friend of Sebastian's. I take it that he is here?'

The countess relaxed her suspicion now she knew Helen was nothing to do with her son and heir. 'I think he is by the doors to the terrace.'

The viscount stood up to peer over the heads of the dancers. 'Oh yes, I see him, surrounded by a bevy of beauties. Come, my dear, time you reclaimed your sweetheart before the maidens of Somerset set their caps at him.'

The crowd cleared and Helen could now see Sebastian,

sitting like a prince at court, absorbed back into the society into which he had been born. A blonde girl perched beside him on a stool. She was holding his hand as if she had every right to it, laughing at his remarks and making it apparent to the other pretenders to her position that she was not surrendering her place. What could a disgraced nurse, a working girl like herself, offer him compared to that cool beauty at his side?

Then, to Helen's horror, she saw the footman offer Sebastian the newspaper. He shook it out and then his expression changed. He began reading the front page avidly.

Oh God. It was too late already.

The panic Helen had barely contained since being wrongly accused broke through. Innocent but condemned. German but British. She couldn't get anything right. Flora had told her already: she had built dreams of matchsticks while all around her the deck was burning. Her sister had been wiser to the ways of the world and Helen had been so, so foolish to hope it would prove otherwise for her.

Chaos such as filled her should not be brought into the ballroom; she, the dingy moth, wings battered and frayed after war's capture, had no place among these refined butterfly women.

She should never have come.

The hunt ball had reached its zenith – wine, food and gossip all in full flood. That was why Sebastian was surprised when the twittering girls gathered round his chair fell silent, allowing the gentle strains of Strauss's Love Songs waltz to wash over him. At least antipathy to Germany had not extended to its music. He was feeling sleepy, tired of conversation and noise after a long convalescence at home, and wished very much that he could excuse himself and go to bed. Jilly kept a hold on his hand to prod him awake when his head nodded, but it was no good. He wouldn't last much longer.

The footman offered him the newspaper. 'This just arrived, sir.'

'Thank you.' He unfolded it and smoothed it out on his lap. 'You can go dance now, Jilly. I'll be quite content reading this.' He was eager to get rid of her; she was far too possessive in a very public context. He didn't want to have to spend the rest of the year explaining to friends and family that there was nothing going on between them.

His eye fell on a headline to an article near the bottom of the page. *German nurse exposed working in British hospital.* How odd. He started reading it with a vague interest which rapidly turned to cold horror. Helen Abendroth Sandford. Her name splashed all over the article. Pills. Black market. Betrayal of trust. No, no, it made no sense.

'Sebastian, is something the matter?' Jilly's eyes dipped to the article. 'Is there bad news?' He wanted to hide it – destroy every paper in the kingdom – but he was too slow. 'Isn't that your nurse? The one you write to?' She twitched the article from his fingers. 'Good Lord! Oh, Seb, I'm so sorry. You must feel so betrayed by her.'

'It's lies.' Sebastian's voice grated in his dry throat.

Jilly gave him a pitying look.

In his shock, it took him a moment to register that the young ladies around him had each subtly reorientated their bodies, sunflowers chasing the sun, moving away from him, the wounded soldier, to the able-bodied heir apparent striding towards them.

'Little Sebastian!' Tolly insisted on calling his nephew 'little' even though Sebastian had an inch on him these days. 'Glad to see you are still in the land of the living.'

'Just about.' Sebastian struggled to remember his company manners. He had to go to Helen – had to help her – but at the moment he was stuck in a stupid ballroom.

The girls parted, dipping curtseys to the viscount, which he acknowledged with an amiable smile for each and every one. He had always dealt with the adulation of the local ladies by being scrupulously charming to all; he reserved his more scandalous behaviour for less observant London society.

'I've brought you a present.' Tolly made a show of patting his pockets. 'Now, where did I put it? Ah, yes.' He turned. 'Good Lord: where's she gone?'

'Who, Tolly?'

'She was here a moment ago, old chap. A darling little nurse by the name of Helen something.'

The blood drained from Sebastian's face. 'Helen! Where?' She was here – but she should still be in France, fighting these accusations. Was Tolly joking?

'Sorry, old boy, looks as though she's run for cover. Shy little thing: she'll turn up again, I've no doubt.' Tolly gave a shrug, dismissing the matter. 'Never mind: plenty more fish as they say.' He cast around him and offered to dance with the nearest lady, who accepted with a jubilant smile.

Damn Tolly for not caring. Sebastian wanted to run from the room before Helen got away, but his wretched leg wouldn't allow him. 'Find her for me, Jilly!'

She paused just for a moment before patting his shoulder reassuringly. 'Of course. I'll do what is necessary, don't you worry.'

Helen had rushed back the way she came, almost colliding with the butler.

'Anything the matter, miss?' he had asked kindly.

Yes, everything. Her courage had fled. The London paper had already arrived. Everyone would turn and look on her with scorn, criticizing Sebastian for having once cared for a traitor. How could she defend herself to Sebastian in the middle of a ballroom, for heaven's sake? He shouldn't be saddled with her disgrace; he needed to move on, be with someone worthy of him. She thought painfully of the girl holding his hand; it seemed he may already have done so.

She choked back a sob. 'My coat, please.'

'Certainly, miss. Shall I phone White Towers and let them know you are coming?'

'No, no, I'll . . . No.'

'Masters, what is this young person doing in the hall? Servants use the side entrance.' A formidable lady came down the stairs with the resolute steps of a general about to review his troops.

'Lady Gertrude, this lady is a friend of the viscount.'

'I think that highly unlikely, though Tolly is likely to try and embarrass us all so perhaps you are right. What do you mean by coming here dressed like that, girl?'

Helen buttoned her coat. 'Mean? I . . . I don't understand.'

Lady Gertrude rolled her eyes. 'If you do not understand, then it is useless for me to explain. He's not going to give a girl like you any serious thought. If you've come here planning to get him to present you to us, then you had better think again.'

'What? Sebastian?'

'No, Tolly! The viscount to you, young lady. Sebastian is already spoken for so you can stop imagining anything from that direction either.'

'He is?'

'Yes. Ah, here she is.'

The girl who had sat at Sebastian's side hurried into the hall.

'Jilly, was this young woman on your guest list?' asked Lady Gertrude.

Jilly Glanville marched up to Helen. 'How dare you come here!'

'I'm here to see Sebastian,' murmured Helen, but that safe haven seemed to be receding – a dream only.

'You are a disgrace. Is it not enough to be dismissed from your position for stealing?'

'What's this?' Lady Gertrude signalled to the butler. He took a firm hold of Helen's arm. 'She's stolen something. Check her pockets.'

'No, you misunderstand, Lady Gertrude,' Miss Glanville said, bristling with outrage. 'It's far worse than that. She's front-page news. A German masquerading as a British nurse who has been stealing medicines.'

Lady Gertrude's face turned pale with fury. 'Then what is she doing here? She should be in prison.'

'She wheedled her way into Sebastian's affections when he was injured – she's come to use his connections and money, I expect, to help her out of her difficulties.'

'I'll call the constable.' Lady Gertrude headed for the telephone on the hall table.

'No, no, please, it isn't like that.' It was happening all over again – condemned with no proof, without even a hearing. Helen felt like she was trapped in a nightmare. 'I'm innocent. I haven't done anything.'

Lady Gertrude's hand hovered over the receiver. 'Are you this German nurse or not?'

'Helen Abendroth Sandford,' supplied Jilly.

'Half German,' said Helen. But what was the point?

'She's been writing to Sebastian for months. You know how vulnerable he is at the moment. It would not be hard for a female like her to get her claws in him. If she's arrested here, he'll find out, try and save her when she deserves everything she gets for what she's done. Boys like Neil are dying, but she abuses her position to cheat them!'

Lady Gertrude stepped back from the table. 'Yes, you are right, Miss Glanville. We must get rid of her immediately. Send her to London, send her to perdition, I don't care as long as it keeps her away from my nephew. Masters?'

'Yes, my lady?'

'Make sure this young person leaves the area at once.'

'You won't let me see him?' Helen glanced back to the ballroom then out at the darkness.

'Over my dead body,' vowed Lady Gertrude.

Masters increased his grip and ushered Helen out of the hall through a door to the servants' quarters. The noise and heat were shocking after the cool marble of the foyer. The driver sat at the kitchen table. 'Innsworth, Lady Gertrude wishes you to take this young person to the village.'

'The station, please,' Helen whispered. Everything had fallen apart. She had been waiting for someone to confirm she wasn't worthy of Sebastian; those who knew him well had done so.

Innsworth sighed philosophically and pushed away the late supper he was enjoying at the scrubbed kitchen table. The other staff ignored Helen, too busy keeping the buffet in the ballroom supplied, a domestic ballet with no time for non-dancers.

'Come along then, miss.' Innsworth buttoned his coat. 'Last train up the line goes in half an hour. We'd better hurry.'

Helen tried to assess her chances of dodging the barrage of the butler, the footmen, the ladies, and throwing herself at Sebastian's feet to beg his protection. Sensing her muscles straining in his grasp, Masters cleared his throat.

'Do not consider it, miss. I have my orders. I have sons at the front and I can tell you it would be a pleasure to enforce them.'

Helen had to accept defeat. Her desperate advance had failed under the counter-attack of Sebastian's family. Perhaps leaving was the only way she could prove her love to Sebastian; he would undoubtedly be better off without her.

'Did you find her?' Sebastian asked Jilly when she returned to the ballroom with a strange expression on her face.

'Yes. Lady Gertrude talked to her, but she didn't want to stay.'

'Rubbish. Whatever's happened, I want her here. Please, go fetch her.' Sebastian got to his feet, determined to hobble in pursuit if no one else was going to catch Helen for him.

Jilly tugged his sleeve. 'But Sebastian, I told you, she's already gone. Innsworth hurried out to meet the last train up the line. You won't be able to catch up with them and, by the time another carriage is harnessed, she'll be half-way to London.'

Collapsing back in his chair, Sebastian hung his head. She was, unfortunately, right. He hit his leg with his fist, close to exploding with frustration. 'I want to see Helen!' His loud voice snagged the attention of those nearest to him, causing them to turn and frown. Gentlemen did not lose their temper in a ballroom.

Jilly knelt by the chair. 'Hush, please. Sebastian, think this through: she chose to leave. It is the first decent thing she's done.'

The very core of his body was shaking. Sebastian took a couple of calming breaths. 'Don't say that, Jilly. She's the most decent person I've met and she is innocent, I know that. She probably panicked. Poor Helen. First Tolly, then Aunt Gertrude – that'd be too much for any girl.'

'Exactly.' Jilly pursed her lips, clamping down on her urge to say more.

'Sorry, Jilly.' Sebastian wished he could control his swings of mood and come up with a sound plan. Be a man, for God's sake. 'I'm ashamed to say I lost it for a moment.'

They sat in silence. Sebastian watched the dancers, feeling as if he were looking at a show staged for his benefit rather than participating in the spectacle. Something was very wrong. He could understand that Helen might creep away and find a less public moment to approach him, but she had fled like . . . well, like Cinderella on the stroke of midnight, not even leaving a glass slipper behind for him to trace her.

Dear Helen, what is the matter? he wondered. *I thought we had an understanding, us against this mad, sad world.*

He couldn't imagine what the charges at the hospital had done to her – she would be crushed. He scrunched up the newspaper article, reminding himself that this was not about how he felt, but what Helen was enduring. She must have thought he would not believe her.

Sebastian's resolve hardened. 'Jilly, would you tell Innsworth when he returns to be ready to take me to the station for the first train?'

'You're following her?' Jilly's mouth curled in disgust.

'Of course.'

'But she's a thief.'

'She is not a thief.' He felt very close to hating Jilly just then.

Jilly wrung her hands. 'But you can't deny that she's German. Can't you see that she wouldn't be loyal to our country?'

He didn't bother to give that question a reply. It was so preposterous.

'Do you even know where to find her?'

'No, but I know where to start.'

'But why? Why is she worth it? You'll share in her disgrace.'

'One doesn't let half one's soul go just because she's afraid.'

Jilly stood up with a huff of exasperation. 'All right, I'll tell him, but you are making a mistake.'

'Thank you.' He dismissed her with a curt nod.

When Jilly had gone, Sebastian tucked the crumpled article out of sight. He had no desire to discuss the news with his family. Like Jilly, they would want to protect him from the scandal. That made no difference, just complicated what he intended to do.

A large grey moth, attracted in by the lights, battered frantically against the glass doors to the terrace. Taking pity, Sebastian used his stick to push them ajar to let it escape back into the night. He stepped outside to take a breath of air, letting the darkness cool and harden his resolution into its new shape.

Helen might have fled, but he loved her far too much to let her go. He was following.

1916 and the darkest days of war are upon us,
Can love survive?

by
Eve Edwards

Coming summer 2014

He just wanted a decent book to read ...

Not too much to ask, is it? It was in 1935 when Allen Lane, Managing Director of Bodley Head Publishers, stood on a platform at Exeter railway station looking for something good to read on his journey back to London. His choice was limited to popular magazines and poor-quality paperbacks – the same choice faced every day by the vast majority of readers, few of whom could afford hardbacks. Lane's disappointment and subsequent anger at the range of books generally available led him to found a company – and change the world.

'We believed in the existence in this country of a vast reading public for intelligent books at a low price, and staked everything on it'
Sir Allen Lane, 1902–1970, founder of Penguin Books

The quality paperback had arrived – and not just in bookshops. Lane was adamant that his Penguins should appear in chain stores and tobacconists, and should cost no more than a packet of cigarettes.

Reading habits (and cigarette prices) have changed since 1935, but Penguin still believes in publishing the best books for everybody to enjoy. We still believe that good design costs no more than bad design, and we still believe that quality books published passionately and responsibly make the world a better place.

So wherever you see the little bird – whether it's on a piece of prize-winning literary fiction or a celebrity autobiography, political tour de force or historical masterpiece, a serial-killer thriller, reference book, world classic or a piece of pure escapism – you can bet that it represents the very best that the genre has to offer.

Whatever you like to read – trust Penguin.